GREAT-GRANDPA'S DIARY

Mary Lu Warstler
4-14-14

Mary Lu Warstler

© 2014 by Mary Lu Warstler
All rights reserved. No part of this book may be reproduced, stored in a retrieval system or transmitted in any form or by any means without the prior written permission of publisher/author, except by reviewer who may quote brief passages in a review to be printed in a newspaper, magazine or journal.

All characters appearing in this work are fictitious. Any resemblance to real persons, living or dead is purely coincidental.

Dedicated to
All my friends at
Copeland Oaks Retirement Community

A Word of thanks

As I have said many times, no book is ever written in a vacuum. God has been teaching me to write through encouraging friends, insightful writers, editors who are willing to take time to point out flaws and point me in the "write" direction, and so many helpful conferences I couldn't begin to name them all.

I have been blessed beyond measure with family and friends who give of their time to help with my editing. I especially want to express my gratitude to my friend Pam Ritchey, who read and reread this story and gave me guidance in things that needed changed.

I have been blessed beyond measure with family and friends who give of their time to help with my editing. I especially want to express my gratitude to my friend Pam Ritchey, who read and reread this story and gave me guidance in things that needed changed and to Don Shilling for his skills in pointing out small errors that are so easy to miss.

I can never thank my family enough for all the encouragement and helpful editing, computer expertise, and many other areas of pushing me forward. Nor can I forget to thank all my friends and "fans" at Copeland Oaks who have praised my work and made me feel like a real celebrity. If I never reach the "best seller list," I know I have made many persons happy and God has placed my work in the hands of those who need it.

A Word from the Author

Several years ago, a friend gave me an old Bible that she found in a box of books destined for the dump. As I turned the pages, I realized that it had belonged to a prisoner in late 1920 and early 1930. He had used the edges of the pages as a diary. The date began with December 23, 1929 and continued daily until April 1930. He began writing again the middle of May 1930 ending the following year in May of 1931.

While I knew nothing about the man, I could see an interesting story developing. Research provided facts about the Ohio Penitentiary in the early years of the Twentieth Century, including a fire in April 1930 in which almost 400 inmates and guards died.

My story takes place in 1999 – seventy years later.

I simply let my imagination go where it would in developing the story. I like animals – especially cats in my stories. I read about the Bengal cat and fell in love with it. Reggie may or may not be a true Bengal cat, but he is close.

Always, my hope is that my written words may give enjoyment and insight into the way God works in a world that is full of both good and evil.

One

Pulled from a sound sleep, Corey Kahlor, heart pounding, reached for the phone and glanced at her bedside clock – 1:30 a.m. Running trembling fingers through her shoulder length auburn hair, cleared her throat and tried to sound awake. "Hello."

"Coral Rae? I'm sorry to wake you in the middle of the night, but…"

"Mom? What is it? Are you all right?" Suddenly Corey was awake and sitting on the side of the bed.

"I'm fine, but your father has had a heart attack. He's asking for us."

"My father?" Corey shook her head and blinked her blue eyes.

"Who is this and what kind of prank are you trying to pull? My father has been dead for years. I should just hang up and call the police."

"Coral Rae, don't hang up. Please. This *is* your mother and this is *not* a practical joke."

It must be my mother. She's the only one who ever calls me by my full name. My friends all call me Corey.

"Mom? I don't understand. You told me my father died when I was about five. So how can…?"

"Oh, Coral Rae, I tried to teach you to always be truthful. Remember how I always said, 'be sure your lies will come back to haunt you'? I should have listened to my own advice. I lied to you when you were young – about your father. I'm so sorry."

"Mom…?"

"He left us when you were about five – just disappeared. I didn't hear from him until last week. He called me from somewhere in Texas. I didn't say anything to you. How could I? Then St. Luke's Hospital here in Masontown called a few minutes ago. He's in the coronary care unit and asked them to call me. He wants to see us."

"How can I go see a complete stranger in the middle of the night and talk to him as if he's my loving father? How can he even ask such a thing? How can you…?"

"I'm sorry Coral Rae. I really am. I shouldn't have lied to you, but I never thought he would return. I know it's awkward, but I had to let you know what's happening now. It's your decision to make about seeing him."

"Are you going?"

"I...there is a part of me that doesn't want anything to do with him, but there's another part that wants to know why he left and where he's been all these years that he didn't communicate with us."

Corey twisted her hair around her finger and chewed on her lower lip pondering the question. *Why should I even consider going? He apparently didn't care much for Mom or me. He made his choice, now he can just live with it – unless he dies. Maybe...Mom needs support.*

"Coral Rae? Are you still there? You didn't go back to sleep, did you?"

"Yes, I'm still here and no I didn't go back to sleep. I'm wide-awake – just trying to sort it all out. I don't want to see him, but I don't want you to go alone. I'll meet you at the hospital in about twenty minutes. Besides, I am curious to know why he left us."

"Thank you, Coral Rae."

Corey heard a smothered sob as her mother hung up the phone. Adrenalin flowing, she glanced at the clock again and started for the kitchen. *Maybe cup of coffee – even instant – will clear my mind.* She turned on the heat under the teakettle and returned to the bedroom to dress while the water heated.

Grabbing her sweat suit that hung across a chair waiting for her morning jog, she dressed quickly, wondering if she should call Roger.

How can I explain a dying father to him when he thinks my father died years ago? Maybe I'll just go with Mom first then...

The teakettle began to sing, so she ran back to the kitchen to turn off the heat. Pouring the water over the coffee crystals in her travel mug, she breathed in the aroma. She took a sip of the hot liquid, letting it slide down her throat as she stared trance-like at the phone, willing it to ring again. Surely, her Mom – or someone – would call to admit this unbelievable story was all a practical joke. The phone didn't ring. She took another sip of coffee, shook her head to clear the confusion and grabbed the phone anyway. Without even thinking about it, she pressed the speed-dial button for Roger.

Sipping her coffee and tapping her foot impatiently, Corey

waited for Roger Trent, her fiancé to answer. One ring…two…five…six… Finally, it stopped ringing and she heard a groggy, "Hullo." Roger sounded as if he had his head covered with a pillow.

"Roger, wake up. It's Corey. I need to talk to you."

"Corey? Corey! It's almost two a.m. Are you all right?"

"I'm fine, but we need to talk."

"Now? At two a.m.?"

"Roger, I'm sorry. I don't have time to explain, but I need for you to meet me at St. Luke's Hospital as soon as you can get there."

"St. Luke's? Corey what's wrong? Your mother?" Roger sounded suddenly alert and anxious.

"No, my father."

"But…, your father is…"

"I know – dead. That's what I've thought for the last twenty years. I just learned he's been alive all these years and now he thinks he's really dying and wants to see me."

There was such a long pause that Corey pulled the phone away from her ear and looked at it as if it were melting or something. "Roger? Are you still there?"

"I'm still here. I'm just trying to figure out if this is my Corey or someone who sounds like her."

"Imagine how I felt when Mom called. I'm meeting her at the hospital. Please come."

"Corey, I don't understand but it sounds intriguing to say the least. I'll be there as soon as I can get dressed. What's the room number or who do I ask for?"

Corey paused, feeling bewildered. "I don't know. He's in the coronary care unit and I'm assuming his name is still Daniel Kahlor. I'll be watching for you."

Corey hung up the phone and hurried to the closet for her coat and purse. Ramming her hand into her pocket, she felt the cold metal keys against her fingers. Clutching them in one hand and her travel mug in the other, she ran down the hall to the elevator and pushed the call button.

Waiting for it to arrive from wherever it had been sleeping, Corey punched the button several more times as if that would speed it up. The doors finally slid open – too slowly for Corey. Stepping inside before they were completely open, she pushed the *close door* button then the one for the ground floor. The doors parted at the parking garage and she dashed to her car. In less than a minute, she was pulling onto the street.

***

Masontown, a quiet town with a population of about 30,000, was located on the Maumee River twenty miles south of Toledo. While benefiting from the closeness of Toledo to the north and Columbus to the south, Masontown seemed to have missed all the crime and corruption of the larger cities. Most life-long residents considered it a typical small town consisting of churches, downtown stores, grade school, junior high school and high school – none of which they shared with other communities. Nothing of importance ever happened in Masontown and life continued day after day with no more trouble than a few inebriated youth playing pranks around Halloween – which was fast approaching.

Along the outer edges of the west, north (across the river) and east, farmers tried to make a living with their crops and livestock. South of town, there was some growth, mostly cracker-box cottages and duplexes. It was a quiet town.

Truth was, while the political leadership saw Masontown as a small stable community, many residents, including younger families and farmers, saw it as an aging, changing community.

Corey had been born at St. Luke's, raised on Walnut Street and graduated from Masontown High School. She received her Bachelor's and Master's in Library Science from Ohio State University. Masontown was her home. She knew every street and alley in it as well as those of newer additions to the area – especially the new Masontown Mall on the east end of town. That had taken some time because of the farmers' protest. But the Mall prevailed and beyond its eastern edge, a number of farmers continued to farm. More farmland edged westward along the Maumee River past the shipping warehouses, many of which were empty. St. Luke's was pretty much in the center of downtown, only a block or two from the Court House and the four major churches – Methodist, Presbyterian, Catholic and Baptist.

Traffic at two o'clock in the morning was slow to non-existent. Only the amber traffic lights blinked as if the signals would never begin again if they stopped completely.

Corey drove through town, avoiding areas where she knew the police sometimes set speed traps either to catch folks from out-of-town or to keep themselves awake in the wee hours of the morning. The temperature had been steadily falling into the upper thirty's and lower forty's over the last few nights – normal for late October in northwest Ohio. Last night's forecast even mentioned snow flurries later in the week. Tonight a cold, wet drizzle that could easily turn to ice, collected on the outside of the car. Corey's mind wandered from the possible treacherous weather to another toxic situation brewing at the hospital.

Mom must be frantic with worry and anger. All these years she assumed her husband, was dead. Or has she lived with the secret of knowing he was alive all these years? Either way, he's back in our lives now. Why? What does he want of us? Does he need someone to take care of him in his old age? Does he really want to make amends? How does one make amends to a child who grew up without her father or to a wife who had to work twice as hard to make a home for her child – be mother and father for her?

Glad to see the security lights that surrounded St. Luke's, penetrating the misty fog like a lighthouse sending a beacon of welcome – or warning – to weary travelers, Corey consciously tuned out her disturbing thoughts. A sense of relief swept over her when she saw the orange-like shroud around the parking deck. As she turned into the parking garage, out of the corner of her eye she caught a glimpse of a shabbily dressed man. He pulled his hat down over his forehead, clutched his coat and ran across the entrance in front of her. Corey slammed on the brake and hit the horn muttering to herself about idiots who don't watch where they are going. The man shook his fist at her and ran into a dark corner of the garage. Trembling with anger and relief, she drove on up the ramp to the second floor where a bridge connected the garage to the hospital. A few cars of various sizes, makes and models occupied slots here and there. She parked her red Ford beside her mother's blue Toyota near the bridge.

***

Forgetting her near accident, Corey ran across the bridge hoping at last to get some answers to a multitude of questions. At the other end of the bridge, her mother waited for her. Sherylee, like her daughter, was dressed in jogging clothes, long blond hair tied in a loose ponytail. The same size as Corey – a slim 5'7" – strangers often mistook them for sisters.

"I waited," Sherylee, said needlessly. "I couldn't face him alone and I didn't think you would want to either."

"You're right," said Corey taking a deep breath and giving her mother a quick hug. "Let's go. I called Roger. He'll be here shortly."

"Should we wait for him? I hope he stands by you in whatever fallout comes from this resurrection from the dead."

"He'll find us and don't worry. It'll be all right. We have the upper hand. The man is ill and we don't have to stay if he becomes abusive or obnoxious in any way." Corey couldn't yet call the man father, or dad and Mr. Kahlor seemed so formal.

Sherylee forced a laugh. "Unless he's changed considerably, he was never abusive. He was always smiling – a hard worker. He had fantasies about his father who died in Korea – always hoping they were wrong and he would find him some day."

"Maybe that's why he left," said Corey, "to find his father – if he thought he was still alive." She glanced at her mother for a hint of understanding. Sherylee turned away and started toward the elevators.

"Maybe," she said. "There's the elevator. He's in the coronary unit on fourth floor."

The doors slid open so quietly that had they not been watching and waiting for the elevator, they would have missed it completely. They hurried inside and Corey pushed the button for the fourth floor. The door closed and within seconds, once again slid silently open, closing behind them with a soft thunk. Hospital smells of antiseptic, alcohol and freshly scrubbed floors, walls and doors rushed at them like a mini-cyclone as they started down the hall. Overhead voices paged doctors, beepers and bells called for attention in rooms and soft rubber soles squeaked on floors. All these sounds competed with the internal pounding of their hearts as Corey and Sherylee approached the nurses' station.

"Can I help you?" The woman in white moved her eyes from the computer screen and smiled at them.

Sherylee took charge as she was in the habit of doing. "I'm Sherylee Kahlor. This is my daughter, Coral Rae. We're here to see Daniel Kahlor. Someone called me about forty-five minutes ago and said he was asking for us."

The nurse looked back at the computer and scrolled down to the name she was looking for. "Yes. He is in room 402. Karen, his night nurse, is with him. She knows you're coming. She's the one who called you."

"Can you tell us his condition?" asked Corey. She wanted to have at least some kind of a hint as to what she would be facing.

"Karen can give you more details, but he is facing a quadruple by-pass first thing in the morning."

"That's sounds serious," Corey mumbled.

"Yes, it is, but he has an excellent surgeon and he seems healthy in other ways. His chances of recovery are very good."

"Thank you," said Sherylee. She took her daughter's hand and led her to room 402 as if she were leading that child left behind so long ago. Corey didn't mind. She knew it was for her mother's sake more than her own.

Instead of a door, the room had only a curtain drawn aside enough that both Corey and her mother could see the man in the bed. Corey didn't remember him, except in pictures of her with him when she was very young. Although Sherylee hadn't seen him in years, she knew him instantly. An IV attached to his arm fed liquids into his veins. While he had an oxygen tube on his nose, at least he had no breathing tube down his throat – yet. He could talk – except he didn't. His mouth opened, but no words came forth.

Two

Corey, Sherylee and the man in the bed, whom Corey assumed was her father, stared at one another, each afraid to make the first sound. The white pillow blended with the thick, wavy white hair to form a soft frame around the man's pale face. His eyes, the same color blue as Corey's, looked from one to the other as the two women moved to the foot of his bed. Corey watched tears form in his eyes and spill over those pale cheeks.

Sherylee sucked in her breath and spoke in a whisper, "Daniel?"

"Sherylee?" Daniel swallowed the lump in his throat, swiped at the tears rolling down his face and looked back at Corey. "And this is Corey? Or should I say Coral Rae?"

"Only Mom calls me that."

"I used to call you Corey, but you were so young when I...when I..."

"Left us?" Sherylee finished for him with a note of bitterness and anger.

"Sherylee, Corey, I'm so sorry."

"Why, Daniel? Why did you leave us?"

"It's a long story, Sherylee..."

The young nurse, who had been checking all the bags and tubes and monitoring the screen that told her many things – blood pressure, heart rate, oxygen level – stepped closer to Corey and Sherylee.

"Hi. I'm Karen. I'll be taking care of Mr. Kahlor through the night and part of tomorrow morning. If you have any questions, I'll be glad to do what I can to answer them."

"Thank you, Karen. I'm Sherylee Kahlor and this is my daughter Coral Rae. Daniel has been away and we haven't seen him for some time."

"Yes, that's what he said when he asked me to call you."

"The nurse at the desk said they'll do a quadruple bypass in the morning."

"That's right. Dr. Jonathan Humphrey, the best cardiac surgeon in this area, will be doing the surgery first thing – about seven.

Sometimes emergencies are inserted into the schedule and we run behind, but Mr. Kahlor is first on the list. There should be no delays. Dr. Humphrey will meet with you before and after the surgery to explain what he is doing and why."

Hearing the soft closing of the elevator followed by footsteps in the hall, Corey and Sherylee turned to see Roger move away from the nurses' station and hurry toward them. He took Corey's hand and kissed her forehead. "Are you all right?" he asked.

Corey nodded and Roger turned to her mother, "Mrs. Kahlor?"

"I'm fine Roger. We were just talking to Karen, Daniel's nurse. I guess we need to introduce you to Coral Rae's father. Daniel, this is Roger Trent, Coral Rae's fiancé."

Karen started out of the room. "I'll give you a few minutes alone with Mr. Kahlor. Please don't upset him or I'll be back in a flash. Don't stay too long."

Roger moved to the side of the bed and carefully took Daniel's free hand. "I'm glad to meet you sir. I've never met a ghost before." He grinned and Daniel chuckled.

"I like this fellow," Daniel said to Corey. "They were just asking me why I left, but I need to talk more about why I returned in case I don't make it through the surgery tomorrow."

"The nurse said you have a very good chance because you are healthy in other ways," said Sherylee. "Besides that, if it were urgently serious, you would be on the operating table right now."

"That's what the nurse told me too, but just in case, I need to ask you to put something in a safe deposit box for me. If I make it, I'll have lots of recovery time when we can hash over old times and determine if new times are possible."

Roger gave him a curious look then glanced at Corey who shrugged. "What do you want put in the bank?" asked Roger.

"Look in my locker. There's a Bible and a spiral notebook in my jacket. Get them for me, please."

Sherylee raised her eyebrows in surprise. "A Bible?"

Daniel smiled at her. "My mother used to take me to Sunday School from the time I was little. But, this Bible is different. It belonged to my grandfather."

Roger retrieved the hard-backed, black Bible and spiral notebook from Daniel's jacket. Both were well worn. Casually he leafed through the Bible. As a writer, he knew people often wrote notes to themselves, to their loved ones or to the world in general in books.

He noticed several pages with writing in pencil around the edges of the page. Taped to the inside back cover was a yellowed piece of news print about one inch square.

"Looks like a newspaper clipping about a robbery."

"The one my grandfather was in prison for," said Daniel.

"What does it say?" asked Corey.

Roger read the clipping: "Toledo Bank robbed. Bystander killed. Four men made off with $50,000."

"Not much there. I'll look it up later," said Corey.

"Otherwise, it looks as if someone used this Bible as calendar and diary," said Roger, carefully laying the Bible and the notebook on the bed. Daniel picked them up – one in each hand.

"You're right. My grandfather was in prison for bank robbery. That's his prison number in the front of the Bible and on the outside of the notebook. Some church group gave him the Bible, notebook and pencil early in December of 1929. The following spring a major fire brought about prison reforms to overcrowded prison systems. Inmates, sentenced too severely for their crime, began to receive parole. Grandfather Kahlor was one of them. He sent all his belongings to his wife and told her to keep them safe until he came for them. He received parole, but disappeared before he made it home."

"Sounds like the Houdini act runs in the family," said Corey with a note of sarcasm.

"Coral Rae!"

"It's all right, Sherylee. She's right," said Daniel, smiling at Corey. "She does have a sarcastic sense of humor."

Roger laughed. Corey smiled at her father. Maybe she would learn to forgive and like him after all.

"I know this is all leading somewhere," said Sherylee. "You should remember I'm not the most patient person in the world."

"I remember. I also realize how late it is. I'll be sleeping for several days. You don't have that luxury, so I'll speed this up. I'll give you highlights now and fill you in later on details that you want or need to know."

Sherylee said, "I need to know about when you left. I know your mother called you a few days before she died and you went to see her. She sent that duffle bag home with you. A week later, the day after the funeral, you took it with you to your mother's house. That's when you disappeared. It has something to do with that Bible and diary, doesn't it?"

Daniel sighed. "You're right. I brought the bag home with me and put it in the attic to go through later – much later. At the cemetery the day of the funeral – you had already taken Corey to the car – a stranger approached me. He said his name was Jones and that my grandfather kept a diary while he was in prison and promised it to him when he got out. He never received it and wanted it. I asked him why my grandfather would promise something to someone who wasn't even born yet at the time. The man wasn't much older than I am. He said it was promised to his grandfather who died before he found it."

"Why would he want an old man's ramblings?" Sherylee asked.

"He said he was a writer and planned to write a novel about a bank robber. I told him I knew nothing about a diary. He said it must be in my grandfather's belongings. He knew I had the duffle bag."

"How did he know that?" asked Corey.

"He said he saw me take a duffle bag from my mother's home."

"He was spying on your mother?" Sherylee gave him an incredulous look.

Daniel nodded. "I told him if he didn't leave immediately, I would call the policeman who stood near the grave. He left, but…"

Daniel paused so long they thought he was getting tired.

"Maybe we better leave," said Sherylee. "You need to…"

Karen appeared at the doorway. "Five minutes," she said. "Mr. Kahlor needs rest and we need to check vitals and begin meds."

"I'm all right," said Daniel. He shook his head and continued. "The next day he called me at work. I lied and told him I had been through the duffle bag and there was no diary. It must still be at my mother's house and I would check it out the next day – my day off from the car dealer."

"That's when you took the duffle bag and your backpack. You said you were going to your mother's house to start clearing out some stuff. Corey was coming down with chicken pox. I couldn't leave her to go with you."

"I intended to put the duffle bag back in the attic and leave it there until we were ready to sell the house, but when I got there, the front door was ajar. I cautiously went in. The house looked as though a tornado had spiraled through it. I knew then that the man was serious about wanting that diary. I was afraid he might be dangerous and I panicked. I knew he wanted the diary and he would hound me until he got it – maybe even threaten my family. I had to protect my wife and precious daughter, so I put the Bible and diary in my backpack, left the duffle bag where the man could find it and ran."

"Why didn't you come home and call the police?" Sherylee tried to hide her confusion and anger.

"I thought he would believe I still had the diary. I didn't want to lead him to you and Corey. I ran across the back meadow to the railroad where I hopped a slow moving train. Jones – or whatever his name was – waved from the hill as the train picked up speed."

"Couldn't you have at least called?"

"I was scared, guilty, depressed, angry, but I was more scared for you and Corey. I felt you were safe as long as I was gone, because everywhere I wandered he was there, following me. I drifted from town to town working wherever I could until I would see him watching me. I began to wonder if I was simply paranoid. Surely, he wouldn't follow me that much. But I kept seeing him."

"Didn't he try to talk to you? Get the diary?" asked Roger.

"He did. Several times, he walked into my place of employment. I ran. Once I came home from work and found my mattress cut to shreds. After that, he tried more often to contact me. Since he didn't find what he wanted in my room, he must have known I carried the diary with me.

"Finally, I came to the end of my endurance. I was ready to find a bridge or tall building and jump. Someone saw me and told me about a Christian clinic in Texas that worked with the whole person – body, soul and emotions. I hitchhiked and hopped trains until I found the place in southern Texas. I wasn't sure they would even take me with no money and no home. At least I had sense enough to stay away from booze and I never smoked—couldn't afford either, anyway."

"Your mother told me you never did pick up those habits – even in your difficult youth," said Sherylee. "That's one of the things I liked about you when we met."

"Somehow I got up enough nerve to talk to someone at the clinic," Daniel continued. "They let me check myself in for an evaluation. I learned that I wasn't paranoid, but my fears were grounded in truth. I described the man who followed me. They had an artist draw him. I knew then he was real and I had been a fool to run away. They told me I should contact the FBI. In fact, they contacted them for me. Two agents came to see me at the clinic. They saw the picture and knew immediately he was in their files. They assured me they would look into the matter.

"I stayed at the clinic almost two years. I should have called you from there. They encouraged me to do so, but I was still afraid. The man was still out there and it had been so long. When I left the clinic, I had turned my life around and I felt more in control. I gave myself a few days to get used to the new me, then I made plans. That's when I called you, but I chickened out before I could ask if you would see me."

"You're getting tired," said Sherylee. "We better leave."

Karen returned to the room. "I have to ask you to leave for now. Mrs. Kahlor if you want to spend the night, you can talk to the head nurse. She'll help you with that."

"Give me five more minutes," said Daniel.

"If you don't mind me working while you talk," said Karen, "I'll get started on checking things out."

"Thank you," said Daniel. "I realized I had cheated my wife and daughter of my love and had missed my daughter growing up. I knew Sherylee wouldn't let you suffer, but… I was wrong, so very wrong to leave."

"Daniel…," Sherylee started, but he held up his hand for her to wait.

"That's more or less the short version of why I left and where I was. Now, for why I came back. First, I want to beg your forgiveness – both of you. I know I don't deserve it and it might take some time, but…" His voice choked as tears slid down his face.

"You're right," said Corey. "Mom taught me to be tolerant and forgiving. I'll try – but give me time."

"She's right, Daniel. It's been twenty years. I don't know you anymore and Coral Rae doesn't know you at all. We'll have to learn all over again, but we'll try."

"That's all I ask," he said then paused, sighed and spoke again. "Now, I need help until I can get out of here. Will you hide this Bible and diary in a safe place – preferably a bank box? I don't want to cause any harm to come to any of you, but I can't leave it lying around here. I intended to get a safe deposit box and send the key to the FBI so they could open if anything happens to me."

"Aren't you being a little melodramatic?" said Sherylee.

"No." He said it with such simplicity that Corey felt the hairs on her arms and the back of her neck stand on edge.

"Do you mind if we read it first?" asked Roger.

Daniel gave him a curious look. Corey laughed. "Roger really is a writer," she said. "He writes for the Masontown Gazette and other papers. He's been talking about doing a novel."

"As long as you get it into a safe deposit box as soon as the bank opens tomorrow. When I'm better, we'll talk more about it."

Roger flipped through the Bible's pages again. Then he leafed through the notebook. "They both look like diaries. Why are there two?"

"I've read and re-read both copies a number of times. They look like repeats at first, but there are differences."

"I find it intriguing that he kept a diary in his way. Maybe we can find out why he kept two and what – if anything – he was trying to tell someone. What do you think Corey?"

Corey moved to the side of the bed and took her father's hand. With tears forming on her eyelashes, she said, "Roger and I will work on this while you recuperate from your surgery." She squeezed his hand, leaned over and planted a kiss on his cheek. "When you're better, we'll pool our information."

"Just be very careful. If you even feel like someone is following you, get it to the FBI."

"We'll be careful, sir, I won't let anything happen to my women." Roger grinned at Corey and her mother.

Sherylee ignored Roger and moved to the side of Daniel's bed. "I want to hate you for what you did to us, but I still love you. Welcome home, Daniel."

Roger nudged Corey and nodded toward the hall. "We'll be back before the surgery in the morning," he said.

"I don't think either of them heard us," said Corey as she and Roger left the room. They walked hand in hand down the corridor to the elevator.

Three

The elevator closed behind them and Roger reached for the main floor button. Corey pulled his arm back. "I came across the bridge from the parking deck. That's second floor."

"You look beat. Why don't I drive you home? We can pick up your car tomorrow."

"Okay, but why don't we take my car and pick up yours tomorrow?"

Roger raised his eyebrows, but before he could say anything, Corey grinned and pushed the second floor button. "In case you haven't noticed," she said, "it's raining and my car is inside – right beside the bridge entrance. We won't have to get wet."

Roger laughed. "As long as you don't mind me driving your car to my place after I let you off."

"Why don't you sleep in my guest room? We won't have much time anyway with his surgery scheduled for seven a.m."

Roger grinned. "That'll work. I expect your mom will stay at the hospital tonight."

"She didn't say, but I'm sure she will. She never stopped loving him."

"I know. I heard her tell him."

"Even before he reappeared, I've seen her sitting, staring at his picture and swiping at her tears. She never knew I saw her. She tried so hard to make it easy for me."

Corey and Roger crossed the bridge to the parking garage and were soon buckled into her red Ford. The mist had turned from foggy to a gentle – but cold – rain. Roger at the wheel, they started out of the garage. Suddenly he slammed on the brake and Corey flew forward, saved from hitting her head by the pull of the seatbelt.

"Roger?"

"Sorry, sweetheart. I thought I saw someone run across in front of me. Just a shadow, I suppose."

"I don't know," said Corey. "A strange man did run across in front of me when I drove in. He shook his fist at me as if it was my fault that he almost got hit."

"Lots of nuts out and about. Homeless men looking for a place to sleep out of the rain maybe.

"I suppose. I wonder how many times..." she let her thought fade away.

"He's all right now," said Roger, "or will be eventually – I hope."

They drove the rest of the way in silence. Roger patted her hand as he flipped on the turn signal before he turned on her street. Pulling into the underground garage, he parked in Corey's spot near the sliding glass doors. Corey slid her key card through the lock and the doors opened. They stepped into the small square waiting area and pushed the call button for the elevator. As soon as the doors closed, Roger pushed the button for second floor and the car responded. They walked down the hall to Corey's apartment where she once again used her sliding keycard to open the door. Inside she hung their coats in the closet and sighed deeply. "Do you want a cup of tea or something?" she asked.

"Not unless you need to unwind. I think we need sleep more than snacks. It's already three o'clock and we need to leave here by six fifteen if we're going to see him before they take him to surgery."

"Thank you, Roger," said Corey. "You're right but..."

"You just want to be a good hostess," he said. He grinned and kissed her cheek. "Go to bed. We'll have coffee later before we leave." Roger kissed her again and started for the guest room. "Do you want the diary?"

"No," said Corey. "My eyes won't stay open to read."

"Me either, but I want to look it over. We'll read it together tomorrow – or whenever."

"Maybe while Dad is in surgery. We can take it to the bank when he is in recovery. Mom might have some helpful information."

***

Dressed in their jogging suits from the night before, Roger and Corey were on the elevator moving to the fourth floor of the hospital at six-thirty the next morning. As before, the silent carrier rose and its doors slid open as if it were a well-oiled machine closing softly behind them.

Sherylee was standing outside the pulled curtain/door of Daniel's room. Corey had never seen her mother so haggard and vulnerable. Sherylee, who was always confident and in control, hugged herself as

GREAT-GRANDPA'S DIARY

if her world was suddenly crumbling around her.

Corey rushed to her mother's side and gave her a hug. "Are you all right? Is he…"

Sherylee put on her everything's fine mask and said, "I'm fine. Karen is getting him ready to go down to surgery. She said we could have a few minutes while we wait for the surgery team to come after him."

"Did you get any rest?" Corey asked. "You look like you were up all night."

"I was. We had a lot of catching up to do. "I'll catch a nap while he's in surgery."

"How long will it take?" Roger gave his soon to be mother-in-law a hug.

"They said at least four hours."

"That long? I guess I never thought about it, but it is the heart they're working on," said Corey.

Karen pulled the curtain aside. "You can go in now," she said. "They will be after him in about ten minutes."

"Thank you," said Sherylee as she followed Corey and Roger into the room.

"Dad…" Suddenly, Corey felt a tightening of her stomach. One day she had no father and the next he was back in her life. Now he faced a life-threatening surgery that might remove him from her life again. When she was a child, she had wondered what it would be like to be pulled down the swirling drain after her bath. Now, she thought she knew. Her world was swirling around her.

As if he had read her mind, Daniel reached for her hand and smiled. "You used to watch the bath water drain from the tub with that same expression," he said.

Corey gulped back the urge to fling herself into his arms – an act that would not be good with all the IV tubes. "You remember that?"

He nodded. "It's all right, Corey. There's no time for chitchat, but I'll be all right. The hospital chaplain was in a little bit ago. Your mother and I have come to terms with my despicable behavior. I have you here and I've met the man who will be your life partner. If I don't make it, I'll die happy. If I do make it, I'll live even happier."

At the end of the hall, another elevator – not the one for visitors – opened with a soft swoosh. The distinct sound of a gurney wheels turning followed, one wheel sounding like an off-key instrument at a band rehearsal.

"Sounds like it's time," said Daniel as Corey leaned over to kiss him. Roger reached for his hand and squeezed. Corey moved aside for her mother to give him a final kiss as the surgery team moved the gurney into the room beside his bed. They watched as the team of two nurses in green surgery scrubs transferred Daniel with ease from bed to gurney. They walked with him to the elevator, gave him a final kiss and watched the elevator swallow him – gurney, surgery team and all. Corey stared at the door with a sinking feeling – as if her father were swirling down that long ago drain.

"The waiting room is this way," said Karen who had followed them to the elevator.

"Do you go off duty soon?" asked Corey. "Not that I want to get rid of you." She felt a blush spread across her cheeks in embarrassment.

"Actually, I'm covering a half a shift for another nurse. I'll be here until about one o'clock."

She led them down another long corridor to a large waiting room surrounded on two sides by windows facing the hallways. Another wall of windows faced the outside, overlooking one of the parking lots. A short hallway divided the fourth wall. Restrooms were straight ahead, closets on the left and a small kitchenette on the right.

Corey looked around the spacious room full of soft chairs, couches, love seats and tables with magazines and newspapers stacked neatly on them. She walked over and peeked through the open space above the counter top into the kitchenette and saw a coffee maker, microwave, refrigerator and a vending machine with various kinds of instant foods ready to heat and eat.

"Would you like some coffee, Mrs. Kahlor?" Roger followed Corey to the kitchenette, reached for a Styrofoam cup and moved to the Kuerig single cup coffee maker.

"Thank you Roger," Sherylee answered. "If there is anything in the vending machine, I'd like a bite of something to eat, too."

"How about a breakfast sandwich? I'll microwave it for you. Corey? Want anything?"

"Just some coffee, please."

The three of them sat in a semi-circle of two chairs and a couch with a table between them while Sherylee ate. No one was ready to talk about what had happened and what the future would hold. For now, it was enough to wait for the immediate future – the results of the surgery.

"Why don't you stretch out on that couch?" Corey said. "I'll see if I can find a blanket for you."

"Try that closet across from the kitchenette," said Roger.

She did and found shelves of pillows and lightweight blankets. Retrieving one of each for her mother, Corey took them to the couch and covered her.

"I don't think I'll sleep," said Sherylee, "but it does feel good to stretch out a little." Three minutes later, she was snoring softly.

Roger smiled and Corey cleaned up the table from their *picnic breakfast.*

"Do you want to stretch out too?" asked Roger. "I'll get you a blanket and…"

"No, I think I would like to look at the diary."

"Good idea," said Roger, choosing another couch where he and Corey could sit together. He pulled the Bible from his backpack and leafed through the pages until he came across the first dated page. "It looks like he began reading on December 24, 1929 – Christmas Eve."

"Dad said he'd been there since September and some church group gave all the inmates a notebook and a Bible for Christmas."

"That would make sense. He just put dates in the Bible then wrote in the notebook. Later, it looks like he wrote in both. Let's see what the first entry in the diary has to say. You want to read it, or shall I?"

"Why don't you read it first?"

Roger opened the very much used spiral notebook and read the tiny scrawled words on the first page.

December 24, 1929 – My name is Harry Kahlor # 518713. It's Christmas Eve, 1929. First time I ever missed being home for Christmas. Men don't get all sentimental over a stupid holiday. Christmas is just like any other day. Nice of that church to give us Bibles and notebooks. I ain't much for reading anything but it is something to do. Ain't much for writing neither. That preacher said to read five chapters a day and write a few paragraphs. I'll give it a try. Don't understand most of what I read. Sam reads his Bible a lot. Maybe he can help when he comes back from visiting his family. Thought Mary Sue would come down today and bring the boys, but I guess not. It's getting dark. I hate the dark. Feels like it will smother the life right out of me. Want to scream, but wouldn't do no good. Probably get me in trouble. Sure wish I'd stayed in West Virginia.

Corey grabbed a tissue from the box on an end table and dabbed at her eyes. "It must have been awful for him to be alone like that for Christmas Eve. I wonder why his wife – my great-grandmother – didn't go to see him."

"Maybe she was too far from the prison," said Roger. "I'm assuming he was in the Ohio State Penitentiary in Columbus. Where did your father grow up? Masontown? That would be a far piece to travel in 1929 and in December with the possibility of snow and ice."

"When I was in about the fourth grade, we had to write an essay about our ancestors – when they settled in Ohio, what they did for a living – that kind of thing. Mom told me that Harry Kahlor was born in a coalmining town in West Virginia – Whipple, I think. He moved to Masontown because it was close Toledo and Columbus. Times were hard in the nineteen twenties and thirties. He came looking for work."

"He settled in Masontown?"

"He did, but it was much smaller than it is today. He grew up west of town in one of the little homes that some housing developer built for *transplants* from other states looking for work during the Great Depression. Many of the homes are either gone or caved in. It must have been difficult for my great-grandmother raising two boys with no steady income and their father in prison. But surely, she could have at least called him on Christmas?"

"I doubt they had phones available except for calling out at specified times. She probably sent him a letter or a card, which he might not have received until days later."

"We need to do more research. How long was he there? What happened to the other men involved in the robbery? When did he get out, where did he go?"

Corey stood up and stretched. "I need to move about a little. Maybe I'll run to the library. I need to let my staff know what's happening and that I won't be in today."

"Mind if I tag along?" said Roger, "or do you need to be alone?"

"Thank you for asking, but I don't mind having company. Oh...we forgot Reggie."

"How can you forget something as noticeable as a super-sized Bengal cat?"

"Mom wasn't home last night and I didn't think about running by there this morning. Maybe I better go feed him and talk to him."

Roger grinned. "You're going to spoil that cat."

Corey laughed. "Well, a cat – or any animal as big as Reggie – needs pampering and company for a while. We don't want him to get angry and out-of-sorts with us. He could chew an arm off quite easily."

Roger laughed with her. Reggie, or more specifically, Sir Reginald, was Sherylee's thirty-pound Bengal cat, who looked like a smaller version of his ancient ancestors, the mighty Bengal tiger. Reggie, however, was as gentle as a newborn kitten. Intuitively he knew not to use his claws and was as clean as the fussiest of housekeepers.

"Why don't we tend to Reggie first? You can call the library from your mother's house."

"Sounds like a plan to me," said Corey. "I'll leave a note for Mom. We can check at the desk for word before we leave. I'll call the library after I take care of Reggie."

Corey wrote the note and used a bottle of water to anchor it to the table in front of the couch where Sherylee slept. Then Roger put the diary and the Bible in his backpack and they moved toward the elevator.

"Sometime today we need to get those books to the bank," said Cory.

"Maybe we can copy them first," said Roger hopefully.

Four

"Why don't we both drive?" said Corey. "Your car was left in the outside lot all night. Sometimes the guards mark the tires if they think someone is using the hospital lot to keep from parking on the street in front of their home. Then we can go our separate ways if we have to or I can leave my car in Mom's garage if we come back together."

"Good idea. I'll meet you there."

As Corey drove away from the parking garage, a cold chill sent a shiver across her shoulders and down her back. *What was that all about? I can't afford to come down with a cold now. But…it felt more like someone was staring at me.*

She reached the older section of town with two-story houses and small yards instead of apartment buildings and businesses. Turning on Walnut Street, she drove two blocks then turned left into the driveway of her mother's two-story white frame house. Corey drove her car into the garage then went back to meet Roger who pulled in behind her. They walked up the wooden steps to the front porch. Corey handed the key to Roger while she got the mail from the mailbox attached to the wall beside the door. He opened the door and was face to face with Reggie.

"I think someone came to greet us," he said

Corey laughed and stooped to scratch Reggie's ears "Hi Reggie. Have you been taking care of the house?"

"Meow."

"I'm sorry we're so late with breakfast," said Corey.

Reggie meowed and looked toward the door.

"She's still at the hospital, Reggie. I'm sure she told you last night when she left where she was going. She just didn't know she would stay. Dad is having heart surgery and she needed to be with him."

While Corey washed his dishes then filled them with fresh water and food, she talked to Reggie, who followed her grumbling to himself until she set the food down for him. He began eating while she went to clean his litter box, still talking to him. Roger leaned against the door smiling.

"Mom will be home tonight," said Corey. "But if she doesn't make it, I'll come and spend the night. Is that all right?"

"Meow," answered Reggie around a mouth full of food making it sound more like, "meorf."

"Don't talk with your mouth full," said Corey.

Reggie turned and glared at her then went back to eating.

Roger laughed aloud.

"What's so funny?" asked Corey.

"You are. Talking to that cat as if he was a person."

"Well, he may not be a person, but he is smarter than most people I know. And he needs to know what's going on."

Roger laughed again. Reggie finished his meal, rubbed against Corey's ankles, purred then sashayed past Roger, slapping his legs with his tail. He continued to the living room, found a sunny spot on the carpet and began his after meal clean-up routine.

Roger shook his head. "Maybe we should call the hospital before heading for the library."

Corey picked up the phone. "I'll call the library first in case there are any problems I need to take care of.

"Why don't we stop for a couple of sandwiches before we go back? Your mom might be hungry."

"Good idea – the sandwiches, but see what Mom has in her fridge. We can make sandwiches quicker and more nutritiously." She turned back to the phone and dialed the library and Roger went to the kitchen.

"Everything all right at the library?" he asked as Corey joined him.

"Yes, Betty is there this morning. She is competent and can handle anything. She has my cell number."

"Okay, we have our lunch. The cat's been fed. The library is under control. Shall we head back to the hospital?" Roger picked up the lunch sack and moved toward the front door.

"Maybe I better call first,"

Reggie followed them from room to room with what Corey was sure was a worried frown. "It'll be all right, Reggie," said Roger. "Someone will be back soon."

Corey turned away from the phone looking perplexed.

"Corey? Something wrong?"

"Yes – sort of," she said.

"What? Your father?"

"No, he's fine – still in surgery. But someone dressed as kitchen help took a tray to his room. The nurse at the desk realized Dad wasn't there and shouldn't have a tray even if he was. She went to tell the man to remove it. He was gone, but the tray was still there. He had dumped Dad's backpack and the bedside table drawer. She called security. Of course the kitchen knew nothing about it except a tray was missing from a cart intended for another floor."

"Your mom…?"

"I called her. They told her. She's upset but she's all right. I told her we would be there as quickly as traffic would allow."

"Think he was looking for the diary?"

"Probably. Roger we need to hide it – soon. Maybe we can get to the bank this afternoon, but now we need to get to the hospital."

Reggie stood on his back paws and rested his front paws on Corey's arm, looking into her eyes as if reading her mind through those blue orbs. Then he meowed and dropped to all fours. Not looking back, he ambled into the living room and stretched out almost the length of the couch.

"That is one big cat," said Roger.

"And smart," said Corey.

"Shall we take my car and leave yours in your mother's garage?"

Corey nodded and Roger opened the passenger door for her.

***

Hardly waiting for the elevator doors to open completely, Corey exited and darted down the corridor to the waiting room where they'd left her mother sleeping earlier. Roger was right behind her.

"Mom? Are you all right?" Corey hurried to the couch where Sherylee was sipping a cup of coffee.

"I'm fine, but I don't understand why or how anyone would…"

"The diary," said Roger. "Someone must have been looking for it."

"Would they…?"

"Mom, someone has been on Dad's heels for twenty years. Surely whoever he is knows he's here."

"Oh." Suddenly Sherylee covered her mouth to hold back angry words. Her eyes narrowed. "No wonder he was afraid to call."

"Did they call the police?" asked Roger.

"Security came and talked to me. I checked but as far as I could tell, nothing was taken. I didn't even think about the diary. Since nothing is missing, there didn't seem to be any reason to call the police. Security will file a report with them.

A frown crossed Corey's brow, then she smiled. "Well, whatever, we brought lunch."

"Thanks," said Sherylee. "I'm ready for a bite of something."

Corey, Roger and Sherylee had just finished their lunch when Dr. Humphrey entered the room. His surgery cap still sat on the top of his head and his mouth cover hung like a loose necklace around his neck.

"Mrs. Kahlor?"

"Yes," answered Sherylee trying to get out of the soft couch.

Doctor Humphrey sat in the chair beside her. "Mr. Kahlor is doing just fine. He will be in recovery until he's alert enough to go to his room." He pulled out a picture chart and showed her what he had done. "If you have any questions, don't be afraid to ask the nurse or myself. Someone will come and get you when he's awake. You can see him for a few minutes, but don't be alarmed if he falls asleep while you are talking. It will take a couple of days for all that anesthetic to work its way out of his system."

"Thank you, doctor," said Sherylee.

Another half hour passed before someone came to take them to the recovery room. They only stayed a few minutes because Daniel was still groggy and full of IV tubes and a ventilator tube in his mouth. He couldn't stay awake.

"Why don't you go home and get some rest," said the nurse. "He won't be ready to visit until tomorrow, but you can come back to see him tonight."

"I think that's a good idea," said Corey, placing her arm around her mother. "I told Reggie you would be home later today."

Sherylee smiled, "Did he say 'Okay'?"

"More or less," said Corey. Roger laughed and started for the elevator. "Why don't I take you girls home then I need to check in at the paper to see if they have an assignment for me."

"You can go do whatever," said Corey. "I'll drive Mom home, since my car is in her garage and hers is here. I'll go to the library and get some paper work done this afternoon while Mom rests."

"Shall I fix dinner for us?" Sherylee asked as she gathered her purse and the empty lunch bags.

"You go home and rest," said Roger. "I'll bring some Chinese takeout for dinner."

Now that everything was back on track, Corey felt more relaxed.

They would see her dad tonight and in a couple of days, he would be up to talking a little. Everything was fine – so why did she have the feeling of impending doom? She was sure they hadn't heard the last of her father's pursuer.

Five

True to Ohio weather patterns, the wet, gloomy days that began the week had evaporated into bright sunny days of Indian summer-like warmth. Friday dawned to the singing of birds and the sun highlighting the brilliant red, yellow and orange fall foliage. It had been four days since Daniel's surgery and the doctor was considering sending him home by Monday or Tuesday.

Corey woke and glanced at the clock – 4:00 a.m. *It's early, but I know I won't go back to sleep. Maybe I can read the diary for a while. Roger won't be here until close to 8:00.*

Corey padded to the kitchen to make coffee than showered and dressed while it perked. Coffee and toast before her, she opened her great-grandfather's diary and began reading, sending a nagging voice of concern to the far reaches of her mind. She knew they should have taken the Bible and the diary to the bank. But…well, it was intriguing. What was in it that someone would want bad enough to hound her father for twenty years and still be searching?

Whatever, she ignored her inner voice and began to read and write some passages on her legal pad.

***

<u>December 26</u> *– I opened the Bible. Looks strange – not like most books. Read from a Book titled Numbers – strange name for a book. "Speak unto the children of Israel and take of every one of them a rod according to the house of their fathers, write thou every man's name upon his rod."*

Makes no sense to me. Sam says a rod was like a walking stick used to herd sheep – or people. Only rod I know was my gun and that's part of what got me in here.

<u>December 27</u> *– Everyone else has visitors today. Mary Sue musta forgot me. Thought about Grandma today – rest her soul – used to beg me to go to church with her. Wish I had. I'll try the Bible again but I'm too blue to focus and this is a strange story.*

"And the Lord opened the mouth of the ass and she said to Balaam. 'What have I done unto thee that thou has smitten me these

three times?'

And Balaam said unto the ass, "Because thou has mocked me: I would there were a sword in mine hand, for now would I kill thee."

And the ass said unto Balaam, "Am not I thine ass, upon which thou has ridden ever since I was thine unto this day? Was I ever wont to do so unto thee?"

And he said, "Nay."

Then the Lord opened the eyes of Balaam, and he saw the angel of the Lord standing in the way, and his sword was drawn in his hand...

That's a funny story. Least my mood's lighter. God shoulda sent me an angel. Maybe I wouldn't be here. But...I'd probably be like Balaam and not see the angel.

<u>*January 13, 1930*</u> *– Grandma would be proud. Went to church tonight. Baptist Church is bringing a revival in to us. We use the dining hall. Don't know how much good it'll do, but I owe it to grandma after all the years she raised me when Momma left us Preacher told us we had to repent for the sins we committed. Guess he means robbing a bank. But all I did was drive a car. Didn't even know what they planned to do. Musta been wrong and I sure am sorry I did it, but I still gotta pay my time.*

<u>*January 19*</u> *– Wrote a nasty letter to Mary Sue. Preacher would say that ain't Christian, but he don't have to live in a small cell with no idea about what's going on with his family. Wonder if God really cares? Why should he?*

<u>*January 21*</u> *– Letter from Mary Sue and the boys today. She ignored my nastiness. Said the boys are growing and miss me. Junior and George wrote notes too. Hope they stay in school and out of trouble. Wish I had. Just wanted easy money for my family. Ha! Easy money. The easier it seems, the more trouble it causes! But I get the last laugh. Ha! Ha!*

<u>*January 22*</u> *– Tonight the last night of the revival. I went all ten days. Preacher said God forgives me, so I'm trying to live better. Even started weaving. Hope I can make few dollars for the family.*

<u>*January 31*</u> *– Letter from Oyler today. Said he would visit soon. Wonder why? One from Dolly too. Good to hear from "friends."*

<u>*February 2*</u> *–Oyler came today. Thought we had a friendly visit, but he left angry. Said he'd see me again, but I doubt it.*

<u>*February 28*</u> *– Professor Snook electrocuted tonight at 7:11 p.m. Met him once. Seemed like a nice fellow. Claimed he was innocent.*

GREAT-GRANDPA'S DIARY

Guess they all do, but he seemed so sincere.

<u>March 1</u> – Today started off dark and rainy. Heard by the grapevine, Snook was buried at Greenlawn Cemetery after short service at King's Ave. Methodist Church.

<u>March 26</u> – Mary Sue brought the boys today – in a blizzard! Said it was her day off and she promised the boys, so she gritted her teeth and drove down here. She's a good woman. So sorry I let her down. Part of the Bible verses for today truly speak of her. "The fear of the Lord is the beginning of wisdom; all who follow his precepts have good understanding. To him belongs eternal praise." Psalm 110:10

<u>March 27</u> – Received word from Paris Writers Magazine. Sounds like they want some of my jokes I sent – especially the one about the robber left holding the bag. I may be a loser, but maybe I'll be a published loser. Ha! Ha! "Give thanks to the Lord, for he is good; his love endures forever." Psalm 118:1

<u>April 1</u> – April Fool's Day. Grandpa – God rest his soul – loved this day. He was a jokester.

<u>April 7</u> – Received birthday wishes from Dad, Marie, Mary Sue, George, Junior and Mrs. Warren Zurphy of Wauseon, Ohio. That was a surprise. Wish I could be home to celebrate.

<u>April 8</u> – Sam died today of heart failure. They took him to the infirmary last week. I sure miss him. We used to talk religion. He was a good man – got into trouble with the wrong people – like a lot of us did.

<u>April 12</u> – Junior's birthday today. Can't believe he's 12. He's the man of the house since I'm gone. Hope he does a better job than I did.

<u>April 13</u> – Ezra Goldmeister and his family visited today. Sure was a surprise. Came down from Toledo to spend the Jewish Easter with family.

<u>April 20</u> – Today is Easter. Wish I could go to church with my family. Feel tense today – like something's going to happen. Never held much store in ESP and all that stuff, but I sure feel weird – maybe because I lost 50¢ in a bet on the ball game. Ha! Ha!

"There are no more entries until May 4", Corey wrote at the end of the words she had copied.

<u>May 4</u> – Haven't been able to write much since the fire. So much

confusion. Lota men died – guards too. Called in the National Guard. We were all moved from our cellblock to another. Burned my hands pretty bad trying to help put out the fire. Thought sure I'd seen my last day. Managed to save my Bible and my diary. Have some important things to write before I kick off. Hands are better now, so I'll do better. Tomorrow is George's 11th birthday.

"*But now, this is what the Lord says – he who created you, O Jacob, he who formed you, O Israel, 'Fear not, for I have redeemed you; I have summoned you by name, you are mine. When you pass through the waters, I will be with you; and when you pass through the rivers, they will not sweep over you. When you walk through the fire, you will not be burned; the flames will not set you ablaze. For I am the Lord, your God...Since you are precious and honored in my sight and because I love you.*" Isaiah 43: 1-4

"The next entry is July – two entries, 22 and 28. After that, there is none until the following year."

<u>May 31, 1931</u> – *It's raining at 7:45 a.m. Feeling O.K, but just can't seem to write. Said what I need to say. Will mail my diaries to Mary Sue. God has changed my life, but have a feeling that the Toledo Gang don't believe that. They'll find a way to get to me.*

Corey took a sip of cold coffee, made a face and glanced at the clock. *Roger should be here soon. After we go to see Dad, maybe we can block out some time to work on this diary – if he doesn't have to run down a story and I don't have an emergency at the library.*

Corey frowned. In the four years she had been head librarian at Masontown Public Library, she had never had any trouble with either people or the building. But in the last three nights, the alarm had gone off twice indicating a break in. Of course, no one was there when the police arrived. Several small accidents had occurred to disrupt library use – books falling unaccountably from a shelf nearly landing on an elderly patron, an electrical glitch prevented the use of the new checkout system and just yesterday morning, one of the toilets overflowed creating a watery mess at the back of the library. Nothing serious – just time consuming for her as head librarian and CEO. Hopefully she could take today off without unpleasant consequences.

Corey placed her jacket and purse on the arm of the couch and glanced at the clock above the kitchen sink as the doorbell rang and

Corey hurried to open the door for Roger.

"Am I late?" he asked.

"You're never late," she said. "Coffee is ready. Would you like an omelet this morning? I have some eggs I need to use up."

"That's as good an excuse as any for cooking up a nice breakfast for your hungry fiancé. Are you trying to impress me?"

"Don't need to," she said, flashing the ring on her left hand. "I already have you hooked."

"Ah, yes you do," he said and gave her a very long good morning kiss.

Roger and Corey enjoyed their breakfast as if it would be their last time of leisure. Had they only known!

Six

As if playing an April Fool's joke in October, the sun warmed the air to early June temperatures.

"I thought we were supposed to get snow flurries by weekend," said Corey as she shed her sweater and threw it to the back seat of Roger's car.

"Mother Nature changed her mind," said Roger, "which is fine with me."

Roger parked in the outer hospital parking lot. "We'll park here so we can enjoy the brief walk in the sun," he said.

A few minutes later, they entered Daniel's room and found him sitting in the chair beside the bed. He no longer had the breathing tube or catheter, but still had to drag the IV with him when he walked up and down the hall or went to the bathroom. Thankfully, he was breathing on his own and eating some soft foods. He smiled broadly when he saw them.

"Looks like I'll make it after all," he said.

Corey gave him a kiss on his stubbly cheek. "It looks like it."

"You must still be feeling pretty rough," said Roger, "but I must say you're looking much better than you did in the wee hours of Monday morning."

"Sherylee tells me you have started reading the diary and looking for information. Please remember that someone followed me from east to west and back again because I had that diary, so be careful. Maybe you should make copies and put the original copies where they'll be safe."

"We will," said Roger. "We intended to do it earlier, but time just got away from us. It is intriguing, but we need more information. Just flipping through the pages, he stops about mid-April 1930, adds a few pages in May and July, then nothing until May 31, 1931. From that point on, it's blank."

"I don't know how long he was in prison. He sent his belongings to my grandmother and said he was expecting to be paroled. She never heard from him again."

"On May 31, he mentioned that he had sent his things to Mary Sue, but he had a feeling the Toledo gang would get to him before he could get home."

"It's possible, but his body was never discovered – at least my grandmother never received any word."

"We'll find out, Dad," said Corey.

"I thought Corey and I could go to Columbus Monday and sort through the files and micro-film at the Ohio Historical Society. They have a special section for prisons. We would go today, but we'll probably need a couple of days. Since today is Friday, nothing will be open tomorrow or Sunday."

"I know Sherylee owns and operates *Sherylee's Fitness Center.* She can take the time off because she's the boss. She has dependable employees who can run the shop, but how are you two getting time off for…"

"This is my job," said Roger. "I'm a free-lance writer for the Masontown Gazette and other papers and magazines. I don't have an office, but I work on various assignments at home. As long as I meet deadlines, they don't care where I work. And Corey is head librarian at Masontown Public Library. She has a good staff under her, so she can take a few days off. They can always contact her by phone if they have a problem."

"You said you read the diary," said Corey.

"I did. Several times," said Daniel. "I spent most of the last two decades hiding and running. When I finally found someone who believed me and was willing to help me, I decided that maybe I could come home. One of the themes in the Bible portion of my grandfather's diary was his loneliness and homesickness for his family. Suddenly, it hit me what I'd done to *my* family. He couldn't correct his mistake, but I had to at least try. No matter how scared I was, I had no right to run away and I had to try to do something about it, so I worked my way back home flipping burgers, mopping floors and anything else I could do for a few dollars to get me home, all the while watching over my shoulder.

"I did see that man several times. And every time I saw him, I called the FBI who was keeping track of him."

"I think I hear Mom coming down the hall," said Corey."

Daniel laughed. "She does have a special walk doesn't she – sort of half skipping like she's anxious to see what's around the next corner."

Corey laughed with him. "That's the way she is and that's the way she raised me. There *is* always something interesting to learn, to do and to see."

"Are you talking about me?" Sherylee said as she sailed into the room. "Isn't it a beautiful day? We need to ask the nurse if we can wheel you down the hall to the little visiting area that has floor to ceiling windows, green plants and a huge fish tank in case you want to go fishing. But most of all you can see the sunshine and watch the birds flying around the parking lot looking for crumbs."

"Well, that's better than looking up and finding birds dropping droppings," said Daniel with a touch of sarcasm.

Roger laughed. "Well you two, enjoy the sunshine. Corey and I are going to work on a diary then get it in a box at the bank. We'll see you later."

"Don't spend the whole day working," said Sherylee. "Take time to enjoy this beautiful day."

"We will," said Corey as she waved to her parents, who were already lost in their own conversation.

***

Stepping off the elevator, Roger placed his hand on Corey's arm and led her out the front door of the hospital. "Let's grab a cup of coffee at the donut shop around the corner."

"Why? We can go…"

"I want one of their special donuts and …"

Corey gave him a quizzical look. Roger wasn't much of a sweet eater. She couldn't remember the last time he ever really asked for something like a donut. But, he seemed anxious for some reason, so she started walking to the parking lot with him. "All right," she said. "I could use a cup of coffee. Shall we walk or drive?"

"Let's walk. We can go through the parking lot to the street. Dolly's Donut Den. It's only about a five-minute walk and it's too beautiful a day to waste in a car."

Corey frowned. *Is this my Roger? He never walks when he can ride and he never eats sweets in the middle if the morning. Whatever, it is a beautiful day.*

Hand in hand, Roger and Corey strolled down the street as if they were tourists on vacation and had no deadlines or reason to hurry. Roger stopped, lifted his foot to a low brick wall. He retied his shoe, that didn't need retied, then moved on. They crossed the street and he stopped to look at something in the pharmacy window.

Corey frowned. *There was nothing wrong with that shoelace and Roger never window-shops. What is he up to?* She laughed and said, "Would you rather go into the drug store for a soda?"

Roger grinned. "No. Just looking to see if anyone I know is in there."

Corey gave him another puzzled glance as he took her arm and pulled her to the Donut Den next door. He pulled the door open and set in motion a string of small jingle bells over the door. The aroma of rising dough, fresh baked and fried donuts and strong coffee mingled to bring a Pavlov-type reaction.

Corey found a booth by the window while Roger placed their order at the counter. When it was ready, he carried the two cups of steaming coffee and two fresh glazed apple fritters to the table. She licked her lips and sighed with pleasure, before even taking the first bite.

"Those smell heavenly. I forgot this place was here. Thank you for bringing me."

Roger smiled at her. "It does smell good." He took a taste of fritter and a sip of coffee and declared both as good as they smelled.

"So why did we come here?" Corey sipped her coffee and peered at him across the rim of her cup. "You aren't that crazy about donuts – although they are good – and I could have made coffee at home."

"You're right. I have ulterior motives. Glance out the window – not as if you are looking for someone, but maybe checking the weather."

"Roger, are you..."

"Humor me."

Corey turned her head slightly and checked the sky. "Still sunny. No clouds. No rain."

"Do you see anyone out there just standing as if waiting for someone?"

"Why would...? Yes, as a matter of fact, there is a man across the street just leaning against the lamppost smoking a cigarette. Do we know him? He looks familiar."

"He should. He's the man I almost hit when we left the parking garage the other night. He's been following us ever since. I saw him in the lobby, but didn't think anything of it until I realized he's been there every day. He's either following us, or he's just someone who is doing what we're doing and going where we're going except he's waiting for us to leave rather than coming in here."

"But why? Maybe we should just go ask him if he's looking for someone."

"Corey think sweetheart. Your father has just given us a diary of a man who spent who knows how long in prison for bank robbery. He was only one of four. Suppose he was involved in something evil and harmful – like one of the Mafia-type gangs of the Twenties. Suppose the authorities never recovered the money. Suppose the families of the other three men are still looking for it. And, remember a man *was* killed."

"Roger, you are really getting into this novel you want to write. That was so long ago."

"Not if Harry wrote some damaging information about someone in a position of power in his diary."

"Roger, surely you don't think…How would anyone know?"

"He was in the lobby when I came in Monday morning. You didn't see him because you took the second floor bridge. He must have followed Daniel there."

"Do you think he is the same…?"

"One who hounded your father for twenty years? I think we better see if there's a back door and find a place where we can copy that diary before we do anything else."

The room was empty, except for one other customer at the counter drinking coffee. Dolly came out to talk. She wiped a vacated table then came to the booth where Corey and Roger sat. "Did you folks enjoy the donuts? Did you sign up for the free drawing?"

"We certainly did enjoy the donuts and coffee," said Roger.

"I didn't see a free drawing," said Corey. "What's the prize?"

"A free dozen donuts of your choice."

"Sounds good to me," said Roger.

"Me too," said Corey. "Where do we sign up?"

"Just put your name, address and phone number on one of those cards at the counter and drop it in the fish bowl."

Corey went to sign up for the prize and Roger asked, "Say, I wonder if you have a back door that we could use."

Dolly looked startled, but answered, "That would depend on why you want to go sneaking off. You already paid so can't be that."

Corey listened from the counter while filling out the card for the drawing.

"To be honest, there's a man following us. We don't know why, but it's rather irritating," said Roger.

"You mean that chap across the street?"

"Yes. Do you know him?"

"He's one of the local street bums. Likes to think he's a lady's man. I don't allow him in here because he pesters my girls. You'll find the back door through the kitchen. If you wait about three minutes, you can grab a ride on the truck. We got a delivery to make out at the mall."

"We need to do some shopping for a party later," said Roger. "So that would work."

"There's a party store next door to the café where Mike is making the delivery."

"Thanks Dolly. We appreciate your help."

"You folks just have a good day and enjoy that sunshine."

Roger slid out of the booth and joined Corey, who was just putting the card into the fish bowl.

"There a back door," he said. "Her delivery truck is going to the mall. We can get a cab back."

"I heard her," said Corey.

"Then let's go."

Dolly walked to the back door with them and spoke to the truck driver. "Mike, these kids need a ride to the mall. Do you mind?"

"Not if you don't, Ms. Dolly. Come on folks. I'm ready to roll."

Roger and Corey climbed aboard the truck – an older model with a bench seat.

"We really appreciate this," said Corey.

"Don't mind helping folks," said Mike.

A few minutes later, he pulled the truck to a stop behind Rick's Place at the mall.

"We're here," said Mike. "Follow me and you can go through the restaurant and on into the mall."

"Thanks again," said Roger reaching to shake Mike's hand.

"Any time," he grinned. "Glad to help."

Seven

Like lovers window shopping, Corey and Roger strolled hand in hand around the mall. After several rounds and they were sure no one was following them, they entered The Copy Shop and made their way to the self-serve machines. Roger pulled the notebook from his backpack.

"Maybe we should make two copies," he said. "We can put the original in the bank and keep the copies for working with – one for you and one for me."

"That makes sense," said Corey. "We could put the originals in my safe deposit box. What about the Bible? Should we copy those pages too?"

"There's not much there – much of it is duplicated in the diary. I think it was primarily a way to keep up with the date and his readings for the day. Apparently he promised someone – the church ladies, God or himself – that he would read five chapters a day and found it easier to jot down notes and write in the diary later."

"You're probably right. The diary is all that man – Jones, was it? – wanted. I read the diary and jotted a few notes this morning before you came, but we need to look at it together."

"I have a better idea," said Roger. "Why don't we drive down to Columbus this afternoon and get a head start on some research. I'll drive and you can read the diary to me on the way. We can either spend the weekend there, or drive back tonight and go back on Monday if we need to."

"That sounds like an awful lot of running back and forth. We don't have a car with us remember. Do we want to go by my place and get my car or to the hospital and get yours? And do we want to do any of it before we go to the bank? Either way it will be noon before we can even think about leaving. Two hours to Columbus, we'll only have three hours at the most."

"If we stand around trying to plan it all out, we won't even get home." Roger sounded irritated. He and Corey had had this argument before. She wanted to have some idea of a plan before proceeding

GREAT-GRANDPA'S DIARY

into anything. He just wanted to jump in and do.

"Either way, I better call Mom and let her know what's going on," said Corey. "She needs to know that we were followed?"

"I guess she needs to be aware in case they try to get to her or your father."

"Why don't you call a taxi, while I call Mother?"

Corey pulled her cell phone from her purse and punched in her mother's cell number. No answer. "She must not have it on in Dad's hospital room. I'll give her five minutes and try again. I don't want to leave a message unless I have to."

Before Corey pocketed her phone, it rang. She smiled as she checked the incoming number. "Hi Mom," she said. "I called…" Corey stopped, listened, paled and glanced at Roger. "Do you want us to come back there? ... Make sure the police understand that they need to keep a 24-hour guard on him. I was calling to tell you that someone has been following Roger and me. We managed to evade him, so he must have gone to see Dad instead. We think he's after the diary. Roger's car is in the hospital lot, so we are calling a cab. We'll stop at the hospital before we do anything else this afternoon."

Corey replaced her phone in her purse. Roger grabbed her hand. "What happened?"

"The man who has been following Dad forced himself into his room and began threatening him. He wants the diary. Mom was just returning from the restroom down the hall, when she saw him. She ran toward the room, calling for help, but Dad has suffered a setback. They called security who called the police. They'll keep a guard on him until the man is caught."

"The man who was following him? Wonder if it's the same man who followed us?"

"I don't know, but probably. When he realized we gave him the slip, he tried a different tactic. Maybe I should call Mom back and tell her to tell the police to talk to Dolly."

"He's probably long gone by now. Let's go the hospital first. We'll check on your mom and dad then decide on what to do next. If we still want to go to Columbus, I'll take you to your apartment for your bag. Your father is as safe as he can be where he is – especially if they set a guard outside his room."

***

The taxi stopped at the front entrance of the hospital. Roger paid him and followed Corey who was already almost to the elevator.

47

Minutes later, they were standing beside Daniel's bed.

"Are you all right?" asked Corey.

"I think so. He wanted the diary – insists it belongs to him. It was the same man who followed me so many years." Daniel was pale and his hands shook.

"Do you have the artist's sketch they made for you at the clinic?"

"Yes, it's in my backpack in the closet."

Roger went to the closet door. He turned back to Daniel. "May I look?"

"Sure."

Roger got the picture from Daniel's bag and handed it to Corey.

"That's the same man who followed us all right, but..."

"But what?" asked Roger.

"I don't know. Something isn't clicking, but I'm not sure what. It'll come to me when I'm falling asleep tonight."

"Don't call me," said Roger. "Write it down and tell me tomorrow."

"But why does he keep insisting it's his diary, when it was Harry Kahlor's? Is he somehow related?"

"If I can remember back twenty years," said Daniel, "he said something about my grandfather promising it to his grandfather when he visited the prison."

"That's it," said Corey.

"What's what?" said Roger.

"I remembered what bothered me about the man following us. Dolly said he is one of the local jerks who pesters her girls all the time. She gives him coffee and a donut and sends him on his way."

"So what's wrong with that?"

"I think what Corey is trying to say is that if the man has been following me for twenty years, how can he be a local pest?"

"That's right, Dad," said Corey. "Either he has a twin brother, or someone is lying about something."

"Why does he want the diary so badly?" asked Roger, "and why would Dolly lie about him?"

"Maybe he thinks there's something in it about him or someone he knows," said Corey.

"Oh, he was probably just a homeless person with mental problems," said Sherylee. "And Dolly sees so many homeless people that all begin to look alike."

"Mom..." Corey glanced at her mother. *After all the tension of*

Dad's return and surgery, she is probably weary of it all. "I hope you are right," she finished and looked at Roger. "Maybe we better contact the FBI and wait until Monday to go to Columbus. They need to know where the man is and what he's up to."

"You're probably right," said Roger, disappointment in his voice. "But if the police were here, they are in charge. They'll call the FBI if necessary."

"Maybe," said Daniel, "but I told them I would contact them any time he showed up."

"Well I don't think we have to worry about him coming back," said Sherylee. "The police have set a guard outside the room around the clock and I have Reggie to look after me. We'll be fine, so you can go to Columbus if you want to. The quicker you go get some information, the quicker we'll know what's going on."

Daniel's nurse was checking his vital signs. "You've had quite a morning Mr. Kahlor."

"A little unsettling," he said, "but I'm fine. I got my family. What more can I ask for?"

"My guess is you could ask for a little peace and quiet so your body can recuperate," said Corey. The nurse smiled at her and nodded in agreement.

"Why don't we go down to the cafeteria for a bite of lunch," said Roger, picking up on the need to vacate the room.

"You two go along," said Sherylee. "Besides, you need to get on the road…"

"That can wait. You need lunch. We need lunch. Dad needs rest. They have a guard outside the room. Let's go." Corey took her mother's arm and began pulling her out of the room.

"She's right, Sherylee," said Daniel. "I feel a nap coming on."

"He'll be just fine, Mrs. Kahlor. We'll call you if he needs you."

"Well, all right. I *am* hungry now that I think about it, but what about your trip to Columbus?"

"We won't get much research done today anyway," said Corey. "Today's Friday and all the offices close early and will be closed all weekend."

"We still might go for a fun weekend then start our research early Monday morning," said Roger.

Corey glanced at Roger who ignored her and began filling his tray with food in the cafeteria line. *And just how much time does he think I can take off at the library? We need to seriously talk about his impulsiveness.*

Corey made sure they took a very long lunch break, so it was almost two o'clock when they went back to Daniel's room. He was still sleeping, so Corey suggested that her mom should lean back in the lounge chair and take a nap too.

"We'll call you when we get on the road," said Roger.

"Or not," remarked Corey.

Sherylee raised her eyebrows and mouthed the word *trouble?* Corey just smiled, waved and headed for the elevator.

Eight

In the parking lot, Roger fumbled with his keys. "Roger, are you angry with me for taking time to take mother to lunch?"

"Of course not. I'm the one that suggested it, remember?"

"But you *are* upset about the delay."

Roger sighed, frowned and answered begrudgingly, "It just seems everything is working against us spending time together. I suppose we may as well forget about going to Columbus today."

"If we planned ahead, we wouldn't have all these interruptions," said Corey.

"Oh sure, we can plan for someone to follow us and make an unscheduled trip to the mall without a car and have someone breaking into your dad's room."

"Roger if you're going to get all snarly about it, maybe you better just take me home and let's forget the whole thing."

Roger glared at Corey then peeled out of the hospital lot faster than he should have.

"We didn't stop at the bank to put these originals in my safe deposit box."

Roger threw up his hands and shook his head. His anger was returning. "Make up your mind. Do you want to go to the bank or to your apartment? If we aren't going to Columbus, I have work to do for the paper."

"Roger, the bank closed at two today. I can just hide the originals in my apartment somewhere."

They drove in silence until they were near Corey's apartment.

"Why don't you let me off by the elevator in the parking garage – just in case anyone is watching for me to drive in – or out."

"Getting a little nervous about being alone?" Roger looked as if he wanted her to ask him to stay.

"I'm not afraid, but no use courting trouble. I'll call you later." Corey got out of the car and walked quickly to the glass doors without looking back. She heard tires squeal as she inserted her keycard into the door.

Corey stepped into the elevator and rose noiselessly to the second floor. She wanted to run, slam the door and fling herself across the bed for a good cry. But, she was too tired to run and doubted if she had the energy to slam a door. Settling for a slow, dragging of one foot after the other, she ambled the short distance down the hall to her apartment. She pulled the keycard from her pocket and reached toward the door. Suddenly she pulled her hand back as if the keyhole had been a coiled rattler.

The door was ajar. She backed away from it and pulled her phone from her purse. She punched in 911 as she backed down the hall toward the elevator. The dispatcher answered. Corey reported a break-in and gave directions to her apartment. Then she punched in Roger's number. Three rings. She was about to hang up. *He must really be mad at me.*

"Corey, you know I don't use the phone when I'm driving."

"Sorry, Roger, I just…"

"…changed your mind and want some company?" She could hear the sarcasm in his voice.

"Yes…no…maybe. Someone broke into my apartment."

"Are you in there alone?"

"No. I'm at the elevator. I called the police. The door is ajar. I wouldn't go in. I'm not that dumb."

"Corey, I didn't mean to sound…I'll be right there. If anyone comes out of the apartment, get out of there."

"I will."

She waited. Minutes ticked by in slow motion until she heard sirens outside and footsteps racing up the stairs. Roger burst through the stairwell door just ahead of two officers with guns ready for action.

"You the lady that called about a break-in?"

"Yes," she answered. "I'm Corey Kahlor and I just got home and found the door to my apartment ajar. I stopped to…never mind you don't need all that information. I just thought it would be better to report it before entering, just in case the person who broke in is still in there."

"And who are you?" he asked turning to Roger.

"Roger Trent, her fiancé. She called me after she called you. I was only a couple blocks away."

The officer moved toward the door and called out, "This is the police. Whoever is in there, come out with your hands in the air."

GREAT-GRANDPA'S DIARY

There was no answer.

He called out again. "This is the police. Come out now."

Still no answer.

The officer kicked the door open. Corey gasped. The living room looked like a major tornado had been through it. Chairs and couch were upside down. Curtains hung half on and half off the hooks. Desk drawers were upside down on piles of papers. The television was lying on the floor face down beside a man lying face up, his eyes staring at the ceiling. It was the man who had followed them that morning and threatened her father later.

Corey cried out and turned away into Roger's open arms.

"Looks like the intruder can't come out," said the officer, pulling his phone from his belt to call the coroner and homicide division.

"If he was the intruder," asked Roger, "who killed him? There must have been at least two of them."

"Unless you two caught him in the act, killed him then stepped back out into the hall to call the police and wait for us."

"Now wait a minute…"

"Roger, don't. He has to think of all aspects."

"Don't you think it would be a good idea to check the rest of the apartment?" Roger gripped Corey's arms almost too tightly.

"Joe's doing that, but nobody else touches anything until Detective Turner gets here."

"Is there a cat or dog in here somewhere?" asked Joe poking his head around the bedroom door.

"No," said Corey. "Not right now. I keep cat supplies – litter box, food, dishes – for Reggie, my mother's cat. He stays with me sometimes."

"Must be a big cat. These are pretty big dishes."

"He a Bengal cat – very large."

"Can we at least sit down?" asked Roger nodding to Corey.

"Maybe I could make some coffee," suggested Corey glancing at the small kitchen on the other side of the dividing counter. "You can see me there. I won't touch anything but the coffee maker."

"Well, all right, but don't touch anything else."

Corey tiptoed around the officer into the kitchen, Roger right behind her. They stopped. Roger whistled. Every drawer in the kitchen was upside down on the floor. Cabinet doors stood open, canned good shoved aside. Even the flour and sugar canisters lay empty on the floor.

"Maybe I won't make coffee," said Corey eyeing the coffee canister upside down in the far corner. The coffee maker lay on its side, the glass pot in several pieces. "They must be desperate or crazy."

"At least the chairs are in one piece. We can sit and wait for Detective Turner."

"Do you know him?" asked Corey. Roger had done some crime reporting for the paper and knew many of the police personnel.

"Yes, as a matter of fact, I do." Roger grinned and Corey felt at smidgen bit better.

Nine

The sound of rolling gurney wheels and shuffling feet announced the arrival of the coroner and possibly Detective Matthew Turner. The officer, who had arrived first, suddenly stood at attention. Corey expected him to salute, but he didn't. A tall, broad shouldered man stepped into the room, approached the officer and spoke in a low gravelly voice.

Corey suddenly felt as if her small, adequate apartment was only a dollhouse and a giant had stepped into it. She shook her head and took a deep breath, needing a gulp of air before the space became a vacuum.

"Corey? Are you all right?" Roger's voice brought her run-away imagination back to reality. The room was still adequate for all of them and the air returned in sufficient quantity. She nodded to Roger. "Just..." She shrugged. He patted her hand and turned back to see what Detective Turner was doing.

"Officer Jones? You the first to arrive?" said the detective.

"Yes sir."

"Want to tell me what happened?"

"The dispatcher sent me to check out a call for a B & E in this apartment. The door was ajar and these two persons – he nodded toward Corey and Roger – were waiting in the hall by the elevator. I called for the intruder to come out. There was no sound inside, so I kicked the door open and found the body. I called you and Doc Morrison. They wanted to sit so I let them go in the kitchen where I could see them."

Detective Turner turned toward Roger and Corey for the first time. A broad grin – at least Corey thought it was a grin – crossed his face. Amidst all the facial hair above and below his mouth it was hard to tell. "Roger Trent. How did you manage to get here before I even got the call?"

"Matt, good to see you again. Meet my fiancée, Corey Kahlor."

"You live here?"

"Corey does."

Detective Turner stretched his hand to Corey. She felt her hand lost in his and was glad he was not one of those persons who had to squeeze the life out of a hand in order to greet a person.

"So, is there any reason for this? Anything you can tell me?"

"Actually, we can somewhat," said Roger. "The man staining her carpet with his blood has been following us for several days and apparently shadowed Corey's father for about twenty years."

"Want to explain further?"

"It's rather a long story," said Roger.

"Give me a short version. We'll get the rest later."

"Short version?" Corey glanced at Roger then back to Detective Turner. "My dad, who died twenty years ago, returned, had a heart attack and gave us a diary from his grandfather. Apparently, someone wants it. They followed him for twenty years and us for four days. He attacked my father in the hospital this morning and now this." She swung her arm to indicate the trashed apartment.

Turner stared, mouth open. "You're right. It sounds like a long story. Your dead father returned?" Turner looked at her, eyes full of skepticism – as if she might be trying to make a joke. You will need to come down to headquarters and to give your statement. Do you have someplace to stay for a few days while we go over this place?"

"I'll stay with my mom on Walnut Street."

"Why don't you stop by Mrs. Kahlor's place around six? I'll order a pizza or something and we can talk," said Roger.

"Might just do that. You can give your statement on my tape recorder and someone will type it tomorrow."

"We'll get out of here then," said Roger. "We'll see you around six – or whenever you're free."

"Somewhere in that neighborhood," said Turner.

Corey handed him a slip of paper on which she wrote her mother's address. Then she and Roger left, taking the elevator to the garage level.

"I'll take my car and park it in Mom's garage tonight. I should go to the library tomorrow – too many weird things happening. I wonder..." She stopped, shook her head and finished with, "never mind." *Of course, those minor irritations at the library have nothing to do with what's happening here. Do they?*

***

Roger pulled into the driveway behind Corey then followed her through the garage to the kitchen. Corey went immediately to the coffee maker. Soon it was bubbling and gurgling like a happy brook flowing timelessly with no cares to slow it down.

Reggie padded into the kitchen and rubbed against Corey's legs. She reached down to scratch his ears. "Hi, Reggie. How's my big boy today?"

"Meow," said Reggie then gave her a small purr.

"You don't sound too sure of yourself," said Corey.

Reggie swished his tail and went for a drink of water from his special bowl.

"Roger, what have we gotten ourselves into?" Corey asked as she began to pull things from the refrigerator – beef cubes, onions, mushrooms."

"What are you doing?" asked Roger

"You invited Detective Turner to dinner. I'm making beef stroganoff."

"I said I would order pizza," said Roger with a note of irritation.

"I know, but Mom should be home about six. She hasn't been eating or sleeping very well these last few days. She needs a hot meal."

"You sure she's coming then?"

"No, but I'll call her and tell her we have company coming. She'll be here. But… Roger, what is going on? Who is that man who attacked my father? Why did he follow him for twenty years? Why didn't he just take the books? Why did he trash my apartment? Why did they kill him and leave him on my living room floor?"

"That's a lot of questions. Maybe Turner can give us some answers," said Roger, wrapping his arms around her, holding her next to him.

"Maybe we should contact the FBI like Dad suggested. He's already been in touch with them."

"We need to mention that to Turner. The murder investigation is his territory. If I know Turner, he won't want to share with anyone – even the FBI."

"I don't care about turf issues. I just want them – whoever they are – to leave us alone."

"I know one thing," said Roger.

"What's that?"

"There's more to that diary and Bible than appears on the surface. I wonder if your father knows more than he's telling us, or if he's as much in the dark as we are."

"Maybe that's why he told us to hide them in a safe place. He knows they mean trouble, but he's not sure what's in that diary that's so important to them. He didn't want us to get involved. That's why he told us to hide them in a safe place." Corey pulled away from his embrace and continued chopping beef cubes and onions.

"Are you sure?" asked Roger.

"Sure about what?"

"Well, what do you really know about Daniel Kahlor? He's been gone most of your life."

"You're right. He's a stranger to me, but Mom…"

"Maybe she's seeing what she wants to see."

Corey paused with her knife midair and turned to face Roger. "I can't believe that. Mom is the most level-headed person I know."

"Well, I think so too, but if I find out he deliberately drew you into something that could cause you or your mother harm, he's going to wish he never came back from the dead."

"Roger!"

"I mean it. I don't take too kindly to people setting my girl and her mother up for a big fall."

"But…" Before Corey could protest further, the coffee pot gave one last gasp and gurgle. "The coffee is ready. Why don't you pour a couple of cups while I put this on to cook, then I'll call Mom and let her know what's happening here and make sure there's no more trouble there."

Roger opened the cabinet and removed two cups, filled them with the hot brew savoring the aroma that filled the room. "I don't know which smells best, the fresh perked coffee or the browning beef and onions."

Corey picked up the kitchen phone and dialed her mother's cell phone. She smiled her appreciation at Roger as she waited for her to answer. She turned back to the phone as her mother's voice said, "Hello, Corey."

Roger took the coffee to the dining room and began spreading out the pages of the copied diary while Corey talked to Sherylee. When she joined him, she picked up her cup and took a sip.

"She sounds really tired," said Corey. "She said Dad is doing all right, but they're keeping a close watch on him. She'll be here by six. Maybe we can convince her to go to bed early. Turner shouldn't need her."

"He might have some questions about the attack on your father, but not much beyond that. But if I know your mother, she won't leave until she's heard everything."

"You're probably right. We have about an hour before we need to clear the table for dinner. Why don't we just read aloud? Sometimes hearing the words make them clearer."

***

Reggie met Sherylee at the door and stood on his back paws with front paws on her stomach. "Meow, meow, meow," he said as if trying to tell her that Corey and Roger were there and were messing up her kitchen.

"I'm sorry, Reggie," she said speaking to him as if he were her child instead of her pet. "I know I've been gone a lot. I'm glad Corey and Roger are taking care of you. I understand we'll have another guest, so you be on your best behavior."

"Meow?" said Reggie as if saying, "Who me?"

Sherylee had no sooner hung up her coat and given Reggie some attention when the doorbell rang. "That must be our guest, now."

Reggie's fur bristled and a low growl sounded in his throat. Sherylee glanced at him as she reached for the door and invited Detective Turner in.

"You must be Detective Turner. Corey said you would be coming. I'm Sherylee and this is Sir Reginald – Reggie, for short."

"Is he a wild cat?"

"No, just big. He's a Bengal and very gentle – most of the time." Reggie was standing back, fur on edge, teeth bared like a dog about to attack.

"Cat's don't like me," said Turner. "I guess they know I'm a dog person."

"Probably," said Sherylee, "but he won't attack you. He'll just ignore you, won't you Reggie?"

Roger joined them at the door as Reggie glared at Turner, turned and ambled off, tail swishing. "Corey is putting dinner on the table. We can eat first and work later."

"I appreciate this," said Turner, following Roger to the dining room. "Not being married, I don't often get home cooked meals."

"Corey is a good cook," said Sherylee.

"I learned from the best," said Corey.

The meal passed with pleasantries and no talk about the misfortunes of the day until Corey and Sherylee started to clear the table. "I'll make a fresh pot of coffee," said Roger and we can go to the living room to talk."

They all helped clear the table then Sherylee moved to her favorite gold upholstered overstuffed chair at the end of the rectangular glass-topped coffee table. Sergeant Turner took the matching chair at the opposite end of the table, leaving the couch for Roger and Corey, who sat together, placing their cups on the coffee table.

Turner leaned forward to place his cup on the end of the table. Reggie ambled out from behind the couch, walked between Turner and the table, leaving fur on his pants legs and looked up at him with what looked like a smirk. Turner jerked his hand back, spilling coffee on his knee. Reggie gave a low snarl, slapped his tail against Turner's leg and sashayed over to make himself comfortable on Sherylee's lap.

Turner frowned, brushed at his pants and set the tape recorder on the table. "Now, let's hear this long and complicated story," he said.

"Corey, you tell him since it's basically your story."

"All right." So between sips of coffee, Corey told Detective Turner the story beginning with the phone call from her mother. Detective Turner listened, making sure the tape was recording.

"Let me see if I have this right? You thought your father died when you were five. Now, he's back from the dead, so to speak. He has a diary that he carried around with him for twenty years and now wants you to keep it safe. Some goon apparently learns you have it and follows you. When you evade him, he goes to the hospital and tries to get what he wants from your father. He fails and apparently, with a partner, he trashes your apartment looking for whatever it is he wants, presumably the diary. The partner – or other unknown person – gets rid of the man who had failed at least two to three times – if you count following you this morning."

"That's about it," said Roger.

"Except that man was the same one who followed my father for twenty years," said Corey.

"Maybe," said Turner. "It's not likely it was the same man."

"But the FBI said…"

"Leave the FBI out of it," snapped Turner. "We don't need them. I can handle my own investigation."

"Whatever you say," said Roger. "So where does that leave us?"

Turner took a sip of his coffee as if to give himself time to get his anger under control. He set the cup down slowly and carefully then said, "We have more questions than solutions. The two most important ones for now, are One: What is so important about the diary? And Two: Who killed the man in your apartment? Both questions leave you vulnerable and in danger. They didn't find what they want. They'll be back. They killed once. They won't hesitate to do it again."

"Thanks, Matt. Did you have to scare her?"

"Sorry, but Corey seems like a sensible girl. She will do better knowing the facts than burying her head in the sand and hoping it will go away."

"Of course she's a sensible girl," said Sherylee. "But even sensible people have difficulty dealing with insensitive people who don't follow any rules but their own."

"You're right," said Corey. "I do need to know what I'm facing in order to protect myself, but like Mom said we aren't dealing with intelligent, law-abiding citizens. It seems the best and only way to fight it is to learn what's in that diary that is so important that they will kill for it."

"Maybe I should take the diary for safe keeping," said Turner.

Corey felt a prickle down her back. Fear? Anger? Jealousy? Whatever it was, she wasn't ready to give up the diary to anyone – not even Sergeant Turner, Masontown Homicide Detective. "It's safe where it is," she said.

"And where is that?" Turner gave Corey a cold stare.

"The less people who know, the better the secret," she said. "When you need to know, we'll see that you know."

"I could get a search warrant," said Turner.

Roger laughed as if Turner had made a joke, but Corey bristled with anger. She glared at him then got up and left the room.

"Maybe we should just burn it," said Roger.

Corey stepped back into the room with the coffee pot in her hand. "And how would they know? They haven't even contacted us asking for the diary – only briefly, when that man attacked Dad. They – whoever they are – assume we have what they want – whether we do or not. We assume they want the diary when they might want something else."

"We still need to know more about your great-grandfather, too. He was in prison for robbery, but did he leave any associates on the outside who might want revenge?" said Roger.

"Or maybe a relative who is afraid of being discovered because of something he wrote?" added Corey.

"Maybe he hid the loot from the bank heist and the families of the original gang want it." said Turner.

"It's been close to seventy years. None of them would be around now," said Corey.

"But their families would be," said Turner. "You and your father are here."

"But even if there is some money somewhere, it's stolen money. It wouldn't legally belong to any of them – or us."

"It they found it – or if Harry Kahlor left instructions in the diary as to where it is – do you think they would turn it in to the authorities? Would you?"

"Of course we would," said Corey indignantly.

"I've read the diary several times," said Roger. "He makes no mention of money except a few dollars he made weaving pillows or betting on a game. And the only names he gives are family members and close friends."

"Well if you want to check into the names further, our research department can take care of for you. Since we now have a murder investigation, I will need to know more about it."

"I thought about that," said Roger, "but I know how touchy they are about doing outside research. But you're right. You now have a murder to investigate. We'll examine the diary some more tonight."

"I'll stop by and see Mr. Kahlor and make sure we have a guard on him round the clock."

"What about my mother? Do you think she's any danger?" Corey glanced at her mother who had been silent most of the evening. Reggie lay across her lap, eyes closed, but his twitching ears told Corey he heard everything that they said. While many don't credit animals with intelligence, Corey believed that Reggie not only heard but also understood even more than they did.

"Do you have the diary?" Turner asked Sherylee.

"I believe my daughter just said she has it hidden," said Sherylee, giving Turner a cold stare. Then she added, "I saw it briefly, but I needed to be with Daniel more than I needed to know about a diary his grandfather wrote while he was in prison. Roger and Corey will work on that."

Corey glared at Turner as he turned back to Roger and said, "Please stay out of my way and out of trouble."

"Sure," said Roger grinning at his friend. "Talk to you in the morning."

Turner left and Roger asked, "What's your problem, Corey? We could have given him one of the copies."

"You will need yours for your book. And I need one for research."

"He could take the original. It would be safe in the evidence room at police headquarters."

"Would it?"

"What's that supposed to mean?"

"It means that I don't like Turner. I'm not sure I even trust him."

"Corey! He's a homicide detective. And beyond that he's my friend."

"Fine, I'll work with him, but that doesn't mean I have to like him."

"I suppose you're afraid he'll find the money and you won't…" Corey's cold, icy stare froze the rest of his words.

"Maybe we should start working on these pages, since we've invested so much time and money on getting the copies and since someone seems desperate to get their hands on them," Roger said, changing the subject. "Do we need to go back to your apartment and get some clothes? You didn't have a chance to pack when we were there."

"My apartment is a crime scene so I can't go in it. I doubt there's anything left that's worth wearing anyway. I keep a few things here. Mom and I are pretty close to the same size if I need anything." Corey grinned at her mother, who returned her smile.

"That's amazing," said Roger smiling at Sherylee.

"Not when you consider her occupation. She opened her business to help women think healthy. She raised me to think about my whole body – physical and emotional."

"Then let's get started on these pages."

"Do you need some help?" Sherylee asked.

Corey looked at her mother's tired eyes and sagging shoulders – so unlike her. "I think we can handle it. You need to get some sleep so you can face tomorrow."

Ten

As good as their intentions had been, Corey and Roger, like Sherylee, were exhausted from the unusual and frightening activities of the day. After a half hour of trying to keep their eyes open and make sense of the diary, Corey threw up her hands and said, "That's it. I've had enough. I can't stay awake any longer. You can stay up if you want to, but I'm going to bed. You know where the guest room is."

"I'm with you. We can only do so much and we've passed our limit. Goodnight."

Roger stacked the papers, placed them in a manuscript box he bought at the copy shop, and made his way to the guest room.

***

The night passed without incident as far as anyone knew. Corey woke with a start, forgetting for the moment where she was. A warm lump of something moved at the foot of the bed. She jerked her feet up toward her body then laughed as Reggie stood and stretched. He jumped from the bed with a thud and started for the door.

"Time for breakfast, Reggie?" Corey sat on the side of the bed feeling around for her slippers. She grabbed her robe and followed Reggie. She had closed the door last night, but Reggie with his size and dexterous forepaws had no problem opening closed doors.

Starting down the stairs, she heard voices in the kitchen. *Roger must be up already.* Sherylee greeted Reggie and when Corey got to the kitchen, the cat was happily chowing down on his breakfast, as was Roger.

"Everything is still hot," said Sherylee. "We thought you would be along since it's Reggie's breakfast time and I knew he was on your bed. I called the hospital and they said Daniel had a good night, but we should wait until after nine-thirty to come in. That will give him time to get his bath and breakfast."

"No more attempts to get to him?"

"Not that anyone is admitting to," said Roger. "But, I'm sure we haven't heard the last of that group of losers."

"Should we go down town and sign our reports before going to the hospital?" said Corey.

"We need to spend some time with the diary this morning," said Roger. "Turner recorded our story last night. He'll get it typed this morning, so all we have to do is read and sign it."

"I wonder how often he takes reports that way. Seems unusual," said Sherylee.

"I doubt he does very often. We're friends."

"*You* are his friend."

"Corey, you're being unfair. You haven't given him a chance."

"Maybe."

"Well, eat your breakfast. Yesterday was a little harrowing for all of us," said Sherylee.

"You can say that again," said Roger around a bite of toast.

Corey pulled out a chair, then filled her plate with soft, yellow scrambled eggs, crisp bacon and buttered toast. She hadn't been hungry when she awoke, but the blending aromas set her mouth to watering.

"Maybe Daniel will feel up to spending a little time with you on it later this afternoon," said Sherylee. "It will be better to pick out small sections of the diary rather than trying to discuss the whole book with him."

"That's a good idea," said Corey. "I've started a list of people that my great-grandfather named in the diary. Maybe Dad can tell us who they are and if they were related to his family."

"You and Roger work on the list. I have to run by the shop before I go to the hospital. We can have lunch at the cafeteria while Daniel has his lunch, then go over the names."

"Sounds like a plan," said Roger. "Now that you mention going out, I just remembered that I need to run by my apartment for some clean clothes then drop off an article for the newspaper."

"I have to stop by the center then run a couple of errands before I go see Daniel," said Sherylee. "Will you be all right here alone, Coral Rae?"

Roger laughed. "With Reggie around, I don't she'll be alone. He can protect her from anyone! What do you think Reg?"

"Meow," answered the Bengal and slapped his tail on the floor as if adding an exclamation point.

"We'll be fine," said Corey. "I'll get started on the notes. Roger can double-check them when he gets back."

***

Sherylee and Roger left. Corey sighed, smoothed the top of Reggie's head and said, "Well, Reggie, it's just you and me now. Will we ever get to the bottom of this mess?"

"Meow," Reggie gave her a sage answer as if saying, "of course."

"I hope you're right," she said. "Anyway, we need to get to work on this diary."

Corey cleared the dining room table, gathered pens, pencils and paper then went to the kitchen for coffee. Reggie began to pace back and forth from dining room to front door softly growling and muttering to himself in his special feline sound of discontent.

"Are you all right, Reggie? I know these last few days have upset your routine, but soon Dad will be home and everything will be back to normal – more or less."

"Meow?" Corey could almost hear the words, "Will they?"

She shivered, wondering what could go wrong next. *Maybe I don't really want to know.* She sighed and stroked Reggie from the top of his head to the tip of his tail. "All right, let's get to work," she said. Reggie jumped to a chair to watch her as if he were the supervisor and she the employee.

Corey laughed and was soon re-reading the diary and checking the notes she made yesterday morning before their world began to feel as if it were stuck in the eye of a hurricane. At the end of her notes, she listed related data.

January 21 – Easy money…year
January 31 – Fred Oyler – Dolly
February 2 – Fred Oyler visits
April 7 – Birthday greetings from Mrs. Warren Zurphy
April 13 – Visit from Ezra Goldmeister
April 20 – Easter Sunday

(Who are Fred Oyler, Dolly, Mrs. W. Zurphy, and Ezra Goldmeister?)

Birthdays:
    April 7 – Harry –
    April 12 – Harry Junior 12
    May 5 – George – 11

GREAT-GRANDPA'S DIARY

May 4 – mentions fire.

***

Corey read the last entry aloud, "May 31, 1931 – 7:45 a.m. Rain. Feeling O.K. Just can't seem to write. Guess I said it all. Mailing my belongings to Mary Sue this afternoon – except my Bible and diary. Will hold on to them until sure of parole date. Have a feeling Toledo Gang don't believe I changed. They'll find a way to get me."

Corey glanced up from her paper. "It sounds like he thinks someone is going to kill him while he is still in prison."

"Meow." Reggie gave the sound an emphatic punch.

Corey continued as if she were talking to a colleague. "Turner can find out for us when and how he died. I read somewhere that the prison system went through an overhaul because of so much corruption – sometime in the mid-1930s. I guess I need to research the prison system."

Corey stopped reading and glanced at the clock. "It's almost lunch time. Where is Roger? He was supposed to be back before now. Maybe I'd better give him a call and he can meet me at the hospital. We can check on Dad then take Mom for lunch."

She reached for her phone and noticed Reggie had left her. *Probably went to the kitchen for a snack or to his litter box.* She punched in Roger's number. It rang three times and he answered just as the front door opened.

"I'm here," he said and proceeded to the dining room.

Reggie ran into the room and almost knocked him down, but as Roger tried to pet him, he growled and backed away.

"Sounds like someone is unhappy," said Roger. He reached again to touch the cat, but Reggie backed away still uttering a mixture of grunts and moans.

"Reggie, are you all right, sweetie?" Corey reached for him and he backed away from her, too. He looked at the door as if he would like to bolt.

"I think he wants out," said Roger.

"He's not allowed out unless he's on a leash. He likes high places and might end up sitting on the roof watching the world go by. He's probably upset because Mom hasn't been spending enough time with him. Bengals like company." Corey frowned at Reggie who stared back at her as if trying to speak through mental telepathy.

"I was just calling you to tell you to meet me at the hospital. It's almost lunch time, so I thought we could check on Dad then take

67

Mom to lunch."

"I got tied up down at the *Gazette* office. I meant to be back sooner. We can go to lunch then come back and work on the diary. Did you get much done?"

"I made a few more notes and thoughts. We need to go over them before we take them to Dad to look over. And I have some things for Turner to look up for us."

Reggie began meowing as if he were in distress.

Alarmed, Corey looked at him and said, "Am I going to have to take you to the vet on top of everything else that's been happening?"

Reggie meowed again adding a low growl.

Corey shook her head in confusion. "If he's still acting strange when we get back from lunch, we'll have to take him to the vet. I'll call Mom and let her know we're on our way."

Corey pulled out her cell phone and punched in her mother's cell number. She reached her mother's voicemail. "That's odd. Why does she have the phone off?"

Reggie growled, jumped to the hook by the door, got his leash and sat like a puppy waiting to go out. Corey had to laugh, but felt uneasy – especially since her mother wasn't answering her phone.

"Maybe they asked her to turn it off in the cardiac unit because of all the machinery."

"Could be. She usually puts it on vibrate though. She'll go to the lounge and call me back."

Corey picked up the stack of notes she had made. "Should we take these with us, or put them away here someplace?"

"Let's take one copy in case your Dad wants to look them over and leave rest here. We didn't get to the bank to put the originals in your box. We better hide them, too."

Corey grinned, went to the kitchen and returned with two large gallon sized zip-lock bags. Roger raised his eyebrows in question while she put the copies in one bag and the originals in the other.

"Now what are you going to do with it?"

"Take it downstairs and put it in the bottom of the basement freezer."

Roger laughed and shook his head. "I'll get the car warmed up while you take care of that."

Reggie followed Roger out the door without him realizing it until he opened the car door and a flash of fur flew over his shoulder to the back seat. He had dropped the leash on the steps and Corey picked it up on her way out. *How did this get out here?* When she got to the car, she found out.

"Why is Reggie in the back seat?"

"You tell me. I opened the door and he flew in. I didn't even see him come out the door."

"Come on Reggie, you can't go with us this time." Corey reached for him, but he smacked her hand with a paw, hissed and growled.

"Reggie! He's never done this before."

"Want me to try?" Roger started to get out of the car.

"Have you ever tried to remove a thirty pound cat who doesn't want to be removed?"

"Will he be all right in the car?"

"He's used to riding in the car. Hopefully he'll stay in it while we go in the hospital. Anyway, we can't get him out and we need to go."

Eleven

Almost at the hospital, Corey checked her phone again. "It's been more than fifteen minutes. She should have called back by now."

"Try again. Maybe she didn't have it on vibrate."

"But she should…" Corey punched in the number while she was talking to Roger. "Still just the voice mail. Maybe I'm being paranoid, but I'm worried."

"Meow." The anxious sound came from the back seat. Corey glanced back at Reggie then over at Roger, who didn't say anything. He zipped into an illegal parking spot, cracked the windows a little and jumped from the car.

"Be good Reggie. Stay here and don't let anyone in the car but us," he said as he closed the door and started after Corey who was already running for the door.

"Meow," answered Reggie as if urging them to hurry.

Roger passed her and caught the elevator as it was starting to close.

"Hey, wait for the next one," shouted a large man at the back of the elevator.

"Sorry. Emergency," said Roger as he held the door for Corey, only a few steps behind him.

"The angry man at the back bumped Roger as he got off at the second floor. Roger bit his lip to keep from yelling at him. Instead, he gave the close door button an extra hard jab.

Reaching the fourth floor, they waited only for the door to open enough to squeeze out then they ran to Daniel's room. A nurse that Corey didn't remember seeing before came out of his room as they reached the curtain/door. "I just gave him a shot and he's sleeping," she said. "Don't disturb him."

Corey looked into the room. The chair her mother usually occupied was empty – so was the guard's chair outside the room. Daniel seemed to be sleeping soundly – as the nurse said – and Corey didn't want to wake him, but she felt something was wrong. She pulled Roger's coat sleeve and ran toward the nurses' station.

"Can I help you?" The nurse looked up from the papers and smiled – her nametag said Doris.

"Thank you, Doris. Could you tell me where Mrs. Kahlor went? I mean, did she go down to the cafeteria or…"

"A nurse from downstairs came up and said that her daughter called and was having car trouble."

Marjorie came out of another room. "Is something wrong Miss Kahlor? You look a little pale."

"I don't know. Doris said I called Mom about my car being broken down. I didn't call her. There was no car trouble and where is the guard they left with my father?"

Marjorie glanced across to Daniel's room. "Doris, where is he?"

"He said the nurse in there told him he could go for a sandwich. Do you want me to call him?"

Corey and Roger exchanged startled glances. "He wasn't supposed to leave without Marjorie's permission," said Corey.

"There should be someone on duty at all times," said Roger.

"And who was the nurse that just came out of there? What did she give my father?" Corey's voice felt tight, like she was strangling.

Marjorie looked alarmed. "What nurse?"

"There was a woman in a nurse's uniform came out as we started in," said Corey. "She said she gave him a shot and he was sleeping, so we shouldn't disturb him."

Marjorie ran to Daniel's room then immediately called a Code Blue. Within seconds a dozen or so nurses, doctors, assistants arrived. They all converged on Daniel and began working with him.

Trying to stay out of the way, Corey wanted to see what was happening. Roger pulled his phone from his pocket and punched in 911. "This is Roger Trent. Put me through to Detective Matt Turner. This is an emergency." He waited a few seconds until the growly voice answered. "Better get over to the hospital. There's been another attempt on Kahlor. His wife is missing and your guard left his post." He didn't bother to say goodbye.

***

Roger and Corey met Turner at the elevator. The missing guard got off the elevator with him. His scarlet face made it clear the detective had chewed him out properly for leaving his post.

"Why did he leave?" asked Roger.

"He said a nurse told him it was all right to go grab a sandwich. She was going to be with Mr. Kahlor for at least fifteen minutes," said Turner.

"The nurse who wasn't a nurse," said Corey. "She told us she gave him a shot and he was sleeping and we shouldn't disturb him. I have a vague idea of what she looked like. I didn't see a nametag. I don't suppose the guard could identify her."

"Good point, Corey," said Turner. "I'll ask him as soon as I find out what is happening in there. Maybe between the three of you, we can get a good picture of her."

***

Roger, Corey, Detective Turner and the guard met with Marjorie and Doris in the lounge at the end of the hall. They placed another guard inside Daniel's room.

"All right, let's get this sorted out so we can …"

"Find my mother," said Corey interrupting him.

"The nurse from downstairs said you called her and she left," said Doris.

"What nurse?" asked Marjorie.

"Was she blonde, blue eyes, spoke with a southern accent?" asked Corey.

"Hey, that's the same nurse who told me she would be with Mr. Kahlor about fifteen minutes if I wanted to grab a sandwich."

"She stopped by the desk earlier and asked for Mrs. Kahlor," said Doris. "Said she was from downstairs and had a message for her. Something about someone working on the lines down there and they couldn't call up here. She said Mrs. Kahlor's daughter called and was having car trouble."

"I don't suppose she said where Miss Kahlor was?" asked Turner.

"As a matter of fact, she did. She said she was stuck out near the old warehouses on River Road. I heard Mrs. Kahlor ask her why she didn't call her cell, but they were moving toward the elevator, so I didn't hear her answer."

Detective Turner was on his phone while they talked. "Send at least two or three cruiser out to the warehouse district. Look for a broken down car or – not sure what we're looking for. I'll meet you there."

"Is my father going to be all right? What did she do…?"

"We got to him in time," said Marjorie. "That poor man is having one awful time recovering from heart surgery, which is tough enough by itself. But, he's hanging in there. We'll be more vigilant."

GREAT-GRANDPA'S DIARY

***

"Charlie, you stay *in* the room with Mr. Kahlor. Buster can sit outside the room. No one goes in or out of that room unless Marjorie or her successor, gives you the okay. You can work out some kind of code if you don't want to run back here every time a nurse has to go in."

"We'll move him to the room across from the station. That way we can see everyone going and coming as well."

"We're coming with you," said Roger as Detective Turner started toward the elevator.

"I'm not sure that's a good idea," he said glancing at Corey. "But, I understand your need. Just stay out of our way. We'll handle things by the book. I've put out an APB on the nurse, or acting nurse. Maybe she'll be able to tell us more."

They stepped into the elevator. As the doors slid closed Corey said, "I doubt it."

"Why do you say that?" Roger asked

"Look what happened to the man in my apartment when he failed and they didn't need him any longer. What do you think her chances of surviving are, when they learn that so many can identify her? She practically gave us a map to where Mom is."

"You've got a point," said Turner. "I hope you're wrong, but unfortunately you're probably right."

They left the hospital and headed for their cars. Turner had parked behind Roger in a no parking zone. The hospital security guard was trying to ticket Roger's car for being in the wrong place, but Reggie had opened the door and held the man at bay with his teeth bared and a low growl in his throat.

Roger and Corey ran to the car and Reggie returned to the back seat. "Be careful," called the guard. "There's a leopard loose in there."

"It's all right," said Corey. "He's just our guard cat."

Detective Turner ignored them and ran to his car. He pulled around Roger and left with lights flashing and sirens screaming. Roger whipped out and took off before Corey hardly had her seatbelt fastened. She glanced in the mirror. The guard stood holding his hat and rubbing his head. A frown covered his face.

***

"Looks like we're here," said Roger as he pulled in behind Detective Turner. Three cruisers with lights flashing had the street blocked off. A blue Toyota was crossways at the corner, another car's front end smashed into its frontend. The Toyota's hood was bent in half and the windshield looked like a frozen pond with a boulder sending crisscrosses of cracks across it. A woman's body lay in a pool of blood beside the disabled cars.

"Roger! That's Mother's car." Corey opened the door to get out of the car. Reggie started around her. She grabbed his leash and fastened it. Together they leaped from the car and started toward the body. Roger jumped out of the car, grabbed Corey and wrapped his arms around her to hold her back. Reggie pulled her forward.

"Corey, you can't go over there. It's a crime scene."

"But…that's Mother's car. Is she…?" Her words ended on a sob.

Reggie pulled harder, growling and muttering to himself.

Detective Turner glanced at them then stooped to look at the body. Standing, he motioned for the officers to let Roger and Corey through the tape.

"That isn't Mrs. Kahlor, is it?" Roger asked still trying to hold Corey back with Reggie pulling them forward.

"No," said Turner. "It's the nurse from the hospital. Corey was right. She was no longer useful."

"But where's my mother? That's her car," Corey wailed. "They – whoever they are – have my mother." Reggie was hissing and pulling toward the car.

"Did anyone search the car?" asked Turner.

"No sir, no one touched anything. We only taped off the scene to keep people back."

"Good job, officer. Corey, do you want to take a look inside to see if anything is different in case she left a clue for us? Your fingerprints are probably all over it anyway."

"I think Reggie wants in there," she said.

"Reggie? Why is he…?" He didn't finish.

"He senses something is wrong with Mother. He's very possessive and he's concerned about her. He won't hurt anything."

Corey eased over to the driver's side where the door was hanging by one hinge. She looked inside then slid into the seat. Reggie leaped over her and began sniffing around like a bloodhound. While Corey felt around the creases and spaces between the front seats, Reggie checked out the floors. Corey's probing fingers found what she was looking for – her mother's cell phone. She held it up for the men to see.

"Her cell?" said Turner.

"She's never without it because of her business. It's on."

"So why didn't it ring when you called her?"

"No, you don't understand. It isn't on so I can call her. It is on because she called me. It's still running. She called my answering machine at the apartment."

"I don't understand," said Roger.

"Roger, you should know my mother better than that. She must have sensed or saw something that warned her of danger. She had to let me know what was going on. She couldn't call my cell. I'd want to talk – ask questions. So she called my apartment knowing I wouldn't be there and my answering machine would get the whole message. Then she hid the phone and hopefully got them to talk to her before they took her wherever they took her."

"You really think…"

"I know my mother."

"Why can't you check the message from your cell phone?"

"Two reasons. The phone is still on, meaning the answering machine is still recording. And I never got around to programing that feature. I never needed it before."

"Then let's get over to your apartment and see if we can find anything helpful," said Turner. He called one of the officers to them.

"This is John Pennyworth, my assistant. Take over here John. I have a lead to check out."

"Yes sir."

Reggie, who had stood impatiently listening to the humans talk, suddenly ran for Roger's car, pulling Corey with him. "I think he's ready to go listen to a tape," called Corey over her shoulder.

With lights flashing and siren blaring, Detective Turner led the way to Corey's apartment. Corey and Roger followed close behind him.

Twelve

Detective Turner screeched to a halt in front of the apartment building with Roger right behind. They all jumped from the cars and ran toward the door. People who had gathered at the sound of sirens, began to part like the Red Sea making room for a large cat and three running people.

"What's happening?"
"Another robbery?"
"Is our neighborhood safe anymore?"
"Is anyone safe anymore?"

With Reggie on his leash, Corey left the questions and fearful bystanders behind and followed Roger and Detective Turner into the building. Too anxious to wait for the elevator, Corey and Reggie started for the stairs. "Sometimes it takes forever for that elevator to respond. My apartment is only on second floor."

She opened the door to the stairwell and started up the stairs. Roger and Turner were right behind her. Reggie slipped his collar and loped up the stairs leaving the three humans in the dust – literally. The stairwells were hardly ever used. Before Corey, Roger and Detective Turner reached the first landing they heard the door above them close.

Taking the stairs two at a time, they pushed the door open to the second floor hall and ran to Corey's apartment. Reggie waited, tail swishing in agitation, in front of the door with a big yellow X across it.

"How did he get here before we did?" Turner asked while he began pulling off the crime tape.

"He slipped his collar and took off," said Corey. "It was easy for him to push the door open."

"But how did he know which door was your apartment?"

Corey shrugged and pushed the apartment door open. "He's been here before. He stays with me sometimes."

"But…never mind. Let's check that answering machine."

Corey went to the phone, hoping the intruders hadn't destroyed it along with everything else in her home. The light wasn't blinking indicating a message.

"Is it still recording?" asked Roger. "Most machines will cut off after three or four minutes."

"I set mine to not turn off until the connection is broken because Mother often calls with long messages about something she wants me to do. I left her cell running so my answering machine would continue to record until we break the connection."

Corey pulled her mother's phone from her pocket and pressed the off button. The machine stopped recording and Corey hit the play button. Holding their breath, they waited for Sherylee's voice. When she spoke, Reggie jumped to the table and pawed at the machine.

"He recognizes Mom's voice," said Corey.

They listened.

"Coral Rae, I think I'm moving into a trap of some kind. I wondered why you didn't call me yourself. I should have known it was a way to get me away from Daniel. Please check on him and make sure he's all right. There's a black Mercedes parked crossways on Warehouse Road near River Road. I'm going to try to go around it, but I don't think they will let me. They're pulling guns – two white males, about thirty or so, normal *hood types.* One is about 5'2" the other 6' big brawny type. I can see most of the license number – 58 DC 8? Not sure of the last number. I have to stop, can't go around or turn around. If they take me somewhere, I will try to mark the tires. Don't worry, but help me if you can. I'll hide the phone. Hope they don't find it."

The last few words were not as clear because the phone was no longer at her lips. There was a pause with only a whirring sound to indicate the recorder was still recording. Detective Turner reached to turn it off.

"Wait," said Corey. "There's more."

"How do you know...?"

A male voice came on the recorder. "All right lady. Out of the car."

"What do you want?" Sherylee's voice sounded calm and controlled. "I don't have much money, but I'll give you what I have. I really need to find my daughter. Her car broke down around here somewhere and I need to help her."

The man laughed a harsh sound. "Ain't nobody around here with car trouble but you."

"My car is fine."

"Not anymore it ain't." There was a loud bang and the sound of breaking glass.

"That's how the window got smashed," said Corey.

"Now what did you do that for? If I had my cell phone with me, I would call the police."

"We'll be long gone before the police figure out what's happening."

"You made that call and said it was Corey."

"Yeah, we called Peggy. She went to tell you and took care of Daniel while she was there."

"What do you mean took care of Daniel?"

"Don't be stupid," said another man. "You don't need to talk to her. Just get her out of that car. Peggy will be here soon."

"What did you do to Daniel?" Sherylee asked again.

"She gave him a new medicine," said the first voice and he laughed again. "Now get out of the car."

"You're going to shoot me anyway. Why not right here?"

"We need you for other things sister," said the second voice.

"Like what?"

"Like providing us with a diary."

"That spiral notebook of Daniel's? There's nothing in it but the ramblings of a lonely old man."

"Harry was a smart man. He left Boss holding an empty bag. We want that cash and we want to know who he fingered besides Judge Homer."

"You aren't going to get what you want, because there are no names in that diary except family names and certainly nothing about money except that he was lucky to make a few pennies with his weaving and cigar making."

"So you say. We want that diary and we'll get it if we have to leave your body on your front porch for them to find."

"Suit yourself, but you still won't have what you want. And you're pretty stupid to kill Daniel since he's the only one who might have any answers for you."

"Shut up. No one calls me stupid." A crack that sounded like a slap across the face followed the man's shout. Corey cringed. Roger wrapped his arms around her. Reggie growled.

"Here comes Peggy," said the second voice.

"Tell her to hit the Toyota head on."

Sounds faded, but they could hear another car stop, voices shouting – two men and a woman – simultaneously followed by a gunshot and a crash of metal against metal. There was more shouting then tires squealing. They heard only the soft whirring of the recording until sirens arrived, followed by a jumble of voices until the tape came to the point where Corey found the cell phone. They listened to their own words on the tape then turned off the machine.

"Well, now we know what happened. We have a description of the men who took her, the kind of vehicle they are driving along with most of the license number. If we only had some idea where they took her," said Turner.

"They will contact Corey about the diary. But how? They have her mother and think they have killed her father. Like Mrs. Kahlor said, they are pretty stupid," said Roger.

"They're second and third generation hoods living off their grandfathers' reputations," said Detective Turner. "They see this as a golden opportunity to make a killing – hopefully not literally. Although that's not without possibility since they've already killed twice."

Reggie paced the apartment, looking, sniffing and growling. Corey had not replaced the collar while they were inside. Reggie started for the door that they had not closed.

"Reggie, wait," she called. "We need you and you need us." She grabbed the leash.

"They know where I live – or lived, until they trashed the place. Will they attempt to contact me here? Do they know where I work? Will they terrorize the library?"

"Like you said, these guys are stupid," said Turner. "Hard to tell what they will do next. I'll call the mayor and strongly suggest that he close the library for a few days – emergency repair work or something. In the meantime we have to find your mother."

"What was that she said about trying to mark the tires?" Roger asked.

Corey laughed. "My mother is a mystery buff. She's always coming up with some kind of wild possibility for a story. I tell her she should write mysteries and use her ideas there. But...wait a minute. I remember not very long ago, she came up with this idea of tracking a getaway car in a bank robbery – something about pressing a skinny tube of lipstick into the crevices of a tire. She wondered if it would leave a mark on the road and if it did, how long it would last."

"Did she try it?"

"We never had an opportunity."

"Do you think...?"

"It's a possibility. She bought a couple tubes of lipstick like that, just in case..."

Turner had been listening to them rolling his eyes and shaking his head. "It's a dumb idea – good for a B rated movie, maybe, but..."

"Let's go back to the scene of the abduction and see if we can pick up a trail. Anything is worth a try," said Corey.

Reggie didn't wait for them to decide if it was worth pursuing or not. Catching his paw on the partly open door, he pulled it, squeezed through the opening and ran for the stairs. Corey, right behind him, opened the exit door and he flew down the stairs. He waited for them beside Roger's car, muttering to himself in his special Bengal language.

Still not too keen on the idea, Turner led the way once again with sirens screaming and emergency lights flashing, racing from one end of town to the other.

"I feel like I'm in one of those cheap films that spend more time in car chases than in solving the crime. If it wasn't so tragic, it would be almost funny," Corey said.

"I'm sure your mother would agree with you. The two of you can have a good laugh when it's over," said Roger.

"I hope so," said Corey, her voice catching in a half-sob.

"We'll find her," said Roger.

"Meow," added Reggie and patted Corey's shoulder with a soft paw.

"Thanks guys," she said. "I needed that."

"Looks like we're here," said Roger stopping behind Turner's car.

The coroner had removed the body of the woman and the crime team placed tape around the scene. Corey jumped from the car and began following Reggie as he sniffed the street. She looked and he sniffed looking for anything that would indicate an unusual mark. Reggie stopped and tentatively pawed at a tiny red dot on the pavement.

"Roger, Detective Turner, over here." Corey waved to them excitedly.

They joined her and looked at the street. Turner walked one

direction and Roger another looking for more dots, but Reggie was already following a trail of dots several feet apart.

"It looks like somehow she managed to do it," said Corey.

"But the dots are so small we'll never see the trail it from the car," said Turner.

"Then' we'll have to walk," said Corey and started following Reggie down the street.

"Wait, Corey," called Detective Turner. "You can't walk down the middle of the street with traffic in all directions."

"How about a bicycle or a motorcycle?" asked Roger.

"That might work." Turner looked around. "Over there," he said nodding to a window across the street – Bart's Bicycle Bargains.

Turner called to the two officers who had been guarding the crime scene. "You two wait here until I return," he said then followed Roger and Corey across the street.

When they returned pushing three bicycles, Turner told one of the officers to call another cruiser for backup. Then he introduced the other young officer as Mark Brown. "Mark will follow us with lights for safety. At least it's Saturday. Not as much traffic today."

"Thank you, Mark," said Corey, "Maybe you can call in a check on the owner of that car while we follow the dots."

"Sure, give me the number."

Turner scowled at Corey and pulled his notebook from his pocket. He gave the license number to Mark and said, "Let's get going."

Roger, Turner and Corey pedaled down the street following tiny red dots. Reggie once again attached to the leash loped ahead of Corey following the dots that hopefully would lead to where the kidnappers had taken Sherylee. The police cruiser followed with lights flashing. Even so, there were several narrow escapes from drivers turning to see a leopard in the middle of the street.

Thirteen

"The dots are fading," Turner shouted above the noise of a truck passing through town. He motioned for them to move over.

Roger and Corey nodded. Turner signaled Officer Brown behind them, who put on his hazard lights and eased over blocking traffic so the bicycles could safely move to an empty parking lot. Mark got out of the cruiser. He joined the three bicyclists and agitated cat in the empty lot.

"We can't just quit," said Corey. "We have to find her."

"We will," said Turner, "but the marks are so faint we can't see which way to go."

"It looks like we're moving toward the river," said Corey. "Maybe she's in one of those abandoned warehouses."

"Excuse me, sir," said Mark. "I got the information on that number you gave me. It belongs to a man named Parker, who owns and operates Parker's Wholesale Merchandise, 691 River Road."

"River Road runs along the Maumee," said Corey.

"Why don't you check it out," Roger said to Turner. "Corey and I will return our bikes then pick up my car and meet you at Parker's."

"I'll put your bike in the trunk of the cruiser," said Mark as he picked up the bike Turner had been riding.

"You two be careful pedaling back. Keep your eyes open – even behind you. Will that cat be all right or should we take him in the cruiser? We don't know what those nuts will do next."

"I don't think Reggie will go with you," said Corey. "He'll stay close. If not, I'll carry him."

Turner raised his eyebrows. "You and what tow motor?"

Corey laughed. Detective Turner and Mark headed for the address on River Road while Roger and Corey turned and started pedaling back to the warehouse district where they had left Roger's car and rented the bikes. They hadn't gone far when Reggie began growling and trying to pull Corey to the curb. She glanced back and noticed a black sedan following close to the bikes.

"We better move over," she called to Roger.

GREAT-GRANDPA'S DIARY

He nodded. They moved toward the sidewalk to let the car pass, but instead of passing, the car increased speed and veered toward them. Someone on the sidewalk screamed. Someone else yelled, "Look out!"

"Jump," Roger called back to Corey as he leaped from the moving bike onto the sidewalk. Corey, trying to ensure Reggie was safe, was a little slower in getting off her bike. The car clipped the back tire as she landed on the sidewalk beside Roger. Reggie pulled free of his collar, became airborne, landed on top of the car and slid down the windshield. The driver momentarily lost control. When he got the car under control, Reggie leaped to the sidewalk and the car sped off.

"Are you all right?" Roger pulled himself up and limped to Corey, who had a thirty-pound fur ball across her chest. "Maybe I should ask if Reggie is all right."

"I think we both are," she said.

People gathered around them, wanting to help, but fearing the big cat who was now unleashed. "We're all right," said Roger. "Just a few scrapes and bruises. The cat is ours. He's not wild or dangerous."

"I got it all on my cell phone and called for help," said a young man as sirens sounded closer and then suddenly stopped. An officer jumped from his cruiser, leaving it crossways in the street.

"Officer Berkley, here," he said. "Someone want to tell me what's happening? Several on-lookers spoke at once. "Wait. Stop. Who called the police?"

"I did," said a woman holding her cell phone in one hand, keeping the other hand wrapped around the wrist of a small boy. "I saw that car deliberately sideswipe the bicyclists and called immediately."

"I did, too," said the young man.

"And I," offered several other by-standers.

"Thank you – all of you. Is anyone hurt? Do we need an ambulance?"

"No, we're all right," said Roger. "A few scrapes and bruises, but nothing is broken."

"Does that leopard belong to anyone here?"

"He's mine," said Corey. "He pulled out of his collar to chase the car."

The officer's mouth twitched, but he didn't laugh when he asked, "Did he catch it? Or maybe get his license number?"

"He didn't get a number," said Corey, "but he did catch the car and I think he put the fear of Bastet in him."

"Bastet?"

Corey laughed in spite of her trembling. "Bastet is the goddess of cats."

"Oh, eh, did anyone get a license number?"

"I did sir," answered the teenager standing with a group of boys. "I got it all on my cell phone video mode. That was awesome – that cat flying to the car and landing on the windshield. It looked like the man intended to run over all of them, but the cat saved their lives."

"What's your name son?"

"Joshua. Joshua Perkins. You want me to play it for you?"

"Sure, let's see what you got."

Joshua played the video for Officer Berkley.

"Impressive, Joshua. We'll need this for evidence. If you want to ride down to the station with me, I'll give you a receipt for it."

"Will I get it back? I got other stuff ..."

"You'll get it back as soon as we make a copy."

"Yes, sir," he said and stood aside looking as if he had just won a school trophy.

"The rest of you, if you will write your name, address and phone number on this tablet, I'll contact you for your eye-witness report." Officer Berkley then turned to Roger and Corey. "You were with Turner earlier," he said.

"Yeah, we were on our way back to the bicycle shop across from the warehouse to pick up my car when that jerk tried to run over our bikes with us on them," said Roger.

"Looks like your bikes are ready for the junk heap," said Berkley.

A second cruiser pulled up behind the first. "Need any help here, Joe?"

"Yeah, Paul, would you help me get these bikes, what's left of them, in the trunk of my cruiser then take these two over to the warehouse district to pick up their car. I'll take Joshua to the precinct with his *eye witness account* on video."

"You got it on video?"

"The whole thing, including license number."

"Good job, kid. Now," he turned to Corey and Roger, "the warehouse district?"

"Yeah, you know where Bart's Bicycle Bargains is? Our car is near there."

"Got ya." They all helped get the bikes into the trunk then the Officer Berkley took Joshua and his cell phone to the precinct. Roger and Corey got in the back of the second cruiser for the ride to pick up Roger's car.

Fourteen

"What'll we tell the bike dealer?" asked Corey

"The truth. He'll want us to pay the full amount for the bikes, but we'll have to tell him there was an accident and the police are holding the bikes. We'll settle with him when the police release them."

"He won't like that."

"Maybe not, but…There's the bike shop," Roger said to the driver. "And that's my car across the street near the crime scene tape."

"Someone should be guarding the scene if it's still under investigation," said Paul frowning.

"Guess they figured kidnapping takes precedence over an empty crime scene."

"Maybe, I'll wait until you settle with the bike shop. If he gives you any trouble, I'll come in and set him straight," said Paul. "Then I'll drive you over to your car. This is a rough neighborhood. You might not have any tires."

Roger groaned and headed for the shop door, Corey and Reggie right behind him. They came out minutes later grinning and got back in the cruiser.

"From the looks on your faces, I'd say you didn't have any trouble," said Paul.

"Reggie jumped to the counter and began to explain in his own special Bengalese."

Paul laughed. "I'm sure he did a better job than I could have done. Merchants in this neighborhood seem to resent police interference, as they call it. Let's see if your car is drivable." He stopped the cruiser near the car and got out with Corey and Roger to check it over.

"Looks like all the tires are there and still have air in them, but…"

"You think there's a problem – sand in the gas tank? Missing battery?"

"I don't know," said Paul. "The fellows at the precinct laugh at me, but sometimes I just have a feeling that something isn't right."

"Like ESP," said Corey.

"Something like that. My grandmother was a Gypsy fortuneteller years ago." He laughed. "You see why the guys laugh at me."

"Maybe we ought to check it out," said Corey.

Roger moved toward the car and started to open the driver's side door. Reggie blocked him. "Come on Reggie," he said. "If we want to find Mrs. Kahlor, we have to get in the car and…"

Reggie gave an ear-splitting yowl that sounded a lot like, "No!" He smacked Roger's hand away from the door handle. Corey and Paul glanced at each other.

"Roger, is it possible that something *is* wrong?"

"I'll check it over to make sure it's not booby-trapped," said Roger.

"Maybe I better call the bomb squad to check it," said Paul. "They'd find a needle in a haystack in a few minutes with their equipment. Better'n getting yourself blown up." He was already on the phone with the station.

"He's right, Roger. Detective Turner is looking for Mother. If we get ourselves killed, we won't be much help."

Roger's face screwed up in frustration. Finally, he let out a long breath. "These guys are playing for keeps."

While they waited for the bomb squad to arrive, Roger called Turner. He put the cell on speaker mode so Corey could hear. "Did you find her? Is she…?"

"Nothing here except the car and two dead men lying beside it. Parker claims his car hasn't been out of the parking lot all day. He has no idea where the dead men came from or who they are, but claims a lot of drive-by shootings happen in his neighborhood."

"If my mother was there, she left a clue. Let me look – as soon as we can get there."

"Where are you? Thought you were…"

"Long story," said Roger. "To make it short a car ran us off the road, ran over the bikes and kept going. Young fellow in the crowd got it all on his cell phone. Cruiser brought us to my car and called the bomb squad to make sure we don't get blown to bits when we try to start it. I see them coming now. As soon as they say, we're safe we'll be on our way."

Turner said something they didn't understand. Corey wasn't sure she wanted to. Roger said, "Sorry pal."

"I never expected anything like that or I wouldn't have sent you two off without a chaperone."

"We don't need a chaperone. Paul, the second officer at the scene brought us here and called the bomb squad. And we have Reggie, who seems to sense a lot more than we do. We need to get to the bottom of this mystery and get our lives back together. See you in a little bit – I hope."

Roger folded his phone and placed it in his pocket as what looked like a Sherman tank disguised as a jeep, rolled into the parking lot near the cruiser. Three men dressed like aliens from a far planet, climbed from the *Bomb Squad* truck and walked to the cruiser.

"Hi there, Paul. What's going on? Your ESP acting up again?"

"You might say so," said Paul grinning.

"Well, you aren't often wrong and I would rather listen to your inner voice, than see someone blown to bits."

"Thanks. We're not sure what's going on, but the cat is acting strange and like you said, my ESP is acting up. The car's been here several hours. Not sure when the clean-up crew left the crime scene. It's a long story. Fill you in later. Right now you need to check out that car."

Corey, Roger and Reggie joined Paul with the squad. Paul turned to them. "Roger and Corey meet Pete, leader of this team. That's Bob and Mike"

"Meow!"

"Oh, and that's Reggie. He's a Bengal cat – very smart. He agrees there's something wrong and we thought it would be safer for you to check for bombs than for them to do it."

"You're right. We got the equipment, as well as Duke. He's the best bomb sniffing dog in the state." He turned to the two other men with him. "I'll take Duke and get started. You guys hook up the electronic testers. Let's go Duke."

Reggie slipped out of his collar again and greeted the beagle-bloodhound mix. Together they went to the car. "All right," said Pete. "Let's see if there's anything here that shouldn't be."

Reggie and Duke sniffed around the car, beginning at the driver's door, continuing to the passenger door, around the trunk area and the other side, ending at the front. They both stopped and stared at the hood. Duke began howling and Reggie joined with his own special yowl. Pete gave Reggie a curious glance and called to the others. "Bring that stuff over here. Looks like they found something."

Carrying a box that reminded Corey of a Geiger Counter that she once looked up in the library for a child, the man followed the same pattern that Duke and Reggie had followed, ending at the front of the car. When he reached the hood, the soft ticking on the box went wild like an out of control metronome.

They brought out one more piece of equipment that worked something like an X-ray machine. "We can see through the metal to what's inside the car," said Pete. The three men gathered to read the meter.

"What do you think Bob?"

"Looks like two, maybe three sticks of dynamite."

"How's it hooked up? What will trigger it?"

"Looks like it's wired to the battery. Would probably blow when someone turned the key, drawing juice from the battery."

"Yeah, that's what I thought. Should be safe to lift the hood."

"Should be? You want me to do it?"

"No, take Duke, the cat and all of you get behind the cruiser – just in case we're wrong."

"Reggie," Corey called. "Come here." Reggie nudged Duke and they ran behind the cruiser with Roger and Corey. "Do you think he will be safe?"

"It's all right, Corey," said Roger. "He knows what he's doing – I hope."

As soon as everyone had taken cover, Pete unlatched the hood. He tensed. Nothing happened. He slowly lifted the hood and peered under it. Exhaling loudly, he called to the others, "Need your help guys. It's where we said it was, but it's across the rod that holds the hood up. I'll hold the hood while you disarm the bomb."

Bob and Mike ran to him to help. Duke sat beside Paul's cruiser with Reggie. Three very tense minutes later the two men lifted the bundle of dynamite from the car and Pete let the hood fall into place.

Roger put his arms around a trembling Corey. "It's all right, sweetheart. They took care of it."

"Roger, we would have been blown to bits when we…"

"But it didn't happen. We're all right." He turned to Paul and the bomb squad members. "We can't thank you enough," he said, "especially you, Paul. I wouldn't have thought to call out the bomb squad. I probably would have just checked it out to make sure the car was safe for Corey."

Pete laughed, "I don't think that cat would have let you do that.

He's a smart one. I've heard of Bengals. They're very intelligent. You ever want to get rid of him, I'll take him in a heartbeat. Wouldn't take much to train him."

"I think you're right. Reggie would have done what he could to protect us. Thanks again."

"Just doing our jobs," said Pete. "Glad we could help prevent a tragedy."

"I know you need to meet Detective Turner," said Paul. "I'll escort you there. When you get through dodging bullets, hit and run drivers and car bombs, you can stop by and file a report."

"Sure thing," said Roger then he turned to Corey. "Let's go see if we can find any clues about your mother. I'm with you. I think if she was there – and she must have been since they found the car there – she will find some way to let us know she's all right."

Corey nodded and got in the car. Reggie flew to the back seat. She knew Roger hadn't stated the other possibility – that if her mother was dead, there would be no clues.

Fifteen

"Looks like the troops are leaving," said Roger as they rounded a corner and eased to the curb at the address on River Road.

"Detective Turner waited for us," said Corey. "Maybe they found something. Shall I put Reggie's leash on him? He seems to be out of the collar more than he's in it."

"I think you're right. He'll stay with us unless he senses something that needs him, then it won't matter if he's on a leash or not. He'll go."

Reggie sat turning his head from one to the other then added his own comment, "Meow?" He pressed on the door handle, opened the door and got out as Corey opened the front passenger door. Together they moved toward Turner as he walked toward them. Once again, crime scene tape cordoned off a section of the parking lot at Parker's Wholesale Merchandise and paint marked the spots where the bodies had been. The tow truck had a large hook in the car that Corey was sure had carried her mother away. The driver was ready to tow it to the Police lot where it would receive a good going over. The odor of burnt leaves, diesel fuel and spray paint mingled in the fall air.

"Could I take a look inside before they tow it?" asked Corey.

Turner paused then said, "We gave it a good going over and they'll go over it again at the garage. The car's clean, but go ahead. You *might* find something we missed. It doesn't even look like Mrs. Kahlor was in that car. Parker insists it never left the lot."

"Mother gave a description of this car as well as most of the license number."

"She was under a lot of stress. She could have been mistaken."

"Did she sound stressed to you? My mother was in complete control of her senses. If she said this was the car, then I don't care what Parker says, this was the car and she was in it."

"How does he explain the two dead men?" Roger asked – partly to change the subject and partly out of curiosity.

"He says this is a rough neighborhood. Gangs are always driving by and shooting people."

"Then why aren't there holes in the vehicles?" asked Corey.

"Good question," said Turner. He motioned for the tow truck to hold off for a few minutes. Corey opened the back passenger door and Reggie leaped over her onto the seat. While Corey looked all around the back wondering what her mother would try to hide to show she was in the car, Reggie jumped to the front and gave it a good sniffing. Corey knew the police had already gone over it very carefully – even the trunk and found nothing. *But she's my mother. I know her better than they do. She would not be obvious.*

"We checked everything Corey. It is almost as if they cleaned it out with a sweeper before we arrived," said Turner

"Did you ask them if they did?"

"Yeah. Of course they said no."

"Did you check the sweeper bag or the dumpster for the bag?"

"Eh...Hey Brown. Check out that dumpster. See if there's anything that looks like a sweeper bag."

"Yes sir."

Meanwhile Corey and Reggie continued to gaze around the car, stopping every once in a while to touch the seat, or feel under or around it. Then Reggie moved to the edge of the seat on the back passenger side and began pawing and digging at the side. "Did you find something Reg?" she asked and moved to help him. Reggie caught a piece of the carpet between the back seat and the door with his sharp claws. Corey reached a finger under the edge. A smile spread across her face. She found what she was looking for. "Good boy, Reggie."

"Corey? Did you find something?" Roger peered into the car.

"I think we did," she said and continued to pull at the carpet. "The carpet is loose about an inch worth between the seat and the door. If Mother was sitting on this side of the seat, as she probably would have been, she could have used her nails to rip a small hole. Reggie found the hole. Ah, there it is." Triumphantly she held up what looked like a small piece of plastic.

"What is it?" Turner took the object in his hand and frowned.

"It's one of her fake fingernails. She must have been desperate to give up one of her nails like that."

"You're sure it's hers? Someone else could..."

"Rip the carpet wide enough to insert a fingernail? Only someone else as desperate as my mother and that would mean that another person has been in this car at some time. It's her favorite

GREAT-GRANDPA'S DIARY

color of pale pink that will go with any outfit."

"Well, it might prove she was in this car, but where is she now?"

"Inside the building?"

"Come on Brown, let's search the building for Mrs. Kahlor." Turner started toward the building.

"Want me to call for a warrant?"

"We have reason to believe it's possible the woman is here. If they get nasty, we'll call the judge."

Roger and Corey followed Turner into the building. Albert Parker met him at the door. "What do you want now, Turner? You've confiscated my car, messed up my parking lot and made my employees uneasy. What more can you do before I call the commissioner?"

"We have proof the woman we're looking for was in your car, Parker. Now I want to search the premises for her."

"I ought to make you get a warrant, but go ahead and search all you want to. You won't find anyone here except my employees."

Reggie stopped beside Corey, looked up at the man with a low rumbling growl accompanied by a snarl.

"Where did that come from? Isn't it against the law to have unleashed wild animals in public?"

"We're not in public and he isn't wild. We're in your warehouse," said Corey. "He's better behaved than some people I've met today. But you're probably right. Mother isn't here. I'm sure they've taken her somewhere else by now."

"Turner and Roger both looked at her in surprise, but before they could say anything, she continued, "I'm sorry, Mr. Parker, if we're upsetting your day, but my mother has been kidnapped and I'm really upset and my stomach tends to get upset with me." She clutched her stomach as if in pain. "May I use your restroom?"

"Sure, it's right over there just past a row of boxed merchandise."

Corey, still holding her stomach, hurried to restroom. Roger and Turner watched her go then turned toward Parker's office to begin their search. Reggie loped beside her.

Reggie ran into the restroom ahead of her and Corey closed and locked the door. They hurriedly looked around the room. Reggie sniffed the floor while Corey checked the medicine cabinet. She lifted the lid on the commode tank. Nothing there. Checked the windowsill. Nothing. Time was running out. Reggie began pulling papers out of the waste paper basket – a small, round plastic one in the corner. Corey helped, checking each crumpled piece of paper. She shifted to reach for one when she saw another fingernail lying inconspicuously between the wastepaper basket and the wall. She picked it up. It was a match for the other one. *She'll have to spend some serious time with Tammy at the Nail Palace when this is all over.* At the same time, Reggie, picked up a crumpled paper towel and raised up with front feet on Corey's waist. He garbled around the paper in his mouth. Corey smiled, took the gift, and opened it. Written with an eyebrow pencil were the words, "I'm OK. Taking me to Donut Shop."

Putting the nail and the folded towel in her pocket, she flushed the toilet, turned on the water to wash her hands then reached for a paper towel. She wet it and left the room dabbing at her face as if she had been thoroughly sick. Turner and Roger, their search ended, met her with Parker.

"Thank you," she said to Parker. "I don't know where my mother is, but I know she was in your car. Maybe someone stole it then returned it. If you see anything of her, please call us."

"We aren't done yet," said Turner as he turned to walk out with Roger and Corey following them to Roger's car.

"What was that all about?" he asked Corey.

"Yeah, you have a stomach of iron."

Reggie tugged at Corey's pant leg trying to pull her to the car.

"We're going, Reggie," she said then turned to Turner. "He was too willing to let us search. He knew she wasn't there. Can we go somewhere? He's watching and will get suspicious if we linger too long."

"How about Maurice's Sandwich Shop near the hospital?" said Roger.

"You go ahead and I'll meet you there," said Turner.

"Roger, help me to the car like I'm ready to pass out or something. I want him to think I'm really sick."

"All right," said Roger placing his arm around her and helping her into the car. He ran around to the driver's side, gave her a quizzical look and started the car. "You found something?"

"Yes, another fingernail and a note," she said, "but let's wait for Turner."

"Meow," said Reggie sounding agitated.

"He's anxious to find Mother."

Sixteen

Maurice's Sandwich Shop, about two blocks from the hospital, was just around the corner from Dolly's Donut Den. Without the sirens and flashing lights, they moved a little slower this time.

"We can't take Reggie in with us," said Roger.

"We can't leave him in the car either," said Corey. "He can open your car doors. Maybe I could hide him in my coat."

Roger glanced at her with a look that asked, *"Are you kidding?"*

"No, I guess not. Maybe I could hide him under my shirt and they would think I'm pregnant."

"Corey, we better get some coffee in you. You're losing it."

Corey laughed then brushed at the tears that suddenly rolled down her face. "I'm sorry Roger. You're right. If we don't find Mother soon…" She couldn't finish her sentence.

Reggie opened the door and got out of the car as if he were tired of their prattle. He ambled over to the restaurant, stood and stretched to place a paw on a sign in the window.

Roger and Corey grinned at each other then got out to see what Reggie was up to. Corey read the sign Reggie was pointing to and started laughing.

"Now what?" asked Roger. He read the sign and also laughed. It was a small handwritten sign that said, "Animals prohibited except service animals."

Corey slipped the collar with the leash on Reggie and they all went in.

"You can't bring that wild cat in here," said Maurice.

"He's not a wild cat," said Corey. "He is a Bengal cat. They are very intelligent animals and often trained as service animals."

"You need a service animal? You're blind?"

"Service animals serve more than just the blind," she said. "Some animals help children know when they are going to have a seizure. Some help calm emotionally disturbed persons. Someone just kidnapped my mother and I'm very much emotionally disturbed. Reggie keeps me from going off the deep end."

Maurice stared at her for a minute then laughed. "He scares away customers, you pay."

"Thank you," said Corey and followed Roger to the end booth. Reggie jumped to the corner and Corey slid in beside him. He curled into a ball to wait for whatever happened next.

The server came to take their orders. Roger looked at Corey.

"I'm not hungry," she said.

"Corey, it's after three o'clock. You need something or you won't be able to keep going."

"I can't..."

Roger turned to the impatient server who stood tapping her foot. "We'll both have a grilled cheese and coffee – black. Our friend, who'll be joining us, will have a Reuben and coffee."

"Maybe we should have ordered something for Reggie," said Roger when the server had left.

"He can have mine," said Corey.

"Corey..."

"He likes grilled cheese," she said defensively.

Roger shook his head and glanced at Reggie who had made himself into a fur pillow in the corner beside Corey.

Turner arrived about ten minutes later. Roger moved over for him to share his side of the booth. He raised his eyebrows in question when he saw the fur pillow beside Corey, but he said nothing.

"All right, let's hear what you found." Impatiently, he waited for the server to set the food on the table and fill coffee cups. As soon as she left, he turned back to Corey. "Well?"

"Don't they teach patience in Detective school?" She smiled at him, then pulled the second fingernail from her pocket and handed it to him."

He pulled the first one from his pocket and laid them side by side on the table. "They match all right. Where did you find it?"

"In the restroom. I knew she had to have been there and would probably ask to use the restroom. The nail was lying on the floor almost hidden by the shadows of the wastepaper basket. Reggie moved the basket and began pawing through the paper towels. I picked up the nail and Reggie gave me the crumpled towel. I thought I'd been in there long enough, so I flushed the toilet." She reached into her other pocket and pulled out the towel with her mother's message on it. "This was near the bottom of the basket."

She laid it out on the table for the men to see.

GREAT-GRANDPA'S DIARY

"Your mother must be one smart woman. How could she possibly know you would find this and not someone else?"

"Why would anyone else go in there to rummage through the trash papers? Even if someone else found it, they wouldn't have a clue as to what it was all about, but at least she would have tried."

"So now where do we go? How many donut shops are there in Masontown?"

"Several, but I have a hunch of where to begin," said Corey.

"Dolly's?" Roger gave her a quizzical look.

"The donut shop around the corner?" asked Turner. "Why would you think it would be that one?" Turner looked at her as if she had been withholding evidence from him. "There must be a dozen pastry shops in town."

"But her note didn't say *pastry shop*. It said *donut*. And how many pastry shops actually say Donut Shop?"

"Got a phone book handy?" asked Turner sounding more sarcastic than interested.

"No, but..." Corey turned to Roger. "Remember when we went there yesterday when we realized that man was following us?"

"Yeah, I said I was hungry for donuts," said Roger taking a bite of his cheese sandwich.

"We went to Dolly's Donut Den because it was close and we could walk. The man followed and stood across the street watching the shop. I'm sure he could see us."

Corey picked at her sandwich, giving more to Reggie than to herself.

"We asked Dolly if there was a back door so we could slip out. She wanted to know why and we told her the man was following us and we just wanted to get away from him," said Roger.

"And she said he was a local hood who came around often. Thought he was a lady's man. She said she didn't allow him in the store because he pestered the girls," said Corey. "But it was the same man who followed my father for twenty years. He couldn't have come in often."

"We can't prove he followed your father," said Turner. "After all, Kahlor was a little paranoid at the time. Dolly should know if a man has harassed her girls often."

"Then why didn't she report him to the police?" Corey glared at Turner who glared back.

Roger, sounding annoyed, tried to continue his report. "Anyway, she said her delivery truck was going to the mall in a few minutes and we could ride with him if we wanted to. We did and went to the copy place and made copies of the diary."

"I'm don't understand," said Turner.

"Dolly knew the man who was following us – the same one that someone killed in my apartment and the *same* man who followed my father."

"We've been through this," said Turner. "How could he have followed Mr. Kahlor for twenty years and still be well known to Dolly? Why would she lie about it?"

"Why would my father lie about it?" said Corey. "I don't know what's going on. I just know he was the same man."

"Because of a hand drawn picture that doesn't look like that man at all?" Turner gave her a condescending smile – as if she were a small child insisting she had seen a fairy in her back yard.

"You need to get your eyes examined," said Corey. "That picture is a dead ringer of that man, and you know it."

"But, why would she…?"

"I don't know, but she made it possible for us to be away from my apartment long enough for those hoodlums to trash it. She knew where I lived thanks to the drawing for free donuts. While I was at the counter signing up for that drawing, I realized I could hear everything Roger and Dolly said. She had to have heard us talking about the diary."

"And there is some mention of a Dolly in the diary," said Roger sounding more like he was trying to placate Corey than adding information to the conversation.

"It couldn't have been the same Dolly," said Turner. "The one in the diary was an adult seventy years ago. This Dolly is only in her fifty's – maybe early sixties."

"Close to Daniel's age. She could be a grandchild of someone Mister Kahlor's grandfather knew," said Roger. "Do we know how long Dolly's Donut Den has been around? Maybe Dolly inherited the shop and her name might not even be Dolly at all." Roger looked from Turner to Corey.

"I guess Dolly's is as good a place as any to begin looking," said Turner rolling his eyes and sighing deeply as if getting tired of playing a game with children. At least we can have a donut and more coffee for dessert."

"Shall we walk," said Roger, "It's only around the corner."

"Meow!" answered Reggie.

"He probably thinks the car is faster," said Corey, "– for us anyway. I'm sure he could be there in half the time."

"Well, let's go then," said Roger.

"Give me five minutes head start," said Turner, "so I can check out the place – make sure no one but Dolly is there."

"All right," said Roger. Three minutes later, Reggie was pulling at the leash.

"I think he wants to go, now," said Corey. "He'll go without us if we don't move."

"I think you're right," said Roger, rising and leaving some bills on the table. "Let's go for donuts."

"Maybe we can get the donuts to go – for a bedtime snack," said Corey.

"Meow," said Reggie.

Maurice stopped them as they started out the door. "That is one well behaved service animal," he said. "You can bring him back anytime. And here's a snack for him." He handed her a small doggie bag.

"Meow," said Reggie and sniffed at the bag.

"I think that means, 'Thank you,'" said Corey.

Maurice laughed and went back to his kitchen.

Outside, Corey opened it and found a large portion of sliced turkey. "I'll give you a bite in the car," she said.

"Meow," said Reggie and ran to the car.

Seventeen

Roger drove around the block and parked behind Turner's unmarked vehicle. Corey glanced around the area.

"I think he called back up to be ready. I see a lot of cruisers."

Roger nodded.

As they got out of the car and started across the street to Dolly's, Corey suddenly had a mild panic attack and grasped Roger's arm. "Roger, do you think she's here? Will they hurt her? Is she…"

Taking her hand and squeezing it, Roger said, "Corey don't torture yourself with the what ifs. She has proven resourceful so far."

"You're right, but I can't help worrying. They must keep her tied. Given the slightest chance, she can flatten them both – if there are only two of them."

Roger glanced at her, eyebrows uplifted.

"Didn't you know she has a brown belt in Karate?"

His eyes widened. "No, I didn't know that." Then he grinned. "That takes my worry down a couple of notches."

"The problem is they probably have a gun on her. Karate isn't much good against a loaded gun, especially if they're across the room."

"Turner is in the same booth we had… Was it just yesterday?" She frowned.

"Yeah, it's been a long couple of days and too many emergencies." He squeezed her hand again. "Don't worry. We'll get to the bottom of it soon."

"I know. I just…Something just doesn't feel right. It looked like Dolly and Turner were more chummy than…"

"Corey, he had to make her feel at ease so he can question her."

Feeling the tension that was slowly pressing between them when they spoke of Turner, Corey changed the subject. "That man could see us clearly."

"Unless he could read lips, he didn't know what we were talking about," said Roger.

"But Dolly did. Still, he must have known something before that,

GREAT-GRANDPA'S DIARY

or he wouldn't have been following us. Of course, he'd been following Dad all those years. He must have known Dolly. I wonder if that's how they – whoever *they* are – knew the diary was back in town."

"Good question. We'll ask Turner." Roger took her hand to hurry across the street, missing the sour look she gave him.

"Do you think the Service Animal will work again?" Corey asked.

"We can try, if not, I think Reggie can handle it."

The string of tiny jingle bells tinkled as they opened the door, Dolly looked up from the counter where she was waiting on a customer. Her smile was forced – her mouth curved up, but her eyes were harsh and questioning. The customer left glancing down at Reggie. Roger and Corey stepped up to the counter.

"You can't bring that animal in here."

"He's a Service Animal," said Corey. "I'm having some emotional problems. He was recommended by my counselor."

"Ain't had the drawing yet," she said.

"Oh, I forgot all about that," said Corey. "We just like your donuts and coffee. We thought we'd stop and take some home. We'll just have coffee for now."

"We close at five on Saturdays," said Dolly. "We don't have much of a selection and they're a little stale. We start making fresh ones at three a.m."

"That early?" said Roger. "Glad I don't have a job that starts that early. I'd already be in bed by now."

"We'll take coffee for here and three apple fritters to go," said Corey. "You can go ahead and make preparations for closing. We'll leave when you tell us."

They took their fritters and coffee to a small table next to the booth where Turner was sitting. They nodded to him as they pulled out the chairs. Remembering that Dolly could hear them if they talked, and not wanting her to know they were acquainted with Detective Turner, they refrained from talking to him. Reggie grumbled and chattered to himself. Corey could feel him pulling at the leash and collar. She knew it would be a matter of seconds before he was free – to do what?

Dolly brought the coffee pot over to Turner's booth. "You got a minute?" he asked.

"No, I'm getting ready to close." She started to walk away.

Detective Turner pulled a badge from his pocket. "I suggest that you put a closed sign on the door and sit for a minute."

Dolly flinched and set the coffee pot down on the table. She ambled over to the door, locked it and turned the sign around to Closed. Then she grabbed a cup, filled it and sat down across from Turner, watching him.

"All right," she said. "What do you want? I run a clean place. Never have any complaints – except for the fat ladies who complain because my donuts aren't fat free and sugar-free." She forced a laugh at her attempted joke.

Turner pulled a picture of the man who was outside the day before. "Do you know this man?"

"Sort of. He's one of the neighborhood bums – thinks he's a lady's man. I had to kick him out of here for harassing my girls."

"Known him long?"

"Bout thirty or forty years."

"Does he come around often?"

"Once or twice a week."

"Have you seen him lately?"

"He was following those two yesterday." She nodded toward Corey and Roger. "I helped them get away from him."

"Did he come into the store after they left?"

"Yeah, he said he was looking for that couple who just left. They owed him something and he wanted it."

"Did he say what they owed him?"

"No, but he seemed to think anyone who had more money than he did owed him something – if no more than a couple of bucks for a drink."

"A drinker, eh?"

"Never actually saw him drunk, but aren't most of the street bums drunkards?"

"Did you tell him where they went?"

"I said they went out the back door some time before he came in. I didn't know where they went and didn't care. He got mad and said if he found them, he would teach them a lesson. I told him good luck, gave him a cup of coffee and a donut and sent him on his way."

"You didn't tell him the girl's address?"

"Why would I do that? I didn't even know her."

"But you had her address in the fishbowl. Corey, see if it is still there."

Corey went to the counter and emptied the fishbowl.

"Hey, you can't do that," Dolly shouted and started to get up.

"Stay where you are," said Turner.

Corey returned to the table. "It's not there."

"Let me ask again. Did you give him the girl's address?"

Dolly was beginning to perspire. "He could've looked while I got his coffee."

Reggie, finally free from his collar, took off down the hall.

"Excuse me," said Corey. "But can I use your restroom? I've had too much coffee. Is that the way?"

"Yeah, down that hall where your cat went," Dolly said pointing to the other side of the counter. "The second door on the left."

Reggie was waiting for her between the two doors. When she was out of sight, Corey stopped and listened for any sound then opened the door to the restroom, flipping on the light. Reggie followed her in and while Corey searched for more of her mother's fingernails or some other message, he checked out the wastepaper basket. Then Corey spotted it like before – a pale pink fingernail – in the corner beside the wastepaper basket.

Reggie was only half-heartedly looking through the papers as if he knew there was none with writing.

"No message. That means she either doesn't know where they're taking her, or she's still here," Corey whispered to Reggie who growled in reply.

Deciding she had been in there long enough, Corey flushed the toilet and turned on the water in the sink. Reggie rushed out and sat beside the door across the hall. He clawed at it then rising on his back legs, tried to turn the doorknob with his front paws. Corey eased to the door, put her head against the door and listened. "Mom?" she whispered.

She heard a slight knock, as if a mouse had bumped something in the dark. Taking that as a positive sign as well as Reggie's frantic turning of the doorknob, Corey decided her mother must be in there. *If they tied her hands and put a gag in her mouth, a small thump would be the best she could do.* She tried the door. Locked. Pulling a thin nail file from her purse, she worked at the lock, hoping Dolly wouldn't come looking for her. She heard footsteps and stuffed her hand with the file into her pocket. Roger came around the corner. She put her finger to her lips to warn him not to speak.

He walked past her and knocked on the restroom door. "Corey?

Are you all right?" He waited a few seconds, "All right," he said. "Just making sure you aren't being sick again."

He backed up just as Corey got the door open. Reggie pushed past them into the dark room. Roger and Corey followed. Corey closed the door quietly and felt along the wall for a light switch. Finally, her hand fell on the plastic, oblong cover and she flipped the switch giving life to the sixty-watt bulb hanging from the ceiling. Shelves full of cleaning products filled one wall. In the corner was a deep sink with a mop and bucket resting in it. In the other corner between the sink and more shelves, Sherylee lay in a heap, bound and gagged.

Reggie had already reached her before the light came on and was trying to cut the ropes with his teeth. Corey ran to her and removed the tape across her mouth. Sherylee took a deep breath and whispered, "Thank you."

Reggie ran his sandpaper tongue across the red marks and tried to comfort her. "Reggie, I knew you would help Corey find me."

"Let's get you untied," said Corey.

"Can you handle this?" asked Roger. "I'll go back to Turner and Dolly and wait for your grand entrance." He grinned and winked at Sherylee. She grinned back, then winced because the tape had left her face sore.

"There should be some heavy duty shears here someplace," said Corey as she began looking for something to cut the ropes. She found a package opener. "Here we go," she said, beginning to free Sherylee's hands.

Sherylee held and stroked Reggie who plopped on her chest and purred. Finally, Corey cut the ropes binding her feet.

"Are you all right?" Corey asked as she helped her mother to her feet. "I see bruises. Anything serious?"

"They hit me a couple of times, but I'm all right. Never had a chance to use my Karate skills."

They heard a sound from the end of the hall. "Shhh," whispered Corey. "Someone's coming in the back door. She turned off the light. Heavy steps passed the door moving toward the dining room area. Corey put her ear against the door to listen. Hearing the sound of the steps fade, she eased the door open a crack. They could hear the murmur of voices from the front of the building.

"I don't know how long you've been tied up, but can you walk?"

"I'll make it," Sherylee said. "Did Roger say Turner is here?"

GREAT-GRANDPA'S DIARY

"We followed your signs," said Corey. "We took a chance on this being the donut shop."

Sherylee grinned and whispered back. "We make a good team, don't we?"

"With Reggie's help," said Corey glancing down at Reggie who was weaving around their ankles and purring so loud folks out front could hear him if they listened.

Tiptoeing down the hall to the dining area, Corey whispered, "Give me a few seconds," then she stepped around the corner, leaving Reggie with Sherylee. The unknown man stood midway between her and the table where Roger sat.

"Sorry I took so long," she said, "but it took a while to find what I was looking for."

"I told you where the restroom was. What else were you looking for?" asked Dolly.

"Proof that my mother is here – or had been here."

"Your mother? Why would she be here?"

"She was kidnapped this afternoon."

"Sorry, but I have no idea what you are talking about," said Dolly. "Did you find your *proof*?"

"Yes, as a matter of fact, I did." She held up the third fingernail and handed it to Turner. "I'm sure it will match the other two."

"So someone lost a fingernail in my restroom. Do you know how many women use that room during a day?"

"Not very many with false nails the color of my mother's. It's special ordered for her by Tammy at the Nail Palace."

"She has a point," said Turner. He turned to Corey. "Do you have a picture of your mother with you?"

Corey reached into her purse, drew out a photo holder, opened it to the latest photo of Sherylee and showed it to Dolly.

"Have you seen that woman?" he asked.

"Not that I know of, but like I said a lot of women come in here during the day." Dolly was sweating again. The unknown man, who was never introduced, began backing toward the hall. He turned to run, but was suddenly lying on his back, out cold.

"Oh, by the way," said Corey. "I found better proof than a fingernail. I found the fingers that the nails belong on."

Sherylee stepped around the corner dusting her hands as if she had been working hard. "I have been waiting all day to do that," she said indicating the man on the floor. "Just one good Karate chop –

that's all I wanted."

Color drained from Dolly's face. She grabbed her cup of cold coffee and took a gulp, choked, coughed then took another drink and set the cup down.

"Do you want to change your story," asked Turner, sliding out of the booth to stand beside Dolly. "Kidnapping is a Federal offence. You and your buddy want to take the full credit – including the murder of this man..." – he laid the picture before her again – "...and four others awaiting identification."

"I want my lawyer," said Dolly.

"I think that's a good idea. You can call him from the station. What about him? You want to get him a lawyer too?"

"Let him get his own lawyer – if *she* didn't kill him." She nodded toward Sherylee.

"He's not dead," said Sherylee, "but he will be out for a very long time."

Turner nodded to Roger. "Flip the light switch a couple of times and unlock the door. My men are waiting for a signal."

Roger responded and seconds later police officers filled the room and hall. With the latecomer still out and Dolly subdued, the police were in and out before the neighborhood hardly knew anything had happened.

"If you don't need us," said Roger, "I'm going to get Corey and her mother out of here."

"Good idea. I'll catch up with you later. You going home or to the hospital?"

"I want to go to the hospital and make sure Daniel is all right," said Sherylee. "That woman said she gave him something to kill him."

"He's all right," said Corey. "Roger and I got there just as she was leaving and alerted the head nurse. But, I'm with you. Let's stop by and make sure. We can grab a sandwich from a vending machine until we get home."

"I know you've had a rough day," said Turner, "but I have a feeling you're going to rehash the day's events. Mind if I join you for that?"

"Sure," said Roger. "I'll give you a call when we leave the hospital."

"I'll see you then."

"The car is just across the street," said Roger. "I can..."

"We can walk," said Sherylee. "Reggie is already there waiting for us."

Roger glanced around the room for the cat. "When did he...? Never mind. You're probably right. Let's go."

They walked across the street and Reggie was there. He waited for Sherylee to get in then leaped over her to the other side of the back seat.

Roger started the car. Corey turned around, and handed the bag from the sandwich shop to her mother. "This is a doggie bag from Maurice's for Reggie. It's sliced turkey. Maybe he'll share with you until we can find a vending machine at the hospital."

"No bread?" Sherylee said then laughed.

"Sorry, just plain turkey slices, although we do have a bag of apple fritters if you want..."

"Thanks, but I'll pass on the pastry if you don't mind."

"Meow," said Reggie and nosed at the bag.

At the hospital, Roger parked the car and Corey turned to Reggie. "Sorry, sweetie, but you'll have to stay in the car. We won't be long."

"Meow?"

"It's all right Reggie," said Sherylee. "I'll be right back."

Reggie sat back on the seat, muttering and growling to himself as if to say, "Yeah, sure you will."

Eighteen

As the elevator opened, Roger, Corey and Sherylee stepped out and hurried toward Daniel's room. A new guard outside the door stopped them.

"I'm sorry but visiting hours aren't until seven. I can't let anyone in there without permission from the head nurse."

"You and what army is going to stop me," said Sherylee. "I'm his wife and I will go in there with or without your permission."

She started to push past him but Roger stopped her. "Wait, he's doing his job – for Daniel's protection. We worked that out with Marjorie this morning – afternoon – whenever."

"I'll find her," said Corey and went to the nurses' station. "Excuse me," she said. "I need to speak to Marjorie – or whoever is on duty if she's not here."

"She's with a patient right now. Could I help you?"

"We're Daniel Kahlor's family. After a couple of attempts on his life this morning, guards were placed both inside and outside the room. No one enters without the okay from the head nurse. We need to visit with him for just a few minutes and the new guard doesn't know us."

"Oh yes, we all heard about that. Let me get Dorothy for you." The nurse checked a chart and went into one of the rooms down the hall. A large woman in white hurried down to meet the family.

"Hi, I'm Dorothy. Mary says you want to see Daniel Kahlor. I'm sorry we haven't met and my supervisor told me not to let anyone in to see him except his wife, daughter, daughter's boyfriend and Detective Turner. No one gave me pictures or descriptions."

"How about picture ID's – driver's licenses."

"Sounds reasonable," said Dorothy. They all showed their ID and she smiled. "Sorry to be so picky, but after what happened this morning, I'd lose my job if I let the wrong people in. Marjorie said the wife had been kidnapped before the attempt on Mr. Kahlor's life."

"That's why we're here so early," said Corey. "We just found my mother and freed her. Before she goes home, she wants to make

GREAT-GRANDPA'S DIARY

sure my father is all right and that he knows she is too."

"I understand," said Dorothy. She walked with them to the guard. "It's all right for them to go in for a few minutes. They're family. Thank you for doing your job. Tell your buddy it's all right."

"Yes ma'am," said the guard and opened the curtain. "It's all right, Mike. Family coming in for a few minutes."

Mike nodded. "Would you like this chair?"

"No," said Sherylee. "We won't be staying long. He needs his rest and so do we."

"Sherylee?" Daniel tried to sit up.

"Don't try to move," said Sherylee. "I'm all right. Reggie, Coral Rae and Roger found me. I just wanted to make sure you're okay."

"I feel like I've been run over by a truck, but I think I'm all right. They keep telling me I am anyway. Who is Reggie?"

Sherylee and Corey laughed. "Reggie is my Bengal cat – Sir Reginald. He looks like a miniature leopard – brown with black marble pattern, blue eyes. He's protective of me and very intelligent. You'll meet him soon."

"He's waiting in the car, now – I think," said Corey. "He has a way of opening doors and doing what he pleases."

"I can't wait," said Daniel. 'Maybe when I get in a regular room, he'll find a way to visit me."

"Or before, if he takes a notion," said Corey.

"Have they said when they will move you?" asked Sherylee.

"They keep talking about moving me to a regular room soon as those people – whoever they are – leave us alone. You look like that same truck that hit me, found you. Did they hurt you?"

"Not much. I got the last punch."

Corey and Roger laughed at Daniel's surprised look. "That's right," said Corey." She gave a Karate chop to one of the men at least twice her size."

"You know Karate?"

"Brown Belt. I teach it at the Center."

"I really do have a lot of catching up to do. Twenty years is much too long. I'm so sorry…" Tears formed and began to roll down his face.

"Now cut that out," said Sherylee. "Save those for when we can do it together. For now you need to rest and so do we."

"But we do need to have a long discussion when you feel up to it," said Roger.

"If I had known what a Pandora's Box I was opening with that diary, I would have burned it when I found it."

"That would have been worse," said Roger. "Whoever wants it is taking all kinds of risks – including killing their own people – and they only believe there is a diary. They would never believe you if you said your burned it."

"Maybe you're right. Tomorrow, I'll make myself feel better. We'll talk."

"Tomorrow," said Corey and kissed her father on the cheek. She and Roger left the room so her mother could have a few minutes alone with him – well almost alone, except for the guard.

As they walked to the elevator, Roger called Turner. "We'll be home in about fifteen minutes," he said.

Nineteen

Turner pulled into the driveway behind Roger.

"Shall I make coffee?" asked Sherylee getting out of the car.

"Why don't you take care of Reggie and sit for a while. Roger can make the coffee while I see what I can fix to eat," said Corey.

"There's soup in the freezer. I made a big pot of vegetable beef soup one day last week. There should be plenty of bread and cold cuts for sandwiches. Come on Reggie. I think you deserve a real treat. Want some tuna?"

"Meow." Reggie didn't wait, but trotted ahead of her and was sitting beside his bowl before Sherylee made it to the kitchen.

"I'll get the dishes out," said Roger.

"I'll help," said Turner.

When they were gathered around the table with bowls of steaming soup and platters of cold cuts and bread, Sherylee turned to Corey and said, "All right. You first. You know about my kidnapping. I want to know how you found me."

"Do you mind if I tape this?" asked Detective Turner. "It will make it easier when we write up the reports."

"That makes sense to me," said Sherylee. "Go ahead Coral Rae."

"When we got to the hospital, they told us that you had a call from me saying that I was having car trouble and you went to help. How did you get the message?"

"That fake nurse, as you called her, told me. She said she was from first floor and you called the front desk and asked if someone could give me the message. She said you dropped your cell phone in a puddle and couldn't call on it."

"Didn't you wonder why I didn't call your cell even if mine wasn't working. Had it really been me, I would have had to call from somewhere, so why not to your cell instead of the hospital number – which I don't even know?"

"I asked her that. She said you tried but my cell wasn't on. I remembered it was off while I was in the ICU area. I thought I must have forgotten and turned it off instead of putting it on vibrate.

Anyway, it was almost lunchtime, so I told Daniel I would take care of you and your car then take you to lunch. We'd be back around one or so. The fake nurse left with me. When we got to the main entrance, she went down one of the corridors – I assumed back to her job – and I left to go help you."

"She must have gone back later," said Corey. "But, why did she wait so long before going back to kill Dad?"

"She probably wanted to make sure I left the hospital," said Sherylee.

"Reggie and I found your cellphone," said Corey. "We left it on until we got to my answering machine."

Sherylee continued her story, "The closer I got to the warehouse district, the more I began to realize something was wrong. I pulled out my cell phone and called your home number to leave a message. I assume you got it since I have my phone back and you followed my clues. I didn't call your cell because I needed more time and if you answered, we'd talk and I couldn't give you all the information."

"I thought that might be why you called my apartment knowing I wasn't there."

"One of the men made a phone call on his way to my car. He was near enough that I heard, but didn't give it much thought. He said, 'Did you take care of him? ... Why not? ... Well, do it and get out here. Then he closed the phone and came over to me."

"After we checked your message on my machine, we returned to the warehouse to see if you were able to mark the tires in some way," said Corey

"How did you manage that?" asked Roger, reaching for another thick slice of Italian bread.

"I kicked one of the men and he knocked me down. I fell against the car. It was simple enough to slip the lipstick into the tire groove. They were busy arguing with the fake nurse who had just arrived. He called her stupid again for letting someone see her. But when she said she bribed the guard, told him she would be there a while and he could go get a sandwich, they really got mad and told her she was worse than stupid because now everyone would recognize her. They couldn't have that. So they shot her."

"We heard the gunshot on the cell phone and hoped it wasn't you," said Corey as she got up to refill the soup tureen.

"They took me to Parker's Warehouse and I knew they would change cars again. Parker would look completely innocent, so I planted one of my fake fingernails under the carpet to prove I had been in that car."

Turner helped himself to more soup. Roger and Corey smiled. "I knew you were seriously working at helping us find you when you were ready to relinquish your nails you just paid big bucks for last Friday."

Sherylee rolled her eyes at her daughter and Corey laughed – she could do that now. "Parker said you weren't there and he had no idea what we were talking about. He said his car hadn't been off the lot all day. When Reggie and I found the fingernail in the car, I knew he was lying about that. In the shop, while Turner questioned Parker. I pretended to be ill and asked to use his restroom. I hoped they had let you go in there before moving you."

"I was surprised they let me go to the restroom. I knew I would have to think fast and work even faster. They wouldn't let me stay in there long. I had already sacrificed one fingernail, what was one more? So I tore off another nail and dropped it beside the basket. I used my eyebrow liner to write a note on the paper towel then shoved it to the bottom of the basket in case someone came in after me to check the room. They did, but they weren't very thorough and didn't find anything."

Reggie sat beside Sherylee grumbling and muttering to himself.

"Is he begging for food?" asked Roger.

"Reggie never begs," said Corey. "If he really wants something, he takes it."

"Yeah, I guess he would, but what is he muttering about?"

"He's just adding his two cents worth to the conversation – probably amazed at their stupidity."

"Meow!"

"I think you might be right," said Sherylee. "So how did you find the right donut shop? I didn't know which one, so I couldn't tell you."

"We decided there were only three or four shops in town that made only donuts and similar pastries," said Roger. "Then Corey remembered signing up for a drawing for free donuts at Dolly's and that Dolly knew the man who followed us and Mr. Kahlor. Corey noticed when she signed up for the prize that she could clearly hear Dolly and me talking at the booth and decided that Dolly must have overheard us discussing the diary and sent the man to search her apartment. With it all, we figured Dolly's Donut Den had to be where they took you."

"I checked the restroom and found your third fingernail, so I knew you had been there. There was no message and there hadn't been much time so I figured you were still there. Reggie was pacing and growling. He must have known."

"Meow!"

"I'm sure he did," said Sherylee, petting the top of Reggie's head. "I heard someone go into the restroom and tried to make some kind of noise, but they really had me tied up and gagged. I managed a little thump with my foot."

"I heard it and so did Reggie. I picked the lock with my nail file. The rest is history, as the saying goes."

Turner stood, pushing his chair away from the table. "That soup was marvelous. Thanks for inviting me. I'll need you to sign this statement, after I get it typed, but it can wait a day or two. You all – maybe I should say *we* all need some rest. I hope you don't have any trouble tonight, but I'm placing a guard outside just in case. Call me if anyone gets by him."

"Surely you don't think…," Sherylee looked horrified.

"We're dealing with nuts that are desperate enough to have killed five times. We don't want to take any chances. You all need to sleep well. Who knows what tomorrow will hold."

"Thanks Turner," said Roger as he walked the detective to the door. "We'll see you tomorrow."

Twenty

Once again, Corey woke in her childhood home. Church bells from St. Michael's Catholic Church two blocks away reminded the faithful – and not so faithful – that it was Sunday morning. Time for early Mass. A warm lump moved at the foot of her bed. Reggie stood, stretched then jumped from the bed landing with a thud.

"Time to eat, Reggie?" asked Corey, grabbing her robe and following him downstairs. She stopped to breathe in the aroma of coffee, sausage and maple syrup. *Umm smells wonderful.*

She reached the kitchen, where Roger and Sherylee were just sitting down at the table.

"You're just in time," said Roger. "Your mother made waffles this morning."

"It smells wonderful, but Mom, you should've stayed in bed and let me…"

"We wanted breakfast, not lunch," said Sherylee giving her daughter a good morning hug. "Besides, I'm fine. It could have been worse if you and Reggie hadn't shown up when you did."

Corey glanced over at Reggie. He was eating his breakfast, ignoring them, so she sat down and began to help herself. "Do you think Dolly is the leader? She's the one who sent that man to my apartment. Did they ever find out his name?"

"Turner said he had several aliases, but mostly he was called Barney. As to Dolly being the leader, Turner says it's up to the D.A. Personally, I don't think so. Parker seems more likely, but even there…someone had a lawyer down there to get them out on bail before they even arrived at the station."

"We should go down and sign those reports before going to the hospital – unless you want to go to church first," said Corey to her mother.

"I talked to Pastor Martin the other day when he came to see Dad after his surgery. He understands why we aren't there – even without knowing all we've been through."

"I think I'll go to the early service," said Corey. "I need some quiet meditation time."

"We need to spend some time with that diary this morning," said Roger.

"Maybe Daniel will feel up to spending a little time with you this afternoon," said Sherylee.

"I have a list of all the people that are named in the diary. Dad could maybe tell us who they are and what relation they were to his father."

"You and Roger can work on that list. I need to run to the Fitness Center and do a couple hours of bookkeeping before I go to the hospital. We can have lunch at the cafeteria while Daniel has his lunch, then we can go over the names."

"Sounds like a plan," said Roger. "Do you want me to drop you off?"

"Why not just take my car," said Corey. "Roger and I will be together anyway."

"You were going to go to church."

"I can skip it today, I guess."

"Tomorrow, maybe one of you can take me to get a rental car until I have time to look for a new car," said Sherylee.

Roger's cell phone rang. "Hello...Sure...I'll take care of it right away. The paper wants me to check something out – just a minor story – shouldn't take more than a half hour."

"Why don't you drop me off since you're going out anyway? Then Coral Rae can go to church and meet me at the hospital if you get tied up."

"How will you get to the hospital?" asked Corey.

"It's only a couple of blocks and it's a beautiful day. I need to walk for the same reason you need to go to church."

Corey nodded. She and her mother understood each other's needs.

"Thanks," said Corey. "I'll be back here by ten and work on the diary until Roger gets back." She turned to face him. "Just be back here by eleven so we can meet Mom for lunch. If you get tied up somewhere, you can meet us there."

"I'll be back long before ten."

"Meow!"

"Where did that come from?" said Roger.

"I think he's emphasizing the fact that you better be back here on time."

"Sure he is," said Roger with more than a little sarcasm, but he looked as if he thought she might be right.

Corey cleared the table, loaded the dishwasher and went to dress. The early service wasn't as formal as the later one, so she put on her new rust colored corduroy pants and melon colored blouse. She topped it off with a rust cardigan embroidered with red, orange and yellow leaves.

"I'll be back in about an hour, Reggie. Take care of things while I'm gone. We'll work on the diary when I get home."

"Meow," answered Reggie and headed for his favorite napping spot where the sun would cover him as it rose higher in the sky.

Corey drove to the Methodist Church downtown where she had been baptized as an infant and where she knew everyone. She hurried up the stone steps and opened the large double doors. Strains of *Come Thou Almighty king* greeted her as much as the usher who handed her a worship bulletin.

She smiled and nodded to Tom, the head usher. Luckily, there was room near the back when several friends moved closer together to make space for her. She smiled and joined them in singing the hymn.

When Rev. Barton picked up his Bible, Corey's thoughts flashed back to the Bible with her great-grandfather's notes in it. She mentally shook her head and tuned her mind to hear the message for her today.

"Then Jesus said to his disciples, 'Therefore I tell you, do not worry about your life, what you will eat; or about your body, what you will wear. Life is more than food, and the body more than clothes...Who of you by worrying can add a single hour to his life? Since you cannot do this very little thing, why do you worry about the rest?" (Luke 12:22-26, NIV).

Rev. Barton closed his Bible and began to tell his congregation how much God loves each and every one. He pointed out that life is full of tragedies and unknown fears, but worrying about it won't change the situation. Only God can do that.

"Put your faith in the One who loves you and is with you in the midst of your troubles, not in the hands of those who would lead you into the troubled waters of the soul."

Corey sat quietly, letting the spirit and the holiness of the place renew her soul. She was beginning to understand that she could not change the evil around her, but she could endure it with the help of

God. When she left the church, she felt a peacefulness she had not felt for several days. *I really needed this time. Maybe my thinking will be clearer when I get back to work on the diary.*

***

Corey returned home, gave Reggie a little playtime then stacked the pages of the copied diary on the table and gathered pens, pencils, markers and legal pads. Of course, Reggie wanted to play with the pencils. He was three years old and still as playful as a young kitten. Corey didn't mind. She had plenty of extra pens.

Opening the diary to page one, she made a list of names and how often they were mentioned.

Letters:
Mary Sue   (Jan. 20, 21, 28; Feb. 11, 21, 24; Mar. 12, 20, 25, 31; Apr. 7, 16)
Hannah (Jan. 23; Feb. 14; Mar. 3, 21; Apr. 16)
Jane   (Feb. 3, 10, 17, 26; Mar. 8, 17; Apr. 14; July 28)
H.J. Giovanni   (Jan 20)
Marie   (Jan. 24, 31; Feb. 8, 12, 21, 27; Mar. 5, 14, 21, 28; Apr. 2, 3, 11, 19)
Fred Oyler and Marie   (Jan. 31)
Goldmeister (Mar. 22)
Someone from Chicago about Mark Hollister (Feb. 6)
Paris Magazine   (Mar. 27, 28 – ($1.50 for two jokes)
Mrs. Warren Zurphy   (Apr. 7 – birthday card)

Visits:
Fred Oyler   (Feb. 2);
Goldmeister   (Apr. 13);
(Mary Sue and boys   (Mar 26)

Unusual Events
Professor Snook Electrocuted.
Mentions a fire

Birthdays
Harry's Grandfather   (April 1);
Harry – (April 7);
George.—(May 5);
Harry Jr. – (April 12)

No entries between April 20 and May 4.
Two short entries in July
Nothing else until May 31, 1931
***

By the time Roger returned, Corey, with Reggie's help, had made three copies of the list. Reggie's contribution was to throw the page to the floor as she finished. Of course, she now had to pick them up and sort all the pages. She had learned early on to number them.

"There isn't much to go on with names," she told Roger. "Most repeats – family members I assume. Dad will be able to tell us for sure. I did come up with a short list of one-time entries or three at the most."

He picked up the lists Corey had made and read over them twice then folded them and placed them in his pocket. "Maybe your father can clue us in on who these people are."

"There has to be something there. Even criminals don't go around kidnapping and killing people just for an old man's diary."

"Remember Harry Kahlor wasn't an old man when he wrote those words. And there is still the question of why two diaries?"

"Maybe we need to double check the Bible with the diary," said Corey.

"I don't think that will change anything, but maybe later. Now, let's go see if your father knows anything that will help us."

"You can stay home and rest today, Reggie. I think the excitement is over," Corey said as she got her jacket from the closet. When she turned to open the door, Reggie stood beside it with his leash in his mouth.

"I think he wants to go," said Roger. "Do you think…?"

"I don't want to think. Hopefully, he'll stay in the car. Most cats do as they please and Reggie is more Cat than most cats."

When they arrived at the hospital, Roger lowered the window an inch or two and Corey said, "Reggie, will you wait in the car? I don't think I can pull the Service Animal gimmick on the hospital staff."

Reggie glared at her.

"If he gets out, he might get hurt – by a car or someone who thinks he's wild," said Corey "It's a nice day. Maybe we can eat at the outside tables where the nurses eat on sunny days."

"Where is that?"

"Around back. Mom knows where it is. She's volunteered here

for several years."

"All right, you go around there with Reggie and wait. I'll bring you a sandwich and something to drink."

"Bring Reggie a ham sandwich – no mayo or mustard – and a bottle of water. Might be a good idea to get a bowl, too."

Roger rolled his eyes and walked toward the hospital entrance while Corey walked with Reggie around the back of the hospital to the picnic area.

Twenty-one

Roger glanced over his shoulder several times, as he made his way to the front entrance. The sun was shining, but he felt a definite chill. *Must be catching Corey's paranoia.*

He walked through the lobby, glancing around for familiar faces – as in followers. He saw no one that looked like they were biding their time, waiting for one of the family to appear.

He reached the elevators, pushed the call button and waited. The door slid open and he was face to face with Sherylee. "They just brought Daniel's lunch, so I thought I might catch you down here. Where is Corey?"

"She took Reggie to the picnic area."

"Reggie? Why is he…?"

"He joined us uninvited and was reluctant to stay in the car. He was acting strange – like he did yesterday when he knew you were in trouble. Corey wouldn't leave him in the car alone."

"He would just follow you anyway," said Sherylee.

"That's what Corey said."

"Reggie is a wonderful companion. He's so intelligent that sometimes I feel inferior to him. We can go to the cafeteria on the first floor and out the side door to the picnic area."

They went through the cafeteria line, picked up sandwiches, drinks and some bananas for dessert. Sherylee led the way to the picnic area where Corey and Reggie had found a table.

"Was everything all right at work?" Corey asked.

"Mostly. The windows were spray-painted with *We want what's ours. Now!* I called Turner. They took pictures then had the windows cleaned for me."

"Maybe they've run out of hoods to do their dirty work since they killed so many the last couple of days."

"Possible but not probable," said Roger

"How is Dad today?" asked Corey.

"He seems more alert and anxious to talk. We just need to watch that we don't tire him too much."

"Is Detective Turner joining us?" Sherylee asked as she picked apart the ham sandwich and broke up pieces of ham and bread for Reggie.

"He said he would try to make it about one," said Roger. "This isn't bad for hospital food."

"It's okay," said Corey, abandoning her sandwich and peeling a banana, enjoying the flavor of the fruit.

"Something bothering you, Coral Rae?" asked Sherylee.

"Nothing I can put my finger on. I'm like Reggie. I just feel uneasy like there's one more spider web in the just cleaned room. Maybe I'm just picking up on his strange behavior, which probably isn't strange at all for a cat."

"We're all on edge," said Roger, "but we'll get to the bottom of this, one way or another."

"It's the other that concerns me," said Corey. "These people are so unpredictable. What will they try next? I can't believe they've given up."

"Nor can I," said Roger, "but worrying about it won't help. I wonder if your father is finished with his lunch."

"Probably," said Sherylee. "I'm anxious to get started on this diary business, too. Let's go."

"What about Reggie? Will he stay in the car?"

"Reggie, you stay in the car like a good kitty. We are all fine, see?"

Reggie rubbed against Sherylee's ankles and purred.

"I'll take him back to the car," said Corey, "and meet you in Dad's room in a few minutes. He should stay in the car now that he knows you're all right."

But Reggie apparently had other ideas. He slipped his collar – again – and took off like a cat with a mission. Corey ran after him, but like his namesake ancestors, he moved much faster – dodging bushes, people and anything else that got in his way. At the front entrance, he jumped, hit the handicap opener and slipped inside. Corey followed close on his heels, but not close enough to stop him. Finally, she caught him at the elevator. But before she could slip his collar and leash on, the shiny doors opened. People got off and Reggie weaved between legs and planted himself in the back corner. Corey got on and tried to coax him off, but Roger and Sherylee got on behind her and pushed the button for four. The elevator began to rise and Sherylee turned to say something to Corey. She threw her hand over her mouth to hold back the scream.

"Coral Rae, what is he doing here? I thought you... He can't..."

"Tell him that," said Corey still trying to catch her breath from chasing him.

Before Sherylee could say anything further, the elevator stopped and the doors opened. Reggie was out in a flash. Corey started after him.

The kitchen staff was gathering empty lunch trays and placing them on the cart. Sherylee's face lost its color as a young man emerged from Daniel's room with the empty tray. She forgot all about Reggie and ran toward the young man. "Stop," she called to him.

He turned to face her but kept easing to the cart. "You aren't the same one who brought that tray up here."

"No ma'am, I'm not. We often trade around."

"Not on this floor," said Marjorie who came running when she heard Sherylee call out. "What's your name and..."

The man, who was much older than the youth who had come earlier, threw the tray at her and started to run for the exit.

"Stop him," said Roger to the guard outside Daniel's room. Reggie didn't wait for the guard, but ran after the man, landing on his back before he reached the exit door. Roger was on the man before he could catch his breath. The guard following on Roger's heels pulled his gun and handed the handcuffs to Roger. Reggie got off the man and slipped away.

The other kitchen aide froze to the spot, afraid to even let the scream flow through her open mouth. She stood against the wall watching. Marjorie took her tray, pulling her from her statue-like stance. "Pick up that tray and gather up everything. Get it to the lab on the double. I'll call and tell them you're coming."

"Yes, Ma'am," said the girl suddenly coming to life. She gathered dishes and spilled food as if her life depended on it.

Corey ran into her father's room and grabbed the water he was about to drink and anything else on his bedside table. "Sorry Dad. More trouble."

She ran back to the girl who was getting on the service elevator. "Here," she said placing the water pitcher and glass on the tray. "Take these too."

The girl nodded, still too dazed to speak.

In the meantime, Marjorie signaled a Code Blue and the team

came running to check Daniel for any signs of poison, distress or anything else out of the ordinary.

The elevator opened and Turner stepped out in the midst of the excitement. "Oh great, here we go again. Now what?"

While the Code Blue Team worked with Daniel, who really wasn't in any distress, Marjorie called down to the kitchen and talked to the Dietitian. Roger tried explained to Turner, who wasn't really listening.

Marjorie hung up the phone and said, "She'll check on Doug, the kid who brought the tray up here and give us a report in a few minutes. Tracie took the tray to the lab for them to analyze everything."

"Will someone tell me what's going on?" Turner glared at Corey as if she were the cause of the disturbance. She turned away to go see Marjorie.

Roger frowned and tried again. "It looks like we arrived just in time to prevent another attempt on Mr. Kahlor's life. Mike has him in custody. We were just going to call you."

"All right, I'll take it from here. Mike hold on to that would-be killer until someone from downtown comes for him. Pulling his phone from his pocket, Turner punched in some numbers and barked orders. "Get up here ASAP. Would be killer apprehended. Need transport."

The phone rang and Marjorie ran for it. "Yes…Thank you Marie. Send him to ER. We sent everything left on the tray to the lab, so we're under control here. Not your fault or Doug's either."

She hung up and turned back to Turner. "They found Doug, the kitchen worker, in a back closet unconscious. The man must have hit him over the head with something heavy. There's no way any of us could have predicted that. It will be a while before we hear from the lab, but…"

"At least he's not dead," said Corey.

"That's a good…"Roger's words were cut off by the sound of the elevator opening. Two armed police officers stepped off.

"You called for a cruiser?" asked one of them.

"That was quick," said Turner.

"We were just around the corner on our way back to the precinct. You got something for us."

"Yeah, take this bum down and lock him up until I get back there to question him. Read him his rights and book him on assault, attempted murder and resisting arrest."

The two officers took the handcuffed man by the arms and led him into the waiting elevator. Corey caught a smirk on the man's face as the door slid shut.

"Do you know those officers?" she asked Turner.

"Not personally. Why?"

"I don't think they are real police officers and I think your prisoner will never see a prison cell – or the light of another day."

"Corey you're getting paranoid," said Roger.

Turner glared at her. "Are you saying I don't know what I'm doing?"

Corey reacted to the anger in his voice and responded in kind. "You haven't kept too many prisoners from this case have you? Five dead – and I would guess number six is coming up. And what about Parker and Dolly? Out on bail? Or off the hook for lack of evidence?"

"Look, *Miss Kahlor*..."

Corey turned her back and started toward her father's room. She heard Roger trying to placate Turner. She didn't care. For a homicide detective he wasn't very good at his job – at least not in her opinion.

The phone rang again at the main desk. Marjorie hurried to answer and Corey turned to listen. "Yes...Thanks Jody...check the rest as well. I don't think he got any of that – not much anyway. At least we know what we're looking for."

Marjorie turned back to Turner, who had followed her to the desk, but included the rest, "The lab says the water glass was contaminated with a barbiturate of some kind. Granules of the not fully dissolved tablets were still in the bottom of the glass. Thanks to Corey's quick thinking, we got it before he drank it. But, I'm afraid the excitement has been a little much for him. According to the monitors, he needs to rest before you try to question him or get much out of him. I'm sorry."

"No problem, Marjorie," said Sherylee. We'll come back in a couple of hours."

"Where's Reggie?" Corey glanced up and down the hall.

"Reggie? What's that cat doing here?" Turner glared at Corey again.

"Catching a would-be killer for the police to..." She didn't finish her accusation. She had been about to say, "For the police to let him get killed."

"Come on Reg. We're going home for a while," called Sherylee and started for the elevator.

Reggie crawled out from under the medicine cart parked outside Daniel's room. One of the nurses held back a scream, but her throat was so tight she squeaked, "How did he get in here? You can't…"

"Never mind, Nancy," said Marjorie. "He did his part in capturing the imposter who tried to poison our patient."

Corey slipped the collar and leash on Reggie. "Come on, Reg. You did a good job. Now let's get you out of here. We'll go home and work some more. You can help keep my papers in order."

The elevator began its descent. "You two can take him home. I'm going back to work for a while," said Sherylee. "Shall we meet back here at four? We'll visit a while then go for a bite to eat."

"Why don't we drop you off and you give us a call when you are ready to go," said Corey. "We'll pick you up. It's supposed to rain. Call us."

"All right," said Sherylee.

Twenty-two

Roger was too quiet as he and Corey walked to his car. Corey glanced sideways at him. *He's upset with me, but I can't help it. After all these years with no father, he finally shows up and Turner is going to let him get killed with his incompetence.*

"Thanks," said Sherylee when Roger dropped her off at her work place. "I'll call you."

"Okay," said Corey.

"Meow," said Reggie.

"You be a good boy and stay home tonight," said Sherylee patting Reggie on his head before she got out of the car.

"Meow," he said again and it sounded more like, "Okay."

The drive to Sherylee's house was not only silent, but also so chilled by the frost between them that Corey shivered. Roger reached to turn on the heat.

"That won't do any good," she said. "The chill isn't in the weather."

"You think it's me?"

"I think we need to talk. If you're angry, say so."

"And why wouldn't I be angry?"

"Why would you?"

"Corey you practically accused Turner of being incompetent. He's a homicide detective and he's my friend."

"And I'm your fiancée. Does his friendship take precedence over that? And did I say anything that's not true?"

"Corey, you're being childish."

"Am I? Then call the police headquarters and ask if that fake kitchen worker is there?"

"Of course, he's there. Those two cops took him in."

"Did they?"

"You're being impossible."

While Corey and Roger argued, Reggie added his mutters and growls in the back seat.

"Even Reggie agrees with me," said Corey as they pulled into the driveway. Roger turned off the engine and Corey reached for the door.

"Corey, can we just forget it. We are both tired and..."

"You're right. Our arguing isn't going to change..." she was about to say Turner, but instead finished with "...anything."

Reggie was already out of the car and loping up the steps to the front porch. Corey followed, opened the door and moved toward the kitchen. Roger was right behind her, hands in his pockets, a frown on his face.

"Shall I make some coffee?" Corey called from the kitchen then lowered her voice when she realized Roger had joined her. "Mom might have some cookies in the freezer. I'll put something in the crockpot for supper while I'm at it. It won't take but a few minutes and we can relax better here than at a restaurant."

"Sounds like a good idea – both of them. But why don't I make the coffee while you get the crockpot meal started."

"Okay." Corey got a freezer bag of beef cubes from the freezer and put it in the microwave long enough to separate the pieces. Then she set about chopping and cutting vegetables. Putting the meat and vegetables in the crockpot, she set the temperature on High and turned to pick up the cup of coffee Roger had poured for her.

With coffee in hand, she and Roger moved to the dining room table with diary pages, notes, writing tools and laptops.

"Why don't we look up some of the events that the diary mentions – specifically someone named Snoop or Scoop or something like that who was executed. See if he was a real person or just a name Harry threw in," said Roger.

"He mentioned a fire after a long absence of writing. I'll look that up while you do Professor Snook," said Corey. "Might help to know a little about the robbery, too."

Two hours later, Roger stood and stretched. "Well this is interesting, but I'm not sure how helpful it is. What about you? What did you find out?"

Corey, with Reggie's help, sorted through the papers from the printer. "Here's an article about the robbery. At three o'clock yesterday afternoon, three armed and masked men robbed the Merchants Bank of Toledo. They killed a bystander who went to the aid of a woman whom one of the robbers knocked down. The three men left with approximately $50,000. A fourth man kept the motor running in the car. Ezra Goldmeister said he recognized the voice of

GREAT-GRANDPA'S DIARY

Harry Kahlor, who was apprehended two hours later alone in his car. Kahlor admitted to driving the car, but said he was not inside the bank. Police are still searching for the other three men."

Corey picked up another printed page. "This one explains the gap in the entries between April 20 and May 4. Actually, there were headlines in a lot of papers – New York Times, Columbus Dispatch, The Times Picayune."

"Really big event?"

"Yes. Listen," she said and began reading from her notes: "April 21, 1930, the Ohio Penitentiary in Columbus, Ohio, experienced the worst disaster not only in Ohio's history, but also in the American prison history. A terrible fire broke out in the early evening, eventually killing 322 prisoners and guards.

"There was little debate about the source of the fire. Apparently, a candle ignited some oily rags left on the roof of the West Block, also known as the Big Block. Although many inmates died from the flames, others perished after breathing poisonous smoke from burning lumber.

"The prison was built in 1834 to hold 1,500 prisoners and was usually overcrowded and notorious for its poor conditions. At the time of the fire, there were 4,300 prisoners living in the jail. Construction crews were working on an expansion and scaffolding was set up along one side of the building. The fire broke out on the scaffolding.

"The cellblock adjacent to the scaffolding housed 800 prisoners; most of them were already locked down for the night. Many reports say that the guards not only refused to release those in jeopardy, but also continued to lock up more prisoners in the upper level as well. Meanwhile the fire spread to the roof endangering the upper levels as well.

"Finally, two prisoners forcibly took the keys from the guard and began their own rescue efforts. Approximately 50 inmates made it out of their cells before the heavy smoke stopped the impromptu evacuation. The roof then caved in on the upper cells. About 169 prisoners burned to death."

Corey stopped reading, cleared her throat and glanced at Roger who sat with his mouth open. Finally, he said, "I can't imagine anything so awful and they didn't even try to save those men. What started the fire anyway?"

"The report says: The reasons why someone started the fire and why it turned into such a tragedy have been heavily disputed. Prison officials claimed that three prisoners, hoping to start a diversion so they could escape, started the fire intentionally. Two of the three accused inmates committed suicide in the months following the fire, seemingly to substantiate that claim. Other observers believed that the fire had been a tragic accident. They felt that prison officials had accused the inmates as a means of diverting attention from the administration's poor handling of the emergency.

"Regardless of the cause, conditions within the penitentiary had been ripe for disaster for years. There had been concern about crowded conditions within the Ohio Penitentiary for more than twenty years. By the date of the fire, the prison held an inmate population twice as large as its original capacity. Responding to this problem after the fire, prison administrators transferred several hundred inmates to a farm in London, Ohio.

"While there were many stories of cruelty and inhumane behavior among both prisoners and guards, there were far more stories of heroism and brotherhood. Two guards, heroes themselves, reported that prisoners saved their lives. Three hundred twenty-two died as a result of the fire.

"The tragedy was roundly condemned in the press as having been preventable. It also led to the repeal of laws on minimum sentences that had in part caused the overcrowding of the prison. The Ohio Parole Board was established in 1931 and within the next year, more than 2,300 prisoners from the Ohio Penitentiary had been released on parole."

"Maybe that's why he stopped writing in May of 1931," said Roger. "Maybe he was one of those released on parole."

"It's possible," said Corey, "but why didn't he contact his family. He seemed to always be lonely and anxious to see his wife and kids."

"Maybe he did – at least his wife. But maybe the former gang got to him first."

"You mean they killed him after he was paroled?"

"If they felt he left them holding the bag or something."

Corey shook her head. "I'm not sure I like where this is going. How about Professor Snook? Was he a real person?"

"Oh, he was real all right. Not much reason to believe Harry Kahlor knew him personally. Probably just knew of him as a prisoner. He was an interesting man and it's an interesting story, but like the fire, I doubt it had a lot to do with what we are searching for."

Roger read from his notes. "James Howard Snook was born in 1879. He was an Ohio athlete and veterinarian. He was a member of the U. S. Olympic Pistol Team that won a Gold Medal at the 1920 Olympics in Antwerp, Belgium. Later, he was head of the Department of Veterinary Medicine at the Ohio State University. He invented the snook hook, a surgical instrument that is still used in spaying animals.

"Snook was convicted of murdering Theora Hix, a 29-year-old medical student with whom he'd had a three-year sexual affair. Snook claimed at his trial in Columbus, Ohio that he had killed Hix because she was threatening to kill Snook's wife and family and that he feared she would shoot him. The trial was considered shocking for the sexual activities discussed. The jury took 28 minutes to deliberate before finding Snook guilty, after which he was sentenced to death by electrocution.

"Snook was executed on February 28, 1930 at the Ohio Penitentiary, by means of the electric chair. He was buried in Green Lawn Cemetery after a short service at the King Avenue Methodist Church. His tombstone, omits his last name, reading only James Howard."

"In the Bible he mentions the death and a burial the next morning in the prison cemetery," said Corey.

"What does the diary say?"

Corey turned to her notes. "This is interesting. The diary says he heard rumors of Snook's burial at Green Lawn in Columbus." She paused, chewing on the end of her pencil. "Maybe I better look closer at the Bible. There might be other discrepancies."

"That's no big deal. Does it matter where a complete stranger was buried?"

"Maybe not, but there might be some other differences that will matter."

"I think it's a waste of time, but help yourself. Shall I make some more coffee?"

"I've had enough. Why don't you separate the names we think are family from the ones we think are friends or acquaintances. Dad can look at them later."

Corey reached for the legal pad and a pencil. Reggie smacked the pencil and it flew across the floor.

"Reggie, what did you do that for?"

Roger laughed. "Maybe he's tired of being ignored."

The cat jumped down and began batting the pencil around the floor, so Corey reached for another one and handed it to Roger. He began dividing the names.

Corey opened the Bible and began writing notes

Jan 13   *Grandma would be proud of me.*
         Wish I could visit her grave up on Maple Hill, Lot # 243, Sect. 87
Jan 15   *If I could only get to the Bank. Ha! Ha!*
Feb 2   *Twenty minute Visit from Oyler today. Said Dolly sent him.*
Feb. 28 *Snook electrocuted*
Mar 1   *Snook buried in prison cemetery*
Mar 22   *letter from Goldmeister. Said Mary Sue might be down Wed. Sounded like he was fishing.*
Apr 1   *Grandpa's birthday – 82 today*
Apr 5   *George 11th Birthday*
Apr 12   *Harry Junior's 12th Birthday*
Apr 13   *Visit from Goldmeister – Supposed to bring Mary Sue and boys, but didn't. Said they would be down tomorrow.*
Apr 7   *Harry's birthday received many cards*

Roger finished his list and handed it to Corey.

Family:
   Mary Sue – wife;
   Harry Junior and George – sons;
   Marie, Hannah and Jane – sisters.

Friends and acquaintances:
   H. J .Giovanni;
   Fred Oyler;
   Mark Hollister,
   Mrs. Warren Zurphy – Wauseon, Oh;
   Ezra Goldmeister;
   Rusty someone;

"Can we cross off the family? Surely they weren't involved in anything illegal – at least the wife and children?" said Roger. "We can get Turner to check out these other names – especially the two from Wauseon, Ohio, as well as Oyler, Goldmeister and Rusty. It would be nice if we had a last name for him."

"Roger?" Corey hesitated, frowning.

"Something troubling you?"

"Yes, but I'm not sure what. I know the police are very busy and we have kept them more busy than usual with all our troubles, but…"

"But what? You want them to do more? Less? Let you handle it?"

"Don't be sarcastic," said Corey. "It just seems that Turner isn't finding any of the information we need about Parker, Dolly and all the others very fast, or else, he's dragging his feet about sharing that information with us."

"Well we aren't exactly law enforcement types," said Roger.

"I know that, but…if he doesn't want to share information with us, that's his privilege as a law enforcement officer, but he could tell us to bug off. Then we could do some research on our own."

"Is that what you want him to do?"

"No, but…"

"What do you want, Corey. The man is busy and you know yourself how much time it takes to look up something on the internet."

"For us, yes, because we don't have the equipment they have and we don't have the kind of information we need to do it faster."

"Corey, are you trying to say that you think Turner doesn't trust us?"

"Maybe, but… maybe I'm asking, if we can trust him?"

"Corey, I think we've been hiding our heads in these files too long. We need to get out of here. It's almost four o'clock. You really need a break."

"Maybe," she said as she turned off her laptop and called her mother. "We're ready to leave," she said. "Are you ready? We can wait if you're not…Okay. See you in a few minutes." She turned to Roger and said, "She'll be waiting for us."

"I wonder if Reggie plans to go with us."

"We won't know until we start out the door," said Corey.

They opened the door. No Reggie. Corey looked in the living room. Reggie was stretched out on the couch.

"I guess not," she said.

Twenty-three

A fine misty rain filled the air as Corey and Roger left the house. "No Reggie this time?" Sherylee asked when they stopped for her.

"No, I guess he was all tired out from the morning," said Roger.

"Well, let's hope Daniel is ready and able to fill in some of the gaps for us," said Sherylee. "We should only stay an hour. They'll be bringing his dinner by then anyway."

"I put some beef stew in the crock pot," said Corey. "I thought it might be more relaxing to go home instead of eating out."

"Thank you Coral Rae. I am getting a little weary of restaurant and cafeteria food."

Roger parked in the parking garage near the bridge since the mist had turned to a steady down pour. They walked across to the hospital's second floor.

"Looks like Turner is waiting for us," said Roger.

"I hope that doesn't mean more trouble," said Sherylee hurrying to meet him.

Roger opened the door and let the women go ahead.

"Good evening," said Turner.

"More trouble?" asked Corey.

"No, I just wanted to be here when you talk to Mr. Kahlor about the diary. I thought you might use the bridge since the weather has turned a little nasty."

Sherylee exhaled a deep sigh. "I was just telling Corey and Roger we can't stay more than an hour. I talked to the nurse a little bit ago. He's still recovering from this morning."

"We'll go back home and hash over any information we get," said Roger. "You're welcome to come home with us," he said. "We aren't trying to cut you out of the action – or eating."

Turner laughed and glanced at Corey. "I don't want to be a bother, but I did think we could compare notes."

"Don't worry about Corey," said Roger as they started walking to the elevator. "She was tired this afternoon."

Corey and Sherylee were walking ahead of the men to the elevator and could not help but hear them. Corey bit her lip to keep from turning around and giving them a blistering retort. Instead, she pretended not to hear them. Sherylee patted her arm and winked at her. Corey relaxed and smiled at her mother. At least someone understood.

The elevator doors slid open. Corey and her mom stood aside to let folks off and then entered. Corey moved to the back and stared straight ahead, saying nothing as if she were the only person on board. When the door opened on the fourth floor, Marjorie met them as they got off.

"You still here?" asked Corey.

Marjorie laughed. "Every once in a while we have to do either a double shift or a shift and a half. Today is my turn for a double. Mr. Kahlor is resting much better. He was just asking when you were coming and how soon it would be time for dinner. I would say he's feeling much better."

"Sounds like it," said Corey.

They went to Daniel's room and Turner told the guards they could have a twenty-minute break to go to the cafeteria if they wanted to. "I'll be here to guard Mr. Kahlor," he said.

"Yes, sir," they said and ran for the elevator.

Daniel smiled as they gathered around his bed. "I'm not sure what all they're giving me in here, but I feel wonderful for the first time in years. If only I had sought medical help instead of trying to find answers on my own…"

"Of course it would help if some jerks would stop trying to keep you from getting better," said Corey.

"Well, yes, but in time…"

"You're right Mr. Kahlor," said Turner. "In time we'll have it all taken care of."

"Yeah, sure we will," Corey muttered under her breath. Roger punched her arm and she turned to stare at him. Then she moved to the other side of her father's bed – away from Roger and Turner.

"Maybe I should have just thrown that diary in the Maumee River and forgotten about it. It really doesn't matter anymore. We can't go back and change anything. Whatever my grandfather did, he did for reasons known only to him. If he wanted us to know, he would have written it in plain English for us."

"That might be so," said Turner, "but he might have been involved in something more than a simple robbery. Maybe he double-crossed his pals and plea-bargained for a shorter sentence by fingering some of them. Some of the people named in that diary, might want to know where he hid the loot – if there was any."

"They would all be dead by now," said Daniel. "Or pretty close to it."

"But their families would still be around," said Turner. "Someone is mighty interested in that diary – enough to try several attempts on your life as well as trashing your daughter's apartment and kidnapping your wife. Who knows what else they will try. If we can find out from the diary, who might be involved, we can run a check on their immediate families and begin to investigate each one."

"If you think it will help, we'll read through the diary again, but I didn't see anything that seemed out of the ordinary for a man to put in his diary," said Daniel.

"Corey has written down all the names from the diary. Maybe you can tell us if they are family, friends or unknown to you," Roger said.

"We know that Mary Sue was his wife, your grandmother. George was your father and Harry, Jr., your uncle."

"That's right."

"How about Marie, Hannah and Jane? They're all mentioned often."

"They were his sisters – my great aunts. I remember my grandmother saying once that Marie visited them often."

"He said something about receiving money from a man named Giovanni," said Corey.

"I know that name. Grandmother said Grandfather did a lot of odd jobs – handyman type of things. Just before he got in trouble, he did some painting for a Harold Giovanni, who must have stopped by the house to give Grandmother what he owed."

"Well, it seems like we can mark him off the list," said Turner.

"How about Fred Oyler? He visited once and was mentioned once with Marie. He says he was disappointed because he thought Oyler was his friend and would have written and visited more often."

"My grandmother mentioned him once or twice. He was one of Great Aunt Marie's many boyfriends. Marie got tired of him and sent him packing. No one in the family liked him except my grandfather. For some reason he thought he was a nice fellow."

"Do you think he might have been into anything illegal?"

"Hard to tell. It was so long ago and I never even knew my

grandfather."

"How about an Ezra Goldmeister? He mentions that he came to Columbus with his family for the Jewish Easter. Once he mentions that Goldmeister told him your grandmother would be down the next day. Was he a friend of the family?"

"I remember my grandmother laughing once when we were talking about church. She mentioned the name."

"If he was a friend of the family, why didn't he offer to take her to see her husband? And why did he just ignore the family after that?" Turner asked.

"I'm not sure he was that good a friend. Grandmother said he wanted her to let George and Junior be taught in the Jewish school. She said no. He was never happy with that."

"How about Rusty? Who was he? There is no last name. He's only mentioned once – something about a letter from Jane and glad she was feeling better and Rusty too."

"Rusty was Great Aunt Jane's son – a wimpy cousin. He never got along with Dad or his brother, Junior. Rusty was a mama's boy – running to the doctor for everything. Grandmother said he died at the hands of a hit-skip driver."

"They never found him – the driver that is?" asked Roger.

"I don't know. That's all she ever said about him."

"Well, we can definitely cross Rusty off the list," said Turner.

"He mentions a couple of people from Wauseon, Ohio. Do you know anything about that place?"

"Nothing other than it's between here and Toledo. I was never there. Who did he mention?"

"A Hollister and someone named Mrs. Warren Zurphy."

"No one I would know. Grandmother never mentioned them. Or I've forgotten if she did.

"Harry says that he received a letter from Chicago about Hollister and Mrs. Zurphy sent him a birthday card."

"She must have been a family friend to send him a birthday card. I have no idea who Hollister was. Nor would I have any idea who is in Chicago who would write to Grandfather."

"That narrows the list down somewhat," said Roger.

"We have Fred Oyler, who was a sister's boyfriend; we have Goldmeister, a Jew from Toledo who was a friend; we have two people from Wauseon – Hollister and Zurphy – who may or may not have been friends." Turner read from his pocket notebook.

Marjorie came in to check Daniel. "The dinner trays will be up in about ten minutes," she said. "I'll need some time to check him and give him his meds. It might be better if you went to dinner and came back around seven. He'll need to rest a little while after he eats."

"I'm all right," said Daniel. "I want my family here."

"I know you do, but we want you to get better so you can go home and be with them all the time," said Marjorie.

"You don't like me here?" Daniel grinned at her.

"We like you just fine," said Marjorie with a serious expression. "But we aren't too fond of the kind of people you attract."

Daniel laughed. "You got a point. I'll see you guys later unless something more important comes up that you have to go and investigate."

"I don't know what that would be. You're here and looking good. We're all here together. We'll see you around seven or so – but just in case, we'll call Marjorie if something comes up," said Sherylee.

Turner walked toward the elevator to wait for them, giving them family time alone. He was just closing his cell phone when the rest came from Daniel's room.

"More trouble?" asked Roger.

"What…? Oh, the phone. No, just checking in with the precinct to make sure .If you're serious about inviting me to dinner, I'll be glad to take you up on it. Maybe we can hash out some more ideas."

"Sure," said Sherylee. "Corey put some beef stew in the crock pot. You're welcome to join us."

Twenty-four

Turner pulled into the driveway behind Roger and they all went up the front steps together. Sherylee reached the key toward the door, then suddenly stopped and pulled her hand back. She sucked in her breath with a gasp.

"Mom?"

"The door is ajar. Did you lock it when you left?"

"Actually, we went out the side door to the garage, but I checked both this door and the kitchen door before we left. They were both shut tight and locked," said Roger.

Turner glanced at the door and pulled his gun. "Looks like someone jimmied the lock. Let me go first. Just be ready to call off your cat. I don't think he likes me."

Stepping into the foyer, Turner took in the living room, dining room and archway to the kitchen in a glance. He put his gun away and motioned for the rest to follow him in.

"Whoever was here is gone," he said, "but they left their calling card."

Corey, Sherylee and Roger stepped inside. Sherylee let out a yelp and Corey had a feeling of deja vu. Upside down furniture, lamps on the floor, knickknacks scattered across the room, the sheers and draperies hung from one corner of the dining room window.

"It looks like a hurricane was through here or else Reggie had one heck of a cat fit," said Roger.

"Where is Reggie?" asked Corey.

"Probably hiding," said Sherylee. "He knows he's been a bad boy."

"Mom, he didn't open the front door."

"He can. He probably took off so I wouldn't scold him."

"He *can* open doors – but he can't unlock doors or jimmy locks," insisted Corey.

Suddenly, Sherylee paled and she began calling him. "Reggie, come on boy. Suppertime. Treat time. Come on Reggie. I'm not mad – much."

There was no answer.

"Someone was in here," said Roger. "They either kidnapped Reggie, or he ran away when they left the door open."

"Why would someone kidnap Reggie? He's a cat. He can't tell them anything about the diary," said Sherylee. "Unless they speak Bengalese."

"Mom, you didn't know anything either, but they kidnapped you in order to force us to give them the diary."

"You mean someone took my Reggie for an old book of someone's ramblings?"

"Looks that way," said Turner who hadn't said anything once they were in the house.

"Well, Corey you go ahead and dish up dinner. I'm going out to see if Reggie is running lose in the streets."

"I'm going with you," said Corey.

"I'll call for some backup, but I think Roger is right. Someone stole the cat for whatever reason. Someone should stay here in case the kidnappers call – for ransom or the diary."

Turner pulled out his cell phone, but before he could dial a number, it rang. "Turner here…Okay…be right there. In the meantime, send a backup cruiser to the Kahlor place…B and E and possible kidnapping of a cat."

"More trouble?" asked Roger as Turner folded the phone and placed it in his pocket.

"Yeah. Possible homicide on the west end. Call me if you get a ransom call."

"I'll stay here," said Roger, "and straighten up the mess while I look for clues," said Roger, "unless you want to check for fingerprints and…"

"And paw prints?" said Turner laughing.

"It *is* a crime scene," said Corey.

"The only crime is allowing a cat that size to throw a tantrum in the first place. I don't have enough manpower to conduct a crime scene investigation caused by a cat. *If* you get a ransom call, let me know." Turner left before Corey or Sherylee could regain their wits and respond.

They grabbed flashlights and treats and started down the stairs to the street. "Why don't we split up?" said Corey. "I'll go right and you go left."

"That's a good idea," said Sherylee.

Corey could hear her mother calling to Reggie as she moved in the opposite direction doing the same. "Reggie. Where are you Reggie? Come on sweetie, treats." One of the children of the street came out on the porch.

"Hi, Miss Kahlor. Is Reggie lost?" All the children in the neighborhood knew Reggie. He would sneak out sometimes and play ball with them.

"Yes, Michael," said Corey. "Someone broke into my mother's house. We think he got out while the door was open."

"Maybe someone kidnapped him," said Michael.

"Maybe," said Corey, "but we have to be sure he's not in the neighborhood."

Michael's mother came to the door to see who her son was talking to. "Reggie's disappeared," he told her. "I'm going to go with her and help look for him."

"You do that Michael. I'll call the other kids and tell them then I'll be along too."

"Thank you," said Corey blinking back the tears. Soon a dozen children and parents were combing the neighborhoods for Reggie. They met Sherylee, who had also gathered a posse of children. Not a street in a four-block area was left unsearched. Reggie was not there – and apparently had not been there.

"We need to go back and check with Roger. Maybe he found something," said Sherylee.

"Thank you – all of you," said Corey. "If you hear anything at all, please call us. We'll let you know when we find him."

"We'll keep looking and call our friends across town," said Michael.

Tears threatening, Corey and Sherylee ran back home, hoping that Reggie was there – maybe hiding because of the mess he'd made.

"But, Reggie has never been destructive," said Sherylee. "He's always been gentle – even when he was a kitten."

As they started up their driveway, Julie, who lived next door, pulled into hers. She called to them. "Sherylee, I had to run to the drugstore for a prescription for Tommy, but as I was leaving a strange car – blue Chevy of some kind pulled into your driveway. Two men got out of it. I told them you were at the hospital and would be back in about an hour or so. They said you gave them a key so they could fix your computer while you were gone. I didn't argue with them, because I had to get Tommy's medicine, but I couldn't believe you would let someone in your house while you were gone – not without telling me."

"You're right, Julie. I wouldn't. Whoever it was seems to have taken Reggie. We've searched the neighborhood. He's gone." Tears began to roll down her face and Julie ran over and hugged her neighbor.

"I'll call all the neighbors. We'll search and search until…"

"We've been searching for the last hour. All the kids and their parents have helped."

"Well, I'll keep a lookout and let you know if I see anything. If you need any of us for anything, call me."

"Thank you Julie. Roger's inside. We'll go see if he's found anything."

***

After Turner left to check out his emergency and Corey and Sherylee ran off looking for Reggie, Roger, not believing they would find him, began putting the place in order – picking up chairs, lamps and anything else that was on the floor where it shouldn't be. He stooped to pick up something that looked like a dart.

This shouldn't be here. Ah ha.

He kept his eyes open for more darts as he righted the living room and dining room. The kitchen had been untouched. He pulled one of the wooden dining chairs over to the window in order the see how much damage was done in pulling the draperies from the corner. *Not much, just pulled out from the hinge.* He got it fastened back up and started to get down when he noticed something that looked like an appointment card on top of the china cabinet.

Mrs. Kahlor must have put it up here and forgot it, but why would she put it way up here?

He climbed off the chair, started to put the card on the table for Sherylee, but couldn't help reading it. *Not a doctor appointment.*

***

Corey and Sherylee came in the front door. "Did you…?" They were empty handed, so Roger didn't finish his question.

"Thank you Roger, for straightening things for me. Reggie must have put up a hurricane of a fight."

"Mrs. Kahlor, did you pick up one of Parker's cards when they kidnapped you?"

"No, I never saw any – not that I would have thought to take one anyway. Why?"

He showed her and Corey the card he found on top of the china cabinet. It was a business card from Parker's Wholesale Merchandise Warehouse.

"How did it get on top of my china cabinet?"

"Take a close look," said Roger.

Sherylee took the card and turned it over and over. "Reggie! There are teeth marks on the card. Reggie somehow got it from one of the men and put it up there."

"Apparently, that's when he tore the curtains down, so we'd have to climb up there to put them back and find the card."

"But what did they do to Reggie? It's obvious they couldn't catch him."

Roger picked up the darts from the table. "They used a tranquilizer dart on him. It must have taken four tries. I found three used darts. Shall we call Turner?"

"You can call Turner if you want to, but I'm going to get my cat," said Sherylee.

"I'm with you," said Corey.

"Let's go," said Roger. "We can call him on the way."

Twenty-five

"This is the second time in two days we've been to that warehouse. If they don't do something more about Parker than a slap on the wrist this time, I'm going to the District Attorney myself," said Corey.

"There's Turner's car. How did he get here so quick?" asked Sherylee.

"He said he was just around the corner," said Roger.

"But, I thought he was called to another murder scene across town."

"So maybe he thought Parker might be involved like he was with your mother's kidnapping. Whatever, he's here, so we can let him do his job."

"If you are suggesting that we go home and wait, forget it. I'll not leave until we find Reggie. Mom and I both know that cat better than Turner does, especially since he doesn't even like Reggie. And the feeling is mutual."

"Don't get pushy, Corey," said Roger. "Turner is a good detective and he has humored us so far. Don't expect him to let us in on his investigations."

Corey said nothing, but got out of the car and caught up with her mother who was talking to Turner. She heard him say, "Look Mrs. Kahlor, I know you're concerned, but he's only a cat. I can't spend a lot of time looking for a cat."

"He's not just a cat," said Sherylee indignantly. "He's *my* cat and he's a special…"

"I've questioned everyone here and they say there's no cat here. Without a search warrant, I can't go in there and search for him."

"You did when my mother was kidnapped," said Corey.

"You mother is a woman – a person. We're talking about a cat. I'm not risking losing my badge over a cat."

"Then I'll go in and search for him myself," said Corey and started toward the door.

"Stop," Turner shouted to her. "You can't just walk in there and start tearing the place apart."

GREAT-GRANDPA'S DIARY

"They didn't mind tearing my apartment up, or my mother's house."

"The cat tore your mother's place apart just acting like a cat."

"He tore the place apart trying to escape from the idiots who were shooting tranquilizer darts at him." Corey took another step to the door.

"I'll have to arrest you for breaking and entering if you go in there," said Turner.

"Really? What time is it?"

Turner looked surprised, than glanced at his watch. "It's a quarter to five," he said.

"The sign on the door says they are open until 5:00."

She opened the door and walked into the large waiting area outside the offices where Albert Parker met her.

"You again. I told you before…"

"We found my mother and she had been here. I'm looking for her cat now. I have reason to believe he's here – or has been."

"I suppose he left a message for you like your mother did?"

"You might say that," said Corey listening carefully for any sound that might be a cat. She heard nothing.

"Well, he ain't here and you don't have a warrant."

"I'm not a police officer. I'm a possible customer here to look around to see if you have what I want."

Corey started toward the back of the warehouse where two large sliding doors were open to the back alley that ran along the river. She heard a muffled yowl and started running toward the open door. Two men were struggling with a burlap sack trying to get it into a small boat at the dock. Once again, she heard the yowl as they dropped the sack in the boat. She ran faster and jumped at the man on the dock. He was ready for her and hit her across the temple. She fell into the boat beside the sack, too dazed to move. Before she could get her wits about her, she heard shouting and the roar of the motor. Suddenly they were moving out into the river.

"Better tie her up," said the man driving the boat.

"She's out. We'll dump her and the cat overboard. They won't know what hit them."

"I still think we ought to just shoot the cat and be done with it."

"Cats hate water. I want to watch this one drown. We'll tie the woman's hands so she can't swim."

"Well hurry up and do it. We'll have a police river cutter after us and I don't plan on getting caught."

The other man laughed. "We got plenty of time, but if you're so antsy, get us to the middle of the river. Corey heard him moving closer to her. Before she could move, he grabbed her hands and tied them in front of her. *Maybe I can still swim a little, but what's he going to do to Reggie?*

She found out sooner than she would have cared to. The man opened the sack and turned it upside down so that Reggie fell out of it into the river. Then he picked her up and threw her in after him. Laughter followed. She heard him yell at the driver, "Hey I want to watch…" The boat was speeding away.

She felt soft wet fur bump up against her as she tried to tread water and pull at the rope with her teeth. "Reggie, swim to the shore before it's too late. I'll keep treading until I get these loose."

Reggie disappeared under the water then slid between her chin and her wrists, which she stretched in front of her. She began kicking her feet and Reggie moved all four paws in a dog paddle stroke. Soon they were at the river's edge on the other side. The ropes were still tied and being wet made it harder to untie them.

"Can you get help, Reggie? My head is throbbing and I can't get the ropes off. Maybe if I just sit here…"

Reggie growled and hissed at some animal that Corey couldn't see. Whatever it was took off when Reggie showed it who was boss.

"Maybe it's not a good idea to stay here," she said. "We'll head across the field and see if we can find someone to help us."

They walked – Corey stumbling several times – for what seemed like several hours, but in reality was probably about twenty minutes. Finally, lights pierced the early evening darkness ahead. "Looks like a farm up ahead, Reggie. Hopefully it will be a friendly place – to both cats and people."

"Meow," answered Reggie.

Another ten minutes and they were nearing the farm's front door. Before they even stepped into the yard, a scrappy little dog of some kind began barking. He ran down the steps from the porch yapping his little heart out. Reggie sat beside Corey, swishing his tail, uttering a low growl.

"It's all right, Reggie. He's protecting his master just like you protect me."

The porch light came on and an older man came out. "Who's there?" he called.

Corey took a couple steps forward into the light. The little dog ran back upon the porch beside his master.

"My name is Corey Kahlor. Some men kidnapped my cat and me and threw us overboard on the river. If you could call my fiancé for me, I would appreciate it."

The man came down the steps and took a closer look at Corey and Reggie. "Are you sure that's a cat? Looks like a baby leopard."

"He's a Bengal cat. He's three years old. His name is Sir Reginald but we call him Reggie."

"Names' Miller – Samuel Miller. My wife, Martha and I own this little farm. This is Scrapper. He's a mutt, but we love him. Come inside. The air is getting cooler and you're wet."

"Thank you," said Corey suddenly realizing how cold she was – and how tired.

"Martha, put the tea kettle on and heat up that soup. This girl and her cat are freezing."

"My goodness, what happened to you? That looks like a nasty gash on your head. Now, you come with me and let's get you out of those wet clothes before you take pneumonia and …why are your hands tied?" She got her sharpest paring knife and began to work on the ropes.

"I'll be all right…" But Corey didn't have a chance to finish her sentence. Martha took her by the hand and led her down the hall to a bedroom – presumably Martha and Samuel's. She reached behind the door and pulled a fluffy robe from a hook. "Take off your shirt, pants and socks," she said, "and put this on. I'll throw your clothes in the dryer." She opened a drawer and pulled out a pair of long, fuzzy slipper socks. "These should warm your feet. Now let's go to the kitchen and take care of that nasty cut and get some hot soup in you."

Corey wanted to resist and protest, but the woman was so insistent and Corcy was cold and hungry. "You really don't have to do all this," said Corey.

"Of course I do," said Martha. "When I became a Christian, I promised God I would listen to Him and take care of strangers if he sent them my way. He did and I do."

Corey blinked at the matter-of-fact faith of this woman. What could she say? She followed her to the kitchen and sat at the table where Martha told her to sit.

While Martha bustled around the kitchen, putting on the kettle, setting a pot of soup on the burner and gathering first aid equipment, Corey took in the homey atmosphere. The kitchen was like many farm kitchens – roomy, warm and cozy. Nothing pretentious, just clean, neat, and uncluttered. Martha's dark eyes missed nothing as she set bandages, tape and alcohol on the table. She wore her dark hair short and her milk chocolate skin glistened in the heat of the kitchen.

While Martha was taking care of her, Samuel brought in a couple of towels. He was at least a foot taller than Martha and darker skinned. The top of his head shone like a polished tabletop. He was a big man – broad shoulders and hands twice the size of Corey's. And yet, he took a towel and gently dried and rubbed Reggie's fur until it glistened in the light of the fireplace. Reggie began to purr. Samuel smiled and stroked the dry fur.

Corey gave them a shortened version of what had happened – telling them only that Reggie had been kidnapped and she tried to save him. Martha clucked her tongue. "What is the world coming to, anyway? Even the poor animals are not safe."

As she listened, Martha was busy dishing up a bowl of hot vegetable soup. She set it on the table in front of Corey and fixed a pot of tea. "Does Reggie like tuna?" she asked as she reached to the cabinet of canned goods.

"Yes, he does," said Corey.

Martha set a bowl of water and a bowl of tuna down for Reggie.

"Meow," said Reggie.

Martha laughed. "How do you like that? He has more manners than most people I know."

"We both thank you very much," said Corey. "If I could use your phone, I'll call Roger to come and get us."

"We would be glad to take you wherever you're going," said Samuel.

"That would be wonderful," said Corey, "but I'm sure he and my mother are driving around looking for us. They'll be worried. It would be easier to call them to come here."

"Whatever's best for you. They probably haven't eaten either," said Martha. "I knew God wanted me to make this pot of soup today for a reason. Don't usually make soup on Sundays. They're welcome to have a bite when they get here."

Corey reached for the wall phone in Martha's kitchen and dialed Sherylee's cell phone. She answered on the first ring, as if she had been holding it in her hand willing it to ring.

"Hello," she answered hesitantly. Corey knew she didn't recognize the number.

"Mom?"

"Corey, where are you? Are you all right?"

"It's a long story. I'm assuming Roger is driving and you're looking for us."

"Yes."

"Tell him I'm all right and some wonderful people took Reggie and me in, got us dry and warm then fed us. They want to feed you too. Mrs. Miller made a pot of delicious soup today."

"And Reggie is all right?"

"He's fine. He's with me." She gave her the address, paused and added, "And Mom, tell Roger to leave Turner out of it for now."

"I'll tell him. You're on the other side of the river, so it will take us a while. The police could get us there faster…"

"Please, no police for now."

"All right."

While Corey waited, the Miller's told her stories about the farming community. "It has changed since we were married almost sixty years ago," said Martha.

"But people are still people," said Samuel.

"I don't suppose you were around in 1929," said Corey. "You are much too young to…"

Samuel and Martha both laughed. "Why thank you for your compliment," said Martha. "Samuel just celebrated his 83rd birthday two weeks ago and my 80th is coming up. In 1929, he was thirteen and I was only nine."

"I would never have guessed. You both are so…so lively."

Samuel and Martha laughed again. "Was there a reason for asking if we were around, or were you just trying to be polite?"

"Meow," said Reggie and smacked Corey's hand.

"Do you remember a big bank robbery in Toledo in the spring of 1929?"

Samuel stared at her for so long that Corey began to feel uncomfortable. "I'm sorry," she said. "I didn't mean to…"

"It's all right," said Martha. "He's tried so hard for almost seventy years to forget that day."

Finally, Samuel swiped his hand across his eyes. "I surely do remember," he said. "I was in Toledo that day. My daddy took us children – five of us – on a rare trip to the city. A friend told him he would help him get a small loan for the farm. It was hard for anyone to get loans in those days, but even harder for black folks.

"He took us to that bank and I never saw such a pretty place in all my life. We went inside for a quick look then he told me to take the little ones across the street to a little park and wait for him. While the youngins played on the swings and slides, I sat on a bench where I could see them and also see the bank across the street. I was responsible for my siblings, but I was worried about my daddy.

"He never believed in second sight, but I knew when something bad was going to happen. I just knew my daddy was in trouble. A very much used Ford pulled up in front of the bank. Three men got out, looked all around, put something over their faces and went inside. One man stayed in the car. That don't look good, I thought. I told my ten-year old sister to watch the little ones and I ran across to see if daddy was all right.

"I didn't go in. I just put my nose to the window and looked in. All three men had guns. Everyone had their hands up, including my daddy. The guard stood with his hand up like everyone else. The tellers filled the bags with money and they started backing out of the building. One of them hit an old woman with the back of his hand. When she fell, he laughed and my daddy started after him, fists balled. Another man standing behind a desk where the guard, couldn't see him, pulled a gun and..."

Tears were running down Samuel's face. Corey sat with her mouth open. "He was the one patron who was killed. I read the account, but they seemed to think one of the robbers shot him."

"No ma'am, it was that big-shot man behind the guard. I tried for years to find out who he was and why they didn't arrest him with the rest. As I remember, only one was ever caught – the man driving the car."

"My great-grandfather," said Corey.

It was Samuel and Martha's turn to stare with mouths open.

"That's really what was behind this kidnapping of Reggie. My great-grandfather left a diary. Apparently, the descendants of the others involved seem to think there is something incriminating in it. They want it. My fiancé and I are just trying to find out what happened to my great-grandfather. Did he die in prison? Or was he paroled and the gang – for lack of a better word – killed him? My dad, who never knew him, inherited the diary from his prison days. He wants to know more about his grandfather and apparently someone else wants to know more about the diary."

"Well, Miss Corey, if I ever saw that man again – or a picture of him – I would know him. It's been almost seventy years since that man killed my daddy. Ain't a week goes by that I don't have nightmares about it. If there is any way we can help you in your search, just ask."

"Thank you, Samuel. You have been a help already. They accused my great-grandfather of pulling the trigger that killed him, but he always claimed he drove the car, but didn't go inside the bank."

"You see, Samuel, I told you the Lord would send someone to give you peace before you die. He's been having those nightmares every night for over a week."

"Have you ever talked to the police about this?"

"I tried to once. They told me to mind my own business. Never went to them again."

Corey gave him her cell phone number. "Call me if you ever have any insight – even second sight. Now, I think I hear my folks." Reggie was already at the door turning the knob and Scrappy was beside him barking.

Corey introduced the Millers. Sherylee looked at the bandage on Corey's head. "You were hurt?

"I'm fine." She gave Sherylee and Roger a short version of their experience. "We'll talk more later," she said. "Right now, I think you're in for a treat. They all sat at the kitchen table and talked like old friends. Corey wasn't ready to tell them about Samuel's father being the man who was killed in the bank robbery. She needed time to digest all the information that seemed to be piling up.

"I thought cats hate water," said Martha. "How could Reggie do what he did if he was afraid of the water?"

"That's what the kidnappers thought too. The one man wanted to watch Reggie drown because he left a lot of scratches on him. But, Reggie is a Bengal cat. One of the characteristics of Bengals is their love of water. They love to play in it. Reggie loves swimming with us."

Corey and Sherylee helped Martha clear the table and wash the dishes. "These warm suds sure feel better than that cold rain water," said Corey.

"And I bet those dry clothes feel better than cold wet ones you arrived with," said Martha.

"Much better. I can't thank you enough for all your help. We'll do all we can to clear the past."

"You just call us if you need help again," said Samuel.

***

Finally, back in the car on the way home, Roger said, "I called Turner and told him you and Reggie were all right and we were going to take you home."

"Did you tell him where we were?" asked Corey.

"No."

"Well, I for one am ready to go home," she said.

"Meow," answered Reggie.

Sherylee laughed. "I think that was a 'me too'."

"Hopefully we'll have an uneventful night. What more can – or will – they do to us. Don't they know if they kill us all they'll never get the diary or Bible?" said Corey.

"Do they even know about the Bible?" asked Sherylee. "All I've heard mentioned is the diary."

Roger and Corey glanced at each other. "Maybe we need to take another look at the Bible part of the diary," said Corey. "Although, what I've read seems to be a repeat of the diary, or vice-versa."

"Did we ever give Turner a copy of the diary?" asked Roger.

"He saw the copies."

"But does he have a copy? And does he know about the Bible?"

Corey was frowning. "I don't think so. We have both the original diary and the Bible in Mom's basement freezer. We never made it to the bank. We've been working on the copies. Whatever, we're home and I'm tired. Our crock pot meal is probably very well done, but the Miller's soup was delicious and filling."

"I'll put it in the refrigerator and heat it for lunch or dinner tomorrow," said Sherylee.

They got out of the car and started to the house. The porch light came on next door. Julie stepped out and called to them. "Did you find Reggie?"

"Meow," answered Reggie as he jumped to her banister and licked her face. Julie laughed and gave him a hug.

"I'm so glad you are all right. I'll call the Kid's Chain," she said. "They'll let everyone know. Goodnight."

"Kid's Chain?" Sherylee and Corey glanced at each other.

Julie laughed. "Yeah, we developed it when one of the children was lost a few years ago. Within minutes we everyone covered and information spread."

"Great idea. We did tell them we'd let them know."

Hesitantly, they moved to the porch and opened the door. Reggie leaped into the foyer and rolled over and over on the carpet.

"He's glad to be home," said Sherylee. "Would anyone like some hot chocolate to relax before we call it a night?"

"Sounds good to me," said Corey.

"Me too," said Roger. "We need to unwind a little. Who knows what we'll face tomorrow?"

Twenty-six

Corey woke to the tapping of rain against the window. Reggie stretched and walked across the bed to lick her face and purr. "How are you this morning, Reggie. You don't seem to be very much affected by your swim in the cold water last night."

"Meow," said Reggie ending in a wide yawn and an "umph."

"I'm glad you think it was a ho-hum experience. I sure didn't enjoy it – except for the time spent with the Millers. We were all too tired to talk about it last night. I should have told Roger and Mom about Mr. Miller's father. Anyway, I am glad you're such a good swimmer."

Reggie jumped from the bed, stretched his front feet forward, then his back feet behind him. Then he continued to the door and pulled it open with his strong front paws.

"Must be breakfast time," said Corey. "I smell the coffee and…that smells like bacon. Mom must be making eggs and toast."

Corey slipped on her robe and slippers and followed Reggie to the kitchen where Roger was already at the table eating. "I thought I smelled bacon, fried eggs and toast," she said.

"We thought maybe you and Reggie might need a little extra rest," said Sherylee.

"Reggie said it was a ho-hum experience," said Corey. "I don't agree with him, but I'm all right thanks to his swimming ability and the kindness of the Millers."

"What do you think they will do today?" asked Sherylee. "We have Daniel surrounded by nurses, aides and police guards. If one of you will drop me off at Martin's Rental Agency, I'll rent a car until I have time to look for a new one. I'll take Reggie with me and we'll go to the Center from the rental agency, unless you two want him."

"Maybe you should take him with you, Roger," said Corey. "You're the only one who hasn't been harassed."

"Are you saying that I might have something to do with all this?" Roger bristled and glared at Corey.

"Of course not," she said. "Don't get so huffy. I'm just stating a fact that you haven't been attacked directly by anyone."

"I can't help it that they haven't come after me. If you had let Turner handle the kidnapping last night, you wouldn't have been attacked either."

"And we wouldn't have Reggie, either. Turner wasn't interested in jeopardizing his precious badge for a cat, as he put it. I could see those men dragging a sack out the back door. He had to have seen it, too, but he wasn't about to do anything and I knew Reggie was in that sack. I heard him. Do you think I could stand there and let them take him to who knows where? And they did intend to drown him. Furthermore…"

Corey threw her napkin on the table and stood so quickly her chair tipped. She grabbed it, continuing to glare at Roger.

"Coral Rae, sit down and eat your breakfast. Stop the arguing. It's bad for your digestion."

"I'm not hungry anymore. I'm going to the library this morning. If he wants to poke around and get himself in trouble, that's his business. I'm…"

"The library is still closed," said Roger. "I don't know what your problem is this morning, but…"

"My problem? You're the one who…"

"Stop it right now, both of you," said Sherylee. "We're all on edge as well we ought to be. It's not normal to be threatened, kidnapped and on the verge of losing our lives. Arguing won't solve anything. Now sit down and eat."

Corey glared at Roger, but realized her mother was close to tears. "I'm sorry, Mom. You're right. We are on edge." She sat down and sipped the coffee her mother set before her and nibbled at a piece of toast.

"Sorry," said Roger. "You're right, of course – both of you. We are on edge and I am the only one who hasn't felt the direct effect of those goons. That not only makes me look guilty, but it makes me feel guilty. Why do I have to watch the ones I love be hurt? Why don't they want me – or are they saving me for the worst?"

"Roger, I would never believe you were involved in any way. And…I was upset with Turner last night. It seems he's dragging his feet for some reason. Does he think this is all a hoax? Does he think it's a waste of time? He hasn't shared any information with us, but he wants to know everything we're doing."

"Well, he *is* the official investigator in this case and he has six murders on his hands. He doesn't have to tell us anything."

"Six murders? The food service man at the hospital? I was right, then."

"Yeah, you don't have to rub it in."

"What happened to him?"

"They found him in the river with his hands still cuffed and a bullet in his back."

"How awful," Sherylee said wrapping her arms around herself with a shudder.

"Anyway," said Roger, "Turner will offer information when he has what he thinks we need."

"But, he hasn't, yet. Anyway, I know all that, but I feel frustrated. Maybe we need to forget him and get on with our own research and investigation like we planned to do before that man – what's his name – trashed my apartment."

"But, Turner can get information for us quicker."

"He can, but will he? He hasn't so far."

"Why would he keep it from us?" Roger was becoming angry again.

"Because, we're not with law enforcement. We are civilians and civilians tend to get in the way of police investigations."

"But, Turner is a friend," said Roger frowning, "and that makes it more difficult for him. We put him in a precarious position. He might want to help, but the rules say he can't. He could lose his job if we got too involved."

"Then why did he say he would help? He could have told us the truth to begin with." Corey took a long drink of coffee to keep from saying more than she intended to say.

"Sometimes friends have a hard time being honest with friends – especially when they are conflicted in their desires to help and their needs to not help," said Sherylee.

"I suppose you're right," said Roger, not sounding like he meant it. "Maybe I'll go have a heart to heart talk with Turner."

"I think it would be a waste of time," said Corey, "but that's up to you. I've had enough for now. The library is still closed, but I've got paper work to do and I need to bury my head in books and forget the world of violence, intrigue and mayhem." She turned to her mother. "Why don't I take you to get a car then I can take Reggie with me to the library. You can go to the hospital when you want to."

"Thanks, Coral Rae."

Roger glanced back to them from his stare into space. "You could leave him here if you want. I have to write a couple of articles for the newspaper or I'll lose my job as a freelance journalist. If I leave, I'll drop him at the library."

"Sounds like a plan," said Sherylee. "We all need a break away from the diary hunters."

"I just hope they need a break away from us," said Corey as she started gathering her laptop and other work related tools to take with her.

Reggie looked from one to the other as they discussed his place for the day. When Roger said he could stay there, he swished his tail and went to curl on the couch for his morning nap.

***

Rain was still falling as Corey and her mother prepared to leave. Corey's car was in the garage, so they could go through the kitchen. But Roger's car was in the driveway. "Do you want to move your car so we can get out?" Corey asked.

"It's pouring down rain out there. I'll get soaked. Why don't you wait a few minutes to see…?"

Corey glared at him, handed her mother her keys, picked up Roger's from the buffet and said, "Mom, drive my car out and pick me up at the end of the driveway. I'll move his car and park it on the street." She turned back to Roger "I'll leave the keys in the car. You can move it when it stops raining."

Corey didn't wait for an answer. She threw a sweat jacket over her head and ran out to move Roger's car. Sherylee had no choice but to drive Corey's car out of the garage, pick her up and continue to Wilson's Rental Agency.

"Corey, don't you think…?"

Corey held up her hand and shook her head. "I don't want to talk about it right now. I need some alone time to think."

"All right, but you know I'm here if you need to think out loud and want a listener."

"Thanks, Mom. I know that and I appreciate it. Rev. Barton said something Sunday – what was it? Oh, yes, he said, 'Put your faith in the One who loves you and is with you in the midst of your troubles, not in the hands of those who would lead you into the troubled waters of the soul.' Right now, I feel like I'm in those troubled waters of the soul. I need to work it through with God."

"I understand," said Sherylee.

A comfortable silence fell between them until they reached the

Wilson's Rental Agency.

"Do you need help choosing?" asked Corey as they got out of the car.

"No, I'll take whatever is available in my price range. When I'm ready to buy, I might need help. See you later." Sherylee gave her daughter a kiss on the cheek and turned toward the door of the rental agency.

"Tell Dad I'll try to get by later," Corey called after her mother .Corey got in her car and pretending to adjust the seat, mirror and seatbelt, waited to make sure her mother was all right and someone was waiting on her. Then she drove away.

At the library's main entrance, she sat for a few minutes in the parking lot. Through the swiping of the windshield wipers, she studied the blurred poster-sized notice that said: Library Closed for Repairs. The rain eased a little and she started to get out of her car, hesitated then started the engine again. *If I go in the front entrance or if anyone sees my car parked here, it will look like we're open. I don't want to be disturbed.*

Corey left the parking lot, drove to the corner of Main Street, turned right on 6th Street and parked her car on the street about a block away from the library. Grabbing her umbrella, she quickly walked back down the street to the alley between 6th and 7th Streets. That led past the back door of the library. Glancing around to make sure no one was watching, she unlocked the door and slipped inside, locking it behind her. She was the head librarian, so there was no reason she shouldn't be there. But she felt an insatiable need to be alone – at least away from anything to with the diary mystery.

Corey hurried up the stairs to the main floor, where her office was semi-hidden among the stacks to the right of the stairs. She liked it there because it was away from browsers at the front of the library and hidden from view of the front windows. Anyone who wanted to see her had to walk down the long hallway created by stacks of books on either side of it. Even though there were windows that gave her a view of the library, she could pull draperies across them for privacy. The back window above the alley also had a darkening shade. She closed them all, not needing to keep out the sun, but she didn't want to view the gloomy, gray sky. Besides, if anyone walked through the alley, she didn't want it known she was in her office.

Setting her laptop on her desk and her briefcase on the floor beside the desk, Corey sat in her swivel chair, leaned back and heaved a long sigh. It felt good to be back where she was comfortable in her surroundings. She loved her mother and her mother's home, but she had been on her own long enough to want – and need – her own space. She loved Roger, but there too, she needed space right now.

I can't understand why Turner isn't telling us some things – like when I can get in my apartment and the names of the men who were killed and why Parker, who looked guilty as sin was never questioned beyond the initial interview. I'm sure he has a lot on his mind and Roger and I have no official reason for him to give us information. But...

She leaned forward in her chair, turned on her computer and waited for it to respond. *There has to be some other way to get the information we need.*

The ringing of her cell phone pulled her out of her contemplation. She considered not answering. It was probably her mother or Roger and she didn't want to talk to either one of them right now. But, she knew if she didn't talk to them, there would be more hurt feelings, so she dug it out of her purse and pressed the talk button without even looking at the Caller ID.

"Hello"

"Corey? This is Dave – Dave O'Riley."

"Dave? This is a surprise. How are you?" Dave was an old boyfriend. Their breaking up was mutual consent. He had been an officer in the Masontown Police Department. He married a very good friend of hers and moved to Washington. They corresponded at Christmas, occasionally during the year and on birthdays.

"I hope I didn't disturb you or interrupt something."

"No, actually, I'm at the library."

"I thought it was closed because of your trouble."

"Are you calling from Washington?"

"No, why?"

"Just wondering how you know about *my* trouble."

Dave laughed. "You always were inquisitive and helped me many times in solving crimes when I was on the force. I'm on vacation. Susie and I brought the kids to visit their grandparents. Is Roger with you?"

"No, I needed a quiet place to be alone to think things through. Why?"

"I need to talk to you – alone. Can you meet me someplace where we won't be seen."

"Why are you being so mysterious? Never mind, you have your reasons and I've always trusted your judgment. Why don't you come to the library? It's closed and no one will be in. Come to the back door. I'll meet you there."

"Five minutes," he said and she was listening to the dial tone.

Now what? I hope he and Susie aren't having troubles and I hope Roger doesn't decide to stop by with Reggie.

Corey left her office and walked downstairs to the back door. She opened it just as Dave ran around the corner. He slipped inside and closed it before saying a word. Corey gave him a questioning glance, locked the door and started up the stairs. He followed. They went into her office and closed the door, creating a more or less soundproof room.

"All right," she said when they were seated across from each other at her desk. "What's all this stealth all about? After the last week, I'm a little edgy about mystery."

"I bet you are. All right I'll explain why I'm here then we can conspire like we used to."

Corey raised her eyebrows. "Maybe we need coffee," she said. He nodded. She opened one of the sliding doors on the cabinet on top of her credenza. Inside was a coffee maker. She filled it with water, measured the coffee and pushed the brew button. While waiting for it to brew they chitchatted about old times, Susie and the kids, her job and her mother's job. The pot began to gurgle its final perk and Corey reached for cups in the cabinet over the small sink. She poured two steaming cups and went back to her desk. "You still drink it black and strong?"

Dave smiled, nodded and breathed in the aroma. Corey sat back in her chair and said, "All right. I'm listening," she said.

Twenty-seven

Corey gave Dave a curious glance as he took a sip of the coffee. She waited, knowing he was putting his thoughts in a succinct pattern. Finally, he took a deep breath and began.

"We've corresponded enough to keep up with family and minor details of our lives. I think I told you when Susie and I were married that we were moving to Washington, D.C. because I had been accepted in the FBI training program."

"And you're still with them?"

"I am, which is why I'm here. As far as my family knows, I'm on vacation. If any of our old friends see me, that's my story."

"But, there's more to it."

"A lot more. I couldn't believe it when my commander asked me to check out a report the FBI has on file concerning a Daniel Kahlor who has been running scared for twenty years. It seemed a relative of someone his grandfather knew wanted a diary his grandfather had written while he was in prison. A mental health clinic in Texas contacted us about a year ago. I flew out to interview Mr. Kahlor. He gave me a picture that a sketch artist at the clinic did with his help of the man who had been following him. That man was in our files.

"We got a background check on Mr. Kahlor to see if there was any validity to his story. He told us all he knew including the name of his wife and little girl – Coral Rae Kahlor. You can imagine how surprised I was. There can't be that many Coral Rae Kahlor's in Masontown, Ohio."

Corey smiled at him and he continued, "You aren't surprised."

"I might be under other circumstances, but I trust you and I am too well aware of all you've said. I might even know more than you do of the situation."

"I thought you might. So what can you tell me? I've talked to a few friends from the force. They say it's Detective Turner's case and he doesn't share information with anyone – not even his partner. But they knew your apartment was trashed and a man was found dead there, your mother was kidnapped, your father has had several attempts on his life and they even kidnapped a cat? Did you know your father was alive all these years? You told everyone he was dead."

Corey smiled, sighed and said, "No. Mom tried to protect me when it seemed he just walked out on us. You have the basics. It's a long story."

"I've got a week – more if I need it."

"Well, it started a week ago – I think. My mother called me at two a.m. and said my father had a heart attack and was in the hospital asking for me. I was confused because I believed my father was dead. It turns out my mother lied because she didn't want to tell me my father deserted us. Anyway, I called Roger and we went to the hospital."

Corey told Dave every detail from that point – except the Samuel Miller story. For some reason she didn't think to tell him about that. "It seems they still want that diary, although we can find nothing in it to be helpful to anyone. Dave, how much do you know about the diary?"

"Only that there is one and it might possibly have names and other vital information about a bank robbery in which a man was killed."

"Do you have any information about who was involved – names for instance?"

"Detective Turner would have all that information. You could…"

"Forget it. Turner is a friend of Roger's. He promised to work with us. We give him information, but we get nothing from him – not even the name of the man who was killed in my apartment."

"If he was the same man who followed your father, I can tell you who he was." Dave shuffled through his briefcase and pulled out he artist's sketch.

"That's him," said Corey.

"Thought it was. He had several aliases, but his real name was Hollister – Robert Hollister. He was the grandson of one of the robbers, Mark Hollister."

"Well, at least that makes sense in a warped kind of way."

"Okay, let's go over this again."

"Roger and I offered to read the diary. Roger is a writer and intends to write a novel about it. My father wondered if his grandfather died in prison or if he was paroled and killed before he could get home. He thinks he was involved with a mafia-type gang and when he was released, he was killed by one of his former pals."

"He's probably right, but I can find out for you. Turner could have given you the information."

"Turner got involved when that man – Hollister – was killed in my apartment. He hasn't even let me know when I can expect to get back in it. I'm staying with my mother right now.

"Anyway, Roger realized we were being followed when we left the hospital last Friday morning. Dad was doing better, but…" Corey continued to tell Dave again all the details of the attempts on her father's life, her mother's kidnapping, the kidnapping of Reggie and the attempt on her life when she tried to save the cat.

"Roger and I had words this morning before I left. I think Turner is dragging his feet and not really trying to find out who is behind all of this. Roger will stand up for his friend and I know Turner likes to work alone. But, I have an eerie feeling that something isn't right – and I don't just mean all the bungled attempts. Everything keeps leading back to Parker, but Turner says there's no hard evidence."

"Your instincts were always good. Let me see what I can find out. As a matter of fact, if I can use the library computer, I can access sites available only to law enforcement. In the meantime, why don't you research these sites and see what you can find out about the robbery. Then we'll compare notes."

"All right, I'll…" the library phone rang. Corey reached for it then pulled back "The library's not open and I don't want anyone to know I'm here," she said. When it stopped ringing, she waited for the answering machine to pick up the message. "Corey, if you are there, pick up the phone. This is Detective Turner and I have information for you."

Corey reached for the phone, but Dave laid a hand over hers. "Wait," he said. "Does he have your cell phone number?"

"No."

"How does he know you are here? Roger?"

"Probably."

"Ignore it. Let Roger call your cell if he really wants to talk to you."

A few minutes later, her cell phone rang. She glanced at Dave then at the phone. She picked it up and pressed the speaker tab.

"Hello."

"Corey, where are you? This is Detective Turner. I need to talk to you. Roger said you were going to the library."

"I was, but it's still closed."

"So where are you?"

"Does it really matter? I need some time alone. I'm tired of people trying to kill me, or my family. I'm tired of mystery and intrigue. If you have some information for me, tell me now. If not, then you can come by the house tonight and talk to all of us."

"Roger said you were a little touchy today. He wasn't kidding."

"Detective Turner, do you have something for me, or not? And how did you get my cell number?"

"Just wanted you to know you can get in your apartment later this afternoon. Forensics is done and we'll send a cleaning crew in early this afternoon and Roger gave me your number."

"Well, thank you very much for the information. I'm sure that will help heal the touchiness. Now if you don't mind I don't like to talk on the phone while I'm driving."

"You didn't say you were driving."

"I don't even tell my mother everything I do. I'll see you tonight. You are welcome to come to dinner – warmed over beef stew that we didn't have last night."

"I would rather see you now…"

"Well, that's impossible, isn't it? Goodbye Detective." Corey closed the phone and gritted her teeth. "The nerve of that man. Who does he think he is?"

Dave grinned and turned back to his searching.

***

"I think I found something," said Corey, pushing the printer command. She got up to grab the paper as it came from the printer.

"What do you have?"

"The *Toledo Times* report of the robbery. There's a very short, one inch square, piece of newsprint taped to the inside cover of the Bible and I ran a shortened version from another paper yesterday – two days ago – last month. The last few days, time has felt like a ball of yarn unraveled and spread around the house by Reggie."

Dave smiled at her frustration. "Let's hear what it says."

Corey read the article which was similar to the earlier version, but contained more facts and information. "At three o'clock Friday afternoon three armed and masked men robbed The Merchants Bank of Toledo. They killed a Negro bystander who went to the aid of a woman whom one of the men knocked down. The men fled with approximately $50,000. A fourth man stayed with the car and took off as soon as the other three were in the car. A bank manager, Ezra Goldmeister, said he recognized the voice of Harry Kahlor, who was apprehended two hours later alone in his car. When it was proven Kahlor's car was used, he admitted to being the driver, but refused to name the others. He claimed they were strangers and forced him to drive the car, saying they would kill his wife and children if he didn't help them. Goldmeister said he could have been mistaken, but the two men had been friends for several years, so it seemed unlikely he would mistake the voice. Three other men who have been seen with Kahlor recently, Mark Hollister, Fred Oyler and Warren Zurphy from Wauseon were questioned and released. They said they were fishing together the day of the robbery. Kahlor refused to name the others or produce the money. He insists they were strangers and he saw no money. Kahlor had a gun but it hadn't been fired."

"That sounds like a lot of circumstantial evidence."

"Harry Kahlor does mention those men in the diary – Goldmeister also. But this still doesn't tell us who the others were and who they're related to today. Maybe if I Google the names it will lead to the present." Corey paused, then said, "I wonder if we could get a picture of Goldmeister."

"I'll try. Any reason?"

Corey told him Samuel Miller's story. "If we had pictures..."

"He could tell us if he...Corey, does Turner know about Miller?"

"No, I didn't even tell Mom and Roger. I guess I wanted to mull it over first."

"Good, let's keep it that way until I can talk to Miller. I think I'm getting close to something, just not sure what," said Dave.

"Shall I put on more coffee? And I think there are some microwave soup containers if you want a bite of lunch."

Before Dave had a chance to answer, Corey's cell phone rang again. She checked her Caller ID. "It's Mom." She pressed the speakerphone button.

"Hi Mom."

"Coral Rae, where are you?"

"Why are you asking?"

"Because Turner called me. He said he was trying to find you. He said Roger told him you were at the library, but he called and didn't get any answer."

"Did he also say he got my cell phone number from Roger, called it and did get an answer?"

"No, he didn't tell me that."

"Well, he did. And he was pretty darn nosey, which is why I wanted to get away by myself today."

"I sensed that this morning. I thought you needed to be alone after you and Roger had a few sour words. Anyway, I told Turner that you said you were going to stop at the library for a few minutes this morning and then run some errands. Of course he wanted to know what kind of errands and where you were going."

"I can't believe the nerve of that man."

"Nor can I. I told him I had no idea where you were going or what you were going to do or who you were going to do it with. I said you are an adult and don't answer to me – or anyone else."

"Thanks, Mom. That man is beginning to irritate me. Have you been to see Dad? There's no more trouble there is there?"

"Well, there was a small incident. Some older man – I won't call him a gentleman – wanted to see Daniel. The nurse told him he wasn't on the list. He got angry and told her to put him on the list. She finally had to call security to remove him from the building."

"Did he give them a name?"

"He said it was Warren Zurphy, Jr. He said he was a friend of Daniel's."

"I don't suppose anyone got an address from him."

"I doubt it, but I'll check with Marjorie. Are you coming by the hospital before you go home? And have you had any lunch?"

Corey grinned at Dave, who reached for the soup in the cabinet over the microwave.

"Just getting ready to put some soup in the microwave," said Corey. "I'm not sure if I'll stop by the hospital or not. Turner says I can get in my apartment later today. They're going to clean it early this afternoon. I'll be home by six for dinner if I don't stop at the hospital first."

"Have you talked to Roger today?"

"No, he hasn't called and I've been busy. He said he was going to work at home and if he needed to go anywhere, he'd bring Reggie to the library."

"He said you weren't there, so he left Reggie with me."

"He didn't call. He must have talked to Turner, whose word is more believable than mine, I suppose."

"Coral Rae, don't let your father's err in judgment cause trouble between you and Roger. Leave the detecting to the professionals,"

"I am, Mom." She winked at Dave who covered his mouth to

hold back the laugh.

"Do you want me to come and get Reggie?"

"No, I'll leave him at the Center. The girls here like to have him around."

"Why don't I stop by there and get him on my way home?"

"That would save me going back. Thanks. See you later."

"Bye, Mom." Corey folded the phone and put it back in her purse.

"I wonder why Turner is so interested in where you are and what you're doing?"

"He's probably afraid I'll uncover something that will make him look bad, or break the case before he can call the shots."

"You might be more accurate than sarcastic," said Dave. "This is a great set-up by the way – almost as good as what I have at my office. What would be the possibility of me coming back here later tonight?"

"I could come with you, but I would have to explain to Roger and Mom why I was going out alone in the middle of the night. It's against the rules, but I could give you a key to the back door. I keep the shades drawn on these windows. They keep the sun out in the morning and it gives me privacy if I want to work after dark."

"I don't want to get you in trouble."

"And I'm not in trouble now?"

Dave laughed. "I mean trouble with your boss."

"I am the boss, except for the Library Board."

"That's right," said Dave. "I forgot you've been promoted since I left for D. C." He glanced at the wall clock. "I'll have to pick up Susie and the kids a little after four, so let's see how much we can accomplish before that."

Dave returned to the computer and Corey pulled out the notes she had made from the both diary and the Bible. Laying them side by side – Bible notes and diary pages – she began to compare.

***

Bible

Jan 13   Grandma would be proud of me. Wish I could visit her grave up on Maple Hill, Lot # 243, Sect 87

Jan 15   If I could only get to the Bank. Ha! Ha!

Feb 2   Twenty minute Visit from Oyler today. Said Dolly sent

him. Angry when he left.
Feb. 28 Snook electrocuted
Mar 1   Snook buried in prison cemetery
Mar 22   Letter from Goldmeister. Said Mary Sue might be down Wed. Sounded like he was *fishing.*
Apr 1   Grandpa's birthday – 82 today
Apr 5   George 11th Birthday
Apr 7   Harry's birthday received many cards
Apr 12   Harry Junior's 12th Birthday
Apr 13   Visit from Goldmeister. Supposed to bring Mary Sue and boys, but didn't. Said they. would be down tomorrow

***

Diary/News

Jan. 13 Mentions Grandma being proud. No mention of grave
Jan. 15 Letter from Hollister with a couple of bucks in it.
Feb. 2   Visit from Oyler. No mention of Dolly
Feb. 28 Snook electrocuted
Mar. 1   Says Snook buried in Greenlawn Cemetery after a service at Kings Ave. Methodist Church in Columbus.
Mar. 22 Letter from Goldmeister. No mention of *fishing* or Mary Sue.
Apr. 1   April Fool's Day. Speaks of Grandpa as if he is dead.
Apr. 5   George's birthday May 5 not April 5
Apr. 7   Received birthday card from Mrs. Warren Zurphy
Apr. 12 Harry Junior's birthday
Apr. 13 Visit from Goldmeister who is in Columbus for Jewish Easter

***

Corey stopped working, rubbed her eyes and glanced at the clock. "I've found a few discrepancies – not sure what they mean, if anything."

Dave looked up from the computer. "People or events?"

"Mostly numbers, like grandpa's 82nd birthday verses grandpa – rest his soul – loves April Fool's Day. Details of grandma's grave, Maple Hill, Lot # 243, Sect 87. Daniel's 11th birthday in April in Bible but May in diary. Twenty minute visit with Oyler. Goldmeister visited on Jewish Easter.

"Jewish Easter?"

"That's what he said. Did he mean Passover? Or is that a clue?" Corey rubbed her eyes again and glanced at the clock. "It's almost four thirty. You need to pick up Susie and the kids."

"Yes, I do, but I'll be back here around midnight. If you need to call me, here's my cell phone number." He wrote the number on a slip of paper and handed it to her. "I'll see you tomorrow."

"Why don't you give Mom a call later and let her know you're in town. I'm sure she'd like to see Susie and kids. They would love Reggie."

"Thanks, I'll do that, but I won't mention that I saw you today."

"Nor will I."

"Where's your car. I didn't see it anywhere. I'm over on 7th Street near some homes."

"I parked on 6th Street and walked down the alley to the back door so no one would know where I was."

"You wanted a little privacy and I messed that up."

"I'm glad there is a *professional* on the case," said Corey and gave Dave a smile. "Why don't you leave now? You have an appointment. All I have to do is pick up Reggie. I'll clean up the kitchenette and then leave."

Twenty-eight

Corey double-checked the locks, restrooms and any other places there might be *accidental destruction,* otherwise known as vandalism. Finding nothing, she left by the back door, making her way down the alley. It was only a little after five, early twilight. The rain had reduced to a drizzle and the alley had no light except the streetlights at either end.

She reached 6th Street, crossed to the other side and passed her car to make sure no one had followed her. Finally, confident that she was alone, she crossed back to her car, drove around the block to Main Street and turned left toward downtown. Sherylee's Fitness Center was four blocks from the library, so Corey was there in less than ten minutes.

Parking in front of the Center, she walked to the door. Reggie, who seemed glad to see her, met her at the door along with two young women in black leotards and blue tops with Sherylee's logo on them.

"Hi Corey," they said together.

"Hi Jane, Pam. How are things going?"

"Better – but your mom is sure getting the business," said Jane, "and we don't mean fitness business."

"Yeah, we all are, but we'll have it all straightened out soon," said Corey.

"Not if that detective guy has anything to do with it," said Pam.

"Turner? Why would you say that?"

"Because he's a jerk – or worse," said Pam.

"Yeah, he came in here acting like a big shot, making veiled passes at us. Your mom took him out to look at the windows that someone spray-painted with graffiti. He said he would take care of it. He did all right. He told the officer who was with him to clean it up. The officer called some of his buddies. They cleaned the windows."

"He is the detective on the case," said Corey, "But he's not the only one."

"Yeah, you and Reggie will get it solved," said Pam.

Corey laughed. "Thanks for the confidence. Are you through for the night? I hope I didn't keep you…"

"Oh, no. We have a half-hour break then we have a Tai Chi class tonight."

"Well, enjoy your break and thanks for letting Reggie visit with you."

"Anytime, Corey. We like having him here."

"Are you ready to go home and see what's happening there, Reggie?"

"Meow," he answered and started for the door.

Corey took his leash off a peg by the door and wrapped it around her wrist. She wouldn't need it in the car.

Reggie wound around her ankles, purred then ran for the car.

"Was your day exciting?" Corey asked as she opened the door for Reggie. He began butting his head against her shoulder and purring as she slid behind the steering wheel.

"I'll take that as a yes," said Corey.

Reggie muttered, meowed and made a variety of sounds as if telling Corey all about his day at the fitness center as they drove home. Corey responded occasionally as if she understood every sound he made. She told him about Dave's visit and Turner's call. Before she hardly knew how far she had gone, she was pulling into the driveway.

"Roger's and Turner's cars are in front of the garage. I wonder if Mom is home or at the hospital. Well if she's not, she'll need to get in the driveway." Corey backed onto the street and parked in front of the house, leaving room in the driveway for her mother when she got home. Reggie jumped out of the car and with two leaps sailed from the car to the banister to the front porch. He was pawing at the doorknob by the time Corey reached the porch. Even though the rain had stopped, clouds still hung very low and everything felt damp and smelled fresh.

"All right, hold your horses. What's your hurry?" Suddenly a chill slithered down her spine. "Is something wrong in there, Reggie – other than the fact that Turner is here?"

Reggie didn't bother to answer. He pushed the door open as soon as she had it unlocked and turned the knob.

"Mom, Roger. Anyone here?"

Reggie ran to the kitchen as Roger called, "In the kitchen, Corey."

Roger was at the stove with an apron around his waist. Detective

Turner sat at the table with a cup of coffee before him. Reggie growled, made a wide arc to avoid walking near Turner and went to his bowls waiting for Corey to fill them with water and food. He looked up at her and Corey was sure he rolled his eyes as if to say, "Is *he* here again?"

"All right, Reggie. I'll fix your dinner." She went to the cabinet and got down a can of kitty food. "Whatever you're cooking smells wonderful," she said to Roger as she dished up Reggie's food and got him some fresh water.

"You're mother said she was stopping by the hospital and would be home around six. I had no idea where you were or if you were even coming home, so I thought I'd better get something going. I was hungry for spaghetti, so that's what I'm fixing. If you want something else, you know where the things are."

"Still angry?"

"I don't like being lied to," said Roger keeping his back to her, concentrating on the pots on the stove.

"And I don't like airing our differences in front of others," she said glancing at Turner.

"Corey, we're all trying to get to the bottom of these murders and the mystery of the diary. It doesn't help when you don't cooperate," said Turner.

"That's funny I thought I was cooperating. I've shared everything I know."

"Then why are you being so mysterious about where you went today?" Roger asked.

Corey glared at him then turned and walked out of the room.

"Miss Kahlor, I need to talk to you," Turner called after her.

She turned around, moved to the doorway and glared at him. "So talk. You have five minutes then I have things to do."

"Corey, don't be so…" Roger began but Turner motioned for him to stop.

"Do you know a David O'Riley?"

"I'm sure you know that I do – or did."

"Have you seen him lately?"

"I don't think that is any of your business. David is an old friend. We correspond once or twice a year. His wife is a very good friend of mine. They live in Washington, D.C. They have two children. Her parents live in Masontown. Is there anything else you want to know if…*I*…know?"

"You didn't answer my question?"

"Like I said it's none of your business who I see or don't see. Your five minutes are about up."

"Miss Kahlor, are you aware that your *friend* is posing as a FBI Agent?"

"What are you trying to say, Detective? Am I supposed to be impressed by your research ability? I might be when you give us some answers about these murders – like who are the murdered men and who is behind the whole scheme?"

"I don't owe you a thing. As a law abiding citizen, you owe the law any help you can give."

"Ah, so now we admit it's all one sided. Detective Turner, if and when, I have any information that will be helpful, you'll be among the first the know. Now, if you will excuse me, I have things to do."

"Corey, dinner will be ready in half an hour. Your mother said she would be home then."

"I'll be in my room preparing my things to move back to my apartment. The clean-up crew should be done by now."

"Miss Kahlor, if you see David O'Riley, I would suggest you use caution in what you say to him. He fancies himself an FBI Agent who is going to solve *my* case and take the credit for it."

"Does it make any difference who gets the credit as long as the case is solved?"

"Like I said, O'Riley is a bounty hunter posing as an FBI Agent. Be careful. You could get in more trouble than you're already in."

Suddenly, Corey burst into laughter. She was still laughing when she turned and ran up the stairs to her room. Reggie, having eaten his fill, went with her.

Corey had no more gotten to her room and sat on the side of the bed, when there was a light tap at the door. Knowing it would be Roger, she was tempted not to open the door. Another tap followed by Roger's voice.

"Corcy, can we talk?"

Corey waited at few seconds. *We need to get this out in the open and over with, I guess.* She got up and opened the door. Reggie glared from the bed, refusing to move to let Roger sit beside Corey who returned to the bed. Roger sat in the chair facing the bed.

"Corey, what has happened between us? We've been snarling like cats and dogs all day."

"I don't know, Roger. I just know that we don't agree on many things that I feel are important. That's not saying that either of us is right or wrong, we just don't agree."

"But that's no excuse for you to lie to me."

"Or for you to jump to conclusions and believe others before even giving me a chance to explain."

"All right, explain."

"What do you want explained?"

"Well, let's start with your attitude. Out of the blue, this morning, you accused me of being in on the attacks to you and your family."

"Roger, I never accused you of anything of the sort. I merely stated the fact that you are the only one who hasn't been attacked by anyone connected with this diary business. You jumped to conclusions and accepted unfounded guilt."

Roger gritted his teeth, took a deep breath and said, "So it's all my fault. Turner said you would turn the tables to make me the scape goat for your bullheadedness."

"Roger, if you want to talk about us, then leave Turner out of it. What we say and do is none of his business."

"Well, at least he's talking sense to me, which is more than I can say for you."

Corey glared and said nothing.

"What about Dave O'Riley?"

"What about him? You know him."

"Are you still…in love…with him?"

"Roger, are you jealous? Dave and I broke up long before I even met you. He's married to my best friend and they have both been my friends since high school."

"Then you have been seeing him?"

Corey shook her head as if trying to clear the cloudiness. "I can't believe how you are jumping from one conclusion to another without any facts in between. How can the fact that Dave, Susie and I are friends give you the conclusion that I've been seeing him? He lives in D.C. and I live in Masontown. You and I see each other every day. When have I had time to visit with him, or he with me?"

"You heard Turner. He's in town and you were secretive today and lied to me about where you were going."

"What makes you think I lied to you? Have I ever lied to you before?"

"No, but you said you were going to the library to work today and the library was still closed and you weren't there."

"You didn't call. Turner told you I wasn't there. Why did you tell him I was at the library, when I said I wanted to be alone for a while? And why did you give him my cell number?"

"He said he had something important to tell you."

"He could have told you, or it could have waited."

"He said he called the library and got the answering machine that said the library is closed for repairs until next week."

"So?"

"If you were there, why didn't you answer the phone?"

"Why would I answer the phone if the library was closed? I wasn't there to do library work except for some paper work. And you know I don't give my cell phone out to just anyone."

"Turner isn't just anyone. He's a friend as well as the detective in this murder investigation."

"He's *your* friend. He didn't need *my* cell number."

"You're evading the subject. Did you see Dave O'Riley?"

"Roger, *are* you jealous? Do I need to prove I'm faithful by denying Turner's allegations? Why do you really want to know? For your own satisfaction or for Turner's benefit?"

"Both."

"Then maybe we better rethink our engagement. If you can't trust me any more than that and his word is more honorable than mine then we have nothing more to talk about. Please leave Roger. I really need to change. I want to go see my father and return to my apartment – that is if I have yours and Turner's permission to go to the hospital."

"Corey, you're being childish."

"Goodnight, Roger."

"Don't be ridiculous, Corey. It sounds like your mother is home and dinner is ready to put on the table."

"I'll grab a bite downtown." Corey turned her back and began gathering clothes from the closet and dresser drawers – clothes she kept at her mother's house. She knew she would have to replace most of her wardrobe eventually. She heard Roger take a step toward her. Reggie jumped between them and growled. Roger left, slamming the door behind him.

Corey picked up her cell phone and dialed her mother's cell phone number.

"Hello."

"Mom, don't let on it's me. Just want to tell you I'm taking some of my things home and will try to stop by to see Dad. Not sure if I'll be back here, or stay at the apartment. I'll explain everything when we can be alone."

"All right, Pam. I'll take care of it in the morning."

"See you later."

"You drink lots of liquids and stay in bed tomorrow. Jane and I will take care of things."

Sherylee disconnected and Corey grinned as she replaced her phone in her purse. She didn't know what was happening between her and Roger, but she knew she didn't like or trust Turner. As long as Roger was close pals with him, there would be friction between her and Roger – at least until these murders and the dilemma of the diary was finished. *Turner is a control freak and I don't fit his mold of a submissive woman.*

Twenty-nine

Corey heard the others in the kitchen eating as she carried her things down the stairs. The aroma of spaghetti spices and garlic bread fresh from the oven almost made her relent and go to dinner – almost. She pictured Turner at the table and continued out to her car. She laid her clothes and briefcase on the back seat and started to close the door. A flash of fur sailed over her head to the front passenger seat.

"Reggie, does Mom know you're coming with me?"

"Meow."

"I'll call her later. We don't want her to worry about you being kidnapped again, do we?"

"Meow." Reggie sat staring ahead as if he wanted to see where they were going and what was happening around him.

Corey gave Reggie a pat on his head and laughed. "All right, I won't stop to see Dad since I don't want to leave you in the car and you can't go in the hospital – or shouldn't."

"Meow?" Reggie looked at her and blinked his eyes.

A half hour later, Corey pulled into her parking spot in the parking garage under her apartment building. She gathered her belongings and walked to the entrance. Somehow, she managed to slide her keycard through the slot without dropping anything. Reggie ran to the elevator raised on his back legs and pushed the call button. When the doors slid open, he bounced inside and pushed the button for the second floor.

When the doors opened again, Reggie leaped out of the elevator and ran ahead of Corey to her apartment. She slid her keycard into the slot and turned the knob. Reggie pushed the door open. Corey, half-afraid of what she might find, lingered at the door. The smell of cleaning agents told her the apartment was clean and caused her to sneeze twice. Reggie turned to look at her as if to say, "Are you all right?"

"I'm fine, Reggie," she said. "I'll open a couple of windows. Might be a little cool, but it will get rid of some of the smell. At least the apartment is clean."

"Meow," answered Reggie and he went in ahead of Corey, sniffed the air then continued on to where Corey kept his bowls. There he waited for her to give him some water and a few crunchies.

"All right, Reggie. Let me put these clothes in the bedroom and open a window or two first."

Once Corey had fed Reggie and put her clothes away, she began a systematic search of the apartment. *I'm getting paranoid, but I just don't trust Turner. He might have had my apartment bugged in case he thinks I'm meeting Dave here or something. Or maybe he's just a pervert who wants to know what a girl thinks and talks about in the privacy of her apartment.*

Reggie watched her and began sniffing and patting things with his paws. Corey grinned at him and started to say something, but thought better of it until their search was through. Suddenly Reggie stiffened. Slowly, he stretched a paw to the phone on the divider counter between the living room and the kitchen. Corey tiptoed over to him remembering the bomb search of Roger's car. She cautiously reached for the phone. Reggie didn't try to stop her. *Must not be a bomb.* She picked it up, turned it over and checked the bottom for anything unusual. She had no idea what she was looking for, but had no trouble seeing the shiny little dot pressed into the groove where the cord should be.

Slowly she set the phone back on the counter top and got a thin sharp knife from the knife holder. She picked the phone up again, eased the shiny button out and set the phone back on the counter top. She wrapped the button in a tissue and started to turn away.

Reggie tapped her arm and took her back to the phone. She lifted the receiver, unscrewed the mouthpiece. There was another one, which she removed and added to the first. *I wonder if there are more, and what do I do with these?*

She laid the tissue on the counter top beside the phone, went to her purse, took out her cell phone and tiptoed to the door. Reggie meowed very loudly just as she opened the door. Corey grinned and turned around to say, "What do you want Reggie? A treat?"

"Meow."

"All right just a minute. I have to put a couple more things away first."

Still smiling, Corey stepped out into the hall and walked away from the room. She found Dave's number and hit send. He answered on the first ring. "Yes."

"I'm at my apartment. I found two bugs in my phone. Do you think there are more and what do I do with these?"

"I'm sorry to hear that Paul. It sounds like a glitch in your internet server. I have some free time tonight, why don't I drop by and take a look at it for you. You still live at the same place?"

"Yes."

"I'll be there in about fifteen minutes. In the meantime I would suggest that you not use your internet."

"Got you."

Corey hung up, slipped her phone in her pocket and went back to the apartment. "All right, Reggie. I promised you a treat and I need something. I was going to go out, but I may as well fix something here. I probably better call Mom and let her know where you are."

"Meow," Reggie answered and leaped to the top of the counter, sat beside the *bugs* and began purring.

Corey laughed as she pulled her cell from her pocket and called Sherylee.

"Hello, Coral Rae."

"Hi, Mom. Just wanted to let you know Reggie came home with me."

"Why are you using your cell phone at your apartment, or are you...?"

"I can't use my apartment phone at the minute."

"Why can't you use your apartment phone? Didn't they clean everything? Hold on a minute." Corey could tell her mother had her hand over the phone while she talked to someone else. "Sorry about that," said Sherylee. "Turner was making a joke."

"Oh?"

"Yeah, when I asked why you couldn't use your phone, he said, 'What's wrong with it? Do you have a spider on it?'"

"Tell him it's worse than that. I have a very large cat on top of it."

"Cat? You mean Reggie?"

"Uh huh. He must think it's a Reggie size toy. He's sitting on it purring up a storm. I would use the bedroom phone, but I'm in the kitchen getting something to eat."

They both laughed then Sherylee asked, "Are you all right, Coral Rae?"

"I'm fine Mom. I'm fixing some chicken stir-fry for Reggie and me then I'll call Dad later and possibly go to bed early. I'll talk to you in the morning."

"All right. You'll feel better after a good night's sleep."

She had no more hung up when her cell phone rang again. "Now what," she said, placing the skillet on the stove and answering it. She saw Dave's name on the caller ID. "Hello," she said.

"I'm outside your door. Didn't want to knock or ring the bell and alert anyone that you have company."

"I'm sorry, ma'am, but you must have a wrong number. There's no one here by the name of Deborah. No, no Sandra Sue either."

She closed the phone and started toward the door. "You, know Reggie if I didn't get wrong numbers once in a while, I wouldn't even know my phone ringer works."

"Meow," he answered as she opened the door as quietly as before.

Dave came in, saw Reggie on the counter top beside the phone and stopped. Corey laughed. "Reggie, I told Mom you were here and I will bring you to the center tomorrow. Would you like to take a nap while I finish cooking? I'll save you some chicken."

"Meow," answered Reggie and jumped to the floor with a very definite thud. While Corey was talking to Reggie, she was leading Dave to the counter top and the *bug-filled* tissue.

Carefully he opened the tissue, rewrapped and placed it in the freezer section of her refrigerator. He motioned and whispered for her to continue what she was doing. Then he began his own systematic search of the apartment using an electronic device not much bigger than a thumb drive for a computer. Reggie followed helping him search. They found another one on the bedroom phone and one in the living room lamp. He added them to the two in the freezer.

"I think you're safe now. Do you have any idea…?"

"Yes." She told him about the conversation she had just had with her mother and Detective Turner's remark.

She turned back to the stove. "Did you eat yet?"

"Grandma and Grandpa Miller took Susie and the kids to McDonalds then to see *Charlotte's Web*. I told them I'd get something later."

"Plates are in the second cabinet from the end. Want to hand me a couple? Second thought, hand me three. I promised Reggie some chicken.

"That is quite some cat," said Dave. "Now I know how he could save your life in the river."

"He's special," said Corey. "Are you doing more research

tonight?"

"Yes, but I think I'm beginning to know what to look for. Is Roger coming over, I'll leave now if…"

"Roger won't be coming over."

"Trouble."

"Until we get this diary business cleared up, Roger is not welcome. Afterward, we'll see."

"I'm sorry if I'm the cause of any…"

"Not you, exactly," she said. She then told him what all had transpired since she left him at the library earlier that evening.

"So basically you're being asked to choose whom you trust – Turner or me? And you're giving Roger a choice between Turner or you?"

"When you put it that way it does sound sort of childish, but yes, I guess that's the way it is. And as far as I'm concerned, it's no contest. I've never known you to lie to me or anyone else. And Roger should know I've never lied to him. If he had asked directly if I were at the library, I probably would have told him. But he didn't. Turner said I wasn't there because I didn't answer the library phone and he chose to believe Turner without even asking me. I can't live with suspicions and innuendoes – not with all that's happened anyway."

"I hope you and Roger will work it out. Don't judge him too harshly. Turner has fooled a lot of people. He has to be in charge and can't stand for anyone to know more about his case than he knows." Dave changed the subject. "What would be the chances of me seeing your father? I called, but the nurse who answered said no one but family and Detective Turner and hospital staff could see him. Do you suppose I could go with you?"

"The nursing staff would report it to Turner."

"Well, I'll have to work around it until I need to blow my cover. Are you going over tonight?"

"I told Mom I thought I would skip it and go to bed early – very early since I have Reggie with me." Before she could say anything else, her apartment phone rang. "Uh oh, we removed the bugs."

"Maybe I can put them back."

"Not before I pick up the phone."

Corey moved to the phone and turned the ringer off. "I can't answer if I don't hear it ring," she said.

Dave laughed as her cell phone rang. "Now we'll find out who it was."

"Maybe," she said looking at the caller ID. "It's Roger, but I almost know Turner is with him." Corey opened the phone and hit the speakerphone mode. Sounding as if she had been sleeping, she answered, "Hello."

"Corey? Is that you?"

"Roger?"

"Corey, are you drunk?"

"Roger, you know I don't drink. What do you want?"

"You said you would be at your apartment, but you didn't answer your phone. Where are you?"

"Roger, you're jumping to conclusions again. I am very tired. I turned off my phone so I could go to bed early."

"You're so grouchy anymore."

"You would be grouchy too if someone kept calling you a liar and waking you up just as you're falling into a deep sleep. If you have something important to say, say it so I can try to get back to sleep. If you are just calling to see if I was telling you the truth because Turner thinks I'm up to something, then you may as well hang up now, because we have nothing more to say."

"Corey, you did say you were going to see your father."

"So why did you call here if you thought I went to see my father?"

"Because the hospital said you haven't been there."

Corey's face began to take on a very red glow, but her voice gave the impression she was in a deep freeze somewhere. "Roger, I'm only going to say this once, so listen carefully. I'm tired of all your jealous checking up to see if I'm lying to you then not believing me when I tell you the truth. I'm tired of you doing Turner's dirty work. If he wants to hound and harass me, I will go to the authorities. If you ever call me again, you had better have a good reason that does not have anything to do with what I have already laid out for you, because one more chance is all you'll get. After that we're through and I will not, let me repeat that, I will NOT answer when I see your number on my caller ID. My answering machine will be taking all my calls at the apartment whether I'm here or not. Good-bye, Roger. And tell Turner I won't speak to him unless he hauls me downtown and he'd better have a very good reason if he does that – and proof to back up his reason."

Corey closed her phone and turned away from Dave. She didn't want him to see the tears that threatened. But he sensed her need and put his arms around her.

"Dave, don't get in trouble because of my emotions."

"You know me better than that. Susie knows me better than that."

"I thought Roger knew me better, but…I'm sorry. That sounds like I'm trying to plant suspicion in your mind. I'm not. I know Susie too well."

"Why don't you come to the library with me? You can help and maybe I can get this cleared up sooner. We'll take my car so if anyone comes around to check, your car will in its spot."

"What about Reggie? I don't want to leave him here alone if someone tries to break in again."

"If they have any sense, they won't tangle with him, but they did kidnap him once. They might try something more violent the next time. Bring him along."

"You sure you don't mind cat hairs in your car?"

Dave laughed. "I have two kids, remember. A few cat hairs are nothing compared to what kids can do to a car."

"Want to go with us, Reggie?"

Reggie, who had been sitting on the couch swinging his head from one speaker to the other during their conversation, jumped off the couch, grabbed his leash from the hook by the door and offered it to Corey.

When they got down to the first floor at the front door, Corey glanced out more to check the weather than anything else. "Dave, someone is watching the apartment building."

"Where?"

"Across the street, near the park see the dark spot by the big oak tree. It's a car."

"Are you sure. Could be just a visitor to one of the apartments."

"Not with a man sitting in it smoking."

"Maybe you better stay here. I'll go alone."

"What if he's following you?"

"He wouldn't be…yes he would if Turner thought I was meeting with you."

"Why don't I take Reggie across to the park for a quick run? Give me five minutes then get in your car and leave. If he's following you, he'll leave and I'll walk down to the corner and take a taxi. I'll meet you at the library when you lose him. If he doesn't follow you, give me five minutes then turn back. I'll return through the front and go out the back, down the alley to the next street."

"I don't know…"

"I'll be fine. I have Reggie. You have to finish that research."

"All right. Go. I'll leave in five minutes.

Corey and Reggie went out the front door, crossed the street and went to the park where she began playing tag with Reggie, while keeping her eye on the car by the oak tree. She saw Dave leave the building, slowly walk toward his car with his hands in his pockets. He lifted one hand, felt the sprinkle of rain, put it back in his pocket and began whistling *Singing in the Rain.*

The man in the car hunched down as if he didn't want anyone to see him. He waited until Dave drove off then leaned back pretending to doze, but Corey felt his eyes watching her.

"All right, Reggie," she said. "Let's see if we can fool the man."

Reggie trotted along beside her like a small dog. Since the elevator could be seen from outside, they went into the building and took the elevator to the second floor. Her apartment faced the park, so she went inside. "Wait here for me Reggie," she said and went to the bedroom, turned the light on so the man would know she was there. She turned back the bed, took as much time as it would take to change to her nightclothes then turned off the light. Hopefully the man would think she had gone to bed.

"Come on, Reggie, we'll go down the back stairs to the alley." When they reached the alley, she walked to the end, stopped at the sidewalk, and looked up and down the street. A car parked in the shadows not far away, suddenly came to life. Lights came on and it pulled away from the curb, stopping beside Corey and Reggie. They got in Dave's car and headed for the library. Hopefully the man in the car out front would take a long nap believing Corey was in bed for the night.

Thirty

Dave drove around the library several times to make sure no one was following or waiting there for them. When it seemed all clear, he drove to the corner of 6th Street and the alley. He stopped long enough for Corey and Reggie to get out of the car then he turned left through the alley to 5th Street. There he parked his car in a darkened corner of an all-night convenience store lot and walked down the alley to 6th Street. He continued through the alley to the back of the library where Corey and Reggie waited inside for him. She opened the door and they all went up the stairs to her office.

With the heavy shades drawn, the computers humming and the coffee pot gurgling, they were ready to work.

"Why don't you do some more comparisons of the names in the robbery and those in the diary?" said Dave. "If there's anything there, it's in code. See if you can decode his writing. I'll keep working on backgrounds. I felt as if I was really close to something this afternoon. I'm just not sure what."

Coffee in hand, paper and pencils beside the screens, Dave and Corey became lost in their work. Reggie explored the stacks for a while then returned to curl up on one of Corey's shelves for a nap.

Corey pulled out the names of the men involved with the bank robbery: Kahlor, Hollister, Zurphy and Oyler.

"Dave?"

"Umm?"

"Didn't you say the man who followed by dad was named Hollister?"

Dave looked up from the computer. "You're right – Robert Hollister – grandson of Mark Hollister."

"Yeah, one of the bank robbers."

"I think we might be on to something. Let's see if anyone else can be traced back to the robbery."

Corey turned back to the list. "I think I'll put a checkmark beside Goldmeister."

"The bank manager?"

"His name keeps popping up. I think it's strange for a man of his standing to know my great-grandfather well enough to claim to know his voice and accuse him of being the one who shot Samuel's father. Then he turned around and visited him in prison and it seemed he was a friend of the family – including Mary Sue and the boys."

"You might be right."

"If we can get a picture for Samuel, we should know if he was the one who fired the shot."

Dave went back to his research and Corey reached for the list from the diary and Googled the names of the men, one at a time, to see if she could find a picture of them. As she found information, she sent it to the printer. Suddenly things were beginning to make sense. Most of the next generation of the families involved had either changed their names or married into other families. She had just pressed *print* on the Goldmeister file when Reggie suddenly woke from his catnap and began prowling. He went out to the stacks and returned to the room softly growling. He tapped Corey's leg.

"What is it Reggie? Are you getting tired? Want to go home?" She glanced at the clock. "It is after midnight."

"Give me five more minutes," said Dave, "and I'll take you home."

Reggie growled and tugged at Corey's jeans. "Dave, something is wrong. Reggie doesn't act like this normally. Maybe…" Before she could finish her sentence, her cell phone rang. She pressed the speaker tab and said, "Hello."

"Coral Rae, where are you? Something is happening…"

"Mom, what is it? Are you all right? Is Dad…?"

"I need you Coral Rae. I need Reggie. I…" a choked sob cut off the rest of her words.

"Where are you?"

"I'm at home, but," she sniffed, "the hospital just called and said Roger and Detective Turner took Daniel out of the hospital."

"What do you mean they took him out of the hospital?"

"They got him into his clothes and left. Detective Turner said he received another threat to his life, so he was going to hide him where he would be safe."

"And they let him go?"

"They had no choice. He's the homicide detective and Roger was one of the family members allowed to see him. They called me, but he was already gone."

"Did they say where they were taking him?"

"No, other than where no one could find him."

"But why didn't he tell you?"

"I don't know. Oh Coral Rae, I'm so worried, but I don't know what to do. I've tried calling both Roger and Detective Turner, but I get no answer. I don't understand why they didn't tell me what they were doing."

"Mom, stay put. I'll be there as soon as I can. If you hear from them and have to go to him, leave me a note or message of some kind. Reggie already knew something was wrong. He'll help and I have another friend who is working on this case."

"Then you didn't listen to Detective Turner."

"Mom, I think we've listened to Turner too much already. Dave and I have pieced together an interesting scenario. I believe Turner is in this up to his eyeballs. I just hope Roger is only being stupid."

"Coral Rae!"

"Be there in about ten minutes." Corey closed her phone and looked at Dave who had been about to tell her his discoveries.

"We'll talk later. If we're right – and I believe we are – then Roger and your father are both in trouble. Let's see if your mother can give us a clue where we should begin looking."

Thirty-one

Ten minutes later Dave pulled into the driveway. As soon as Corey opened the door, Reggie jumped from the car and was at the front door before Corey and Dave could even get their doors open. Sherylee opened the front door to meet them and Reggie flew into her arms. She hugged the cat, sobbing.

"I'm sorry," she said backing into the house so they could all get in. "It just isn't fair," she said. "All these years we lived without him, and now he's back and someone keeps trying to kill him."

"Did anyone call? Do you have any idea where they're going?" asked Corey.

"Only Marjorie from the hospital called. She's really upset. Wondered if she should call his superior or the State Police. I didn't know what to tell her."

"It might be a good idea to call her back and tell her to contact both the Chief of Police and the State Police and tell them he took a patient from the hospital, endangering his recovery from heart surgery," said Dave giving Sherylee a serious look.

"I'm sorry, Mom. I think you remember Dave O'Riley."

"Yes, I do, but Detective Turner said you were pretending to be with the FBI in order to get to Daniel. He said…"

"Mom, whatever Turner said is a lie. Dave *is* a certified FBI Agent and he's here to investigate not only the diary, but the robbery and murder behind the diary."

"Are you sure, Coral Rae?"

Dave pulled out his ID Badge. "Susie and I moved to D.C. so I could enroll in the training program. I've been with them ever since. I talked to Mr. Kahlor in Texas and he has kept in touch. He had no idea I knew his family. When I arrived in town and started talking to some friends on the force, I thought it better to stay out of Turner's way until I knew the lay of the land."

"But that would mean he…and Roger…kidnapped Daniel?"

"I hope Roger is involved against his will. I know he considers Turner a friend, but I sincerely believe he's not a part of Turner's game by choice."

"What are we going to do?"

"Meow!" Reggie went to the door and turned the doorknob as if trying to open it. The phone rang at the same moment. Corey was standing next to it and pressed the speakerphone button. Sherylee answered with a shaky voice, "Hello."

"Mrs. Kahlor, this is Roger." He was whispering. "Find Corey. Tell her I'm sorry. She was right. They are taking us …" There was a loud crack as if someone had slapped him and the phone went dead.

Before anyone could respond, the phone rang again. Turner didn't wait for an answer. He began talking immediately when Corey pressed the speakerphone button. "If you want to see Kahlor and Roger alive, I want that diary and I don't mean a copy. Roger said it's in your safe deposit box."

"The bank is closed until tomorrow," said Corey.

"Find a way. Get your FBI pal to pull strings and get you in. I'll give you two hours."

"Where do you want me to take it? Are my father and Roger all right? Let me talk to them."

"Take it to headquarters and leave it with Sgt. Brown. Tell him it's for me. I've told him I'm expecting a package. He'll take it from there. You have until 3:00 a.m."

"Let me talk to…" The phone was dead.

"What are you going to do?" Sherylee asked her daughter.

"The diary isn't in the safe deposit box. With everything happening, we never had time to take it to the bank. It's in a freezer bag in the bottom of your freezer in the basement. But the diary won't tell him much. There aren't many names in it except for family members. What he needs is the Bible and he doesn't even know it exists. We never got around to telling him about it."

"What happens when we take the diary to the police station? Will he release the men? Will he let us know where they are?" Sherylee looked from Corey to Dave for answers even though she really knew.

Dave and Corey exchanged glances.

"He's going to kill them, isn't he?" said Sherylee.

"Not if we can get to them first," said Corey. "I think I know where they are."

"Where? And how would you know?"

Reggie had been tugging at them and growling. Corey looked down at him and said, "I think Reggie knows too, don't you Reg?"

"Meow!" He ran toward the door again.

"Where did they take you when you were kidnapped? And where did they take Reggie?" asked Corey.

"Parker's Warehouse on River Road," said Sherylee. "They took them there?"

"I think so. I heard sounds in the background that sounded like what I heard at the warehouse."

"Meow."

"I think Reggie believes that's where they are too."

"Then what are we waiting for?" Sherylee grabbed her purse and started for the door.

"Wait, someone has to take the diary to the precinct."

"But…"

"She's right Mrs. Kahlor," said Dave. "It would make sense that you take it. Corey knows where this place is and what to look for. It wouldn't do for me to take the diary."

"You're right, I know you are, but…very well. Take Reggie with you and call me the minute you find out anything. I'll be there as soon as I can."

"Maybe you better…"

"Coral Rae Kahlor, if you think I'm going to sit back and let some killer try to take my Daniel away from me again, you've got another think a coming."

Corey nodded then ran down to the basement to get the diary. She gave it to her mother and said, "Please be careful when you come to Parker's."

"I will. You be careful and don't take any chances – unless you have to."

Corey laughed, opened the door and started to Dave's car. Sherylee went to the garage to get her rental.

"Parker's Warehouse?" asked Dave.

"Yes, near the river on River Road."

"Why would they take him to Parker's?"

"How else could they hide a man they had just taken from the hospital?"

"Maybe I need to get a search warrant."

"Dave, he won't be in the warehouse. And where would you get a search warrant at this time of morning? Parker has boats. What better place to hide him?"

"But…" Dave stopped, a horrified expression spread across his face. "They'd throw him overboard if the police started toward them, wouldn't they?"

Corey nodded. "We need to hurry. I have a feeling Turner means to kill him at 3:00 whether he gets the diary or not."

Thirty-two

Dave began slowing two streets before the warehouse. "Turn down that alley," said Corey. "It runs along the bank of the river behind the warehouse."

Slowly, with no headlights, he turned toward the warehouse. They could see two boats on the river and lights in the warehouse. One boat was just pulling away from a second one that seemed to be anchored near the center of the river.

"That's the boat that they had Reggie on," said Corey, "the one that's returning to shore."

"How do you know it's the same boat?"

"I was in it. I remember sounds and…never mind. I'm sure it's the same one."

"Why would they go to a boat in the middle of the river and then return? Taking supplies for a quick get away?"

"What time is it?"

Corey glanced at the car clock. "It's two-thirty. We only have half an hour to find them." Suddenly she shivered as if a cold breeze whipped across her shoulders. "Dave, we don't have that long," she said.

"Meow," answered Reggie trying to get out of the car.

"What do you mean? He said…"

"I know what he said – that we have until 3:00 a.m. But, Dave he's going to kill them at three whether he gets the diary or not."

"You're probably right, but how can you be so sure?"

"I think the man's a maniac. I'm sure he intends to get the diary and kill us all – one at a time or as many at a time as possible. He knows I've figured things out before and won't stop now. He expects me to be on the boat to try to help them. Then I'll be killed with them and all he has to do is take care of Mom. I've got to try to get to them."

"You can't go alone…"

"If I'm right, there is no time for arguing. Reggie and I will swim to the boat, find them and get them to the side of the boat. If you can swipe one of those boats and be there to help get them off that one and into yours, hopefully, we can get away before it blows. Reggie is already swimming toward the boat."

"All right, go, but be careful. I'll call some back up to help take care of these goons and grab that other boat."

Corey ran to the edge of the river, following Reggie who was already halfway to the anchored boat in the center of the river. She threw off her jacket, kicked off her shoes and swam as fast as she could. Reggie treaded water, waiting for her. Corey pulled herself up and over the side. She grabbed a fishing net and threw it over the side for Reggie to climb aboard. Shivering from fear and cold, she began calling out to them. "Dad? Roger?"

Reggie sniffed around the deck. They started downstairs to the captain's cabin and stopped at the door. Corey called out again. This time she was rewarded – not with an answer per se but by a sound as if someone were pounding on the floor.

"Is it safe to open the door?" she called out to them. "Pound twice if it's safe, three times if there's a bomb attached."

There were two thumps. She breathed a deep sigh and turned the knob. Of course, the door was locked – anything to slow her down and keep her from getting them off the boat in time.

Reggie prowled around looking for who knows what, but he brought her a slim tool like an ice pick. Working with trembling hands, she finally released the lock and opened the door. Reggie, more able to move in the dark, went ahead leading her to a table. Feeling around she found an oil lamp and a box of matches. *They really don't care if I find them as long as we don't get away in time.*

Once she lit the lamp, she saw her father on one of the bunks and Roger on the floor beside him – both bound hand and foot with a piece of duct tape over their mouths.

"This is going to hurt," she said as she yanked the tape off first Roger then Daniel.

"Where's the bomb?" she asked as she began cutting the rope loose with a knife also from the table.

"In the engine room, I think," said Roger as she finished releasing him from his bonds.

"Get Dad untied while I check it out." She lit another lamp and started for the engine room. *If I can disarm it or throw it overboard, maybe we can drive this boat back to shore in case Dave can't get the other one.*

Reggie went with her sniffing as he went. Suddenly, he stopped and stared at the engine itself. Corey held her lantern up to see better. Sure enough, there was a bomb attached to the engine. With a timer on it set to go off at 3:00, but if anyone tried to start the engine, it would also trigger the ignition. The time on the clock read 2:55.

"Come on Reggie, let's get out of here. We'll have to go overboard even if Dave isn't here yet."

"Meow," said Reggie and ran back up to the captain's cabin. Roger had Daniel untied and on his feet. They were moving toward the stairs.

"How are you guys doing," she asked, knowing they would lie to her and tell they were fine.

"Daniel is weak, but we'll make it as long as we can. How much time do we have?"

"About two and a half minutes if' we're lucky. I don't see the boat so we are going to have to jump overboard. The water is cold but it's the only way."

"Corey we can't…"

"Go. You first and catch Dad when I help him over. Reggie will help you. Start swimming with him as fast as you can. I know you think you can't but do it, but you have to – or get blown to bits."

Roger grabbed a life preserver and jumped overboard. Corey wrapped a life jacket around her father's waste tying it as tightly as possible then helped him slip over the edge. Reggie landed in the water beside Roger and was there when Daniel hit the water. Corey was right behind him. Reggie, slipping under Daniel as he had done with Corey, was able to keep his head above water. With Roger and Corey on either side, they began swimming for their lives.

Mentally counting off the seconds with each stroke, Corey expected the explosion to blow them out of the water, but it didn't come. They were almost to the shore when it happened creating a ball of flame on the river and lighting up the shores on both sides, sending waves that helped push them ashore.

Corey, Roger and Daniel sat shivering on the shore. Reggie shook the water from his fur and started down the road toward a house around the bend.

Minutes later, he was leading a group of farmer's back to them. Corey grinned and stood to greet them. "Hello there. We need help. Can you get my father to a warm dry place and call an ambulance. He's recovering from heart surgery and the men who blew up that boat kidnapped him from the hospital."

GREAT-GRANDPA'S DIARY

"Those men from Parker's Warehouse?"

"Yes."

"We been complaining about unusual things happening on the river here, but the authorities never do anything about it. We saw the explosion and were on the way, armed to do something about it this time, when the big cat approached us. I thought he was a wildcat of some kind, but he seemed tame – tried to talk to us – made it very clear he wanted us to follow him."

"The FBI is on the scene, but we might need your help. They should have had things under control and brought a boat out to help us. Something must be wrong."

"Ma'am that's an understatement," said the man who seemed to be the leader. Then he turned to a couple of the younger men. "Joe, you and Randy help the gentleman back to the house. Tell Ma to take care of him and call the ambulance."

"Shall we call the police, too?"

"Call the State Police," said Roger. "I'm not sure we can trust anyone in the Masontown Police Department at this point." Then he turned back to Corey. "Okay, Corey, fill us in on what's happening and how we should proceed."

Corey didn't take time to figure out if Roger was being sensible or sarcastic. It didn't matter. She knew more about what was happening than he did, so she would have to guide them. "David O'Brian, FBI is in charge. He's been investigating all that's happened. We thought my father and Roger were on the boat and assumed a time bomb was planted there somewhere to go off about 3:00 a.m. Dave called for back up and went to take care of the warehouse while Reggie and I swam out to the boat. Dave was going to bring the other boat out to get us once I found them and got them untied. He didn't come. So I'm not sure what's happening in the warehouse."

"Are you sure you can trust that Dave fellow?" the leader of the farmers asked.

"Positive," said Corey not looking at Roger.

"Then if I can make a suggestion," he said, "we have enough men to surround the warehouse until we can find out what's going on inside. We don't want to get anyone killed or hurt if we can help it. If you can find out what happened to the agent and give us a signal of some kind, we'll close in."

"Sounds like a plan," said Roger grinning at Corey.

"I think the best approach would be direct," said Corey. "I'll simply walk in with Reggie like I belong there. When it looks like we need your help, I'll send Reggie. He'll circle the building and when he gets back to the first one, he'll give a signal to attack."

"Will a cat do that?"

"What kind of signal?"

"I'm sure Reggie can do it and you'll know when you hear him." She looked down at the cat who sat beside her like a very docile house cat looking up at her. "You can do that, can't you Reggie?"

"Meow!"

The men laughed and started spreading out to surround the warehouse. Roger walked with Corey and Reggie to the open door.'

"Corey, be careful," he said and kissed her before joining the other men.

"I will," she whispered as she blew him a kiss.

Before she approached the door, Corey recognized her mother's car slowly descending the alley. She ran to the car. "Go to the first farmhouse on the left. Dad's there.

"What about…?"

"No time to explain. We'll catch up with you at the hospital. They've already called an ambulance."

Sherylee asked no more questions, but turned left and continued up the road as if she were looking for a street address. Corey continued to the warehouse. She stopped, took a deep breath then entered into the warehouse as if she belonged there.

Thirty-three

"What are you doing?" cried Corey as she stopped inside the warehouse door.

Two men held Dave while Turner used him for a punching bag. Reggie growled and without waiting for Corey's command, flew at Turner, knocking him to the ground and swiping his claws across his chest and arms. Before anyone could take a shot at him, he flew out the door on the front side of the warehouse. Corey knew he was circling the warehouse. A half minute later, everyone within a mile heard the blood-curdling scream. Even Corey, who knew it wasn't a wild leopard scream, felt goose bumps up her arms and down her back. Turner was still on the ground when Reggie returned to Corey's side.

"What do you think *you're* doing? This time you've gone too far Miss Kahlor. I'm arresting you for assaulting an officer of the law with a deadly animal and for impeding an investigation…"

"Shut up, Turner," said Roger, stepping inside the warehouse behind Corey. "You're the one who's impeding progress and Dave O'Riley is a bona fide FBI Agent."

Detective Turner struggled to his feet and faced Roger. His face had gone white, emphasizing the red blood still flowing from his arms and chest.

"How did you…?"

"How did I get off the boat? My fiancée, whom you tried so hard to turn me against, is smarter than I am. She and her cat can work rings around you and your smultzy gang of thieves anytime."

"Get him," yelled Turner. "Kill them all. They are interfering with the work of a police detective."

The men and women, who included Parker and Dolly, reached for their guns, but in the shadows around the room, the sound of twenty-five guns simultaneously cocked for use.

The big farmer who led the group stepped forward. "The first one to pull a trigger will breathe his last before the sound dies away. In case you think I'm kidding, you are surrounded by twenty-five loaded rifles, shot guns and pistols and one furious feline who would willingly tear you to pieces."

"You can't do this," said Turner. "I'll have you all arrested for kidnapping a police officer."

"We'll let the State Police and/or the FBI make that decision. We have an FBI Agent present and the State Police on their way. I think I hear sirens arriving now," said the farmer.

Turner whirled around, gun aimed at Corey. Roger dived at him and wrapped his arms around his knees while Reggie aimed for the head. Turner fired one wild shot that hit the ceiling. The gun dropped as Reggie clamped his teeth on the soft flesh of the wrist. Turner screamed, "Get him off me. He'll kill me. He's a vicious wild animal. Someone help me."

"Come on Reggie," said Corey. "You don't want to get blood poisoning from him."

Reggie gave one last swipe across Turner's face then ran back to Corey who dropped to her knees to hold him.

"Keep them surrounded until the State Police get here," said Dave and he started over to Corey.

"None of you have any authority," said Turner. "You are just a bunch of outlaws posing as a posse. You can't arrest or hold us. This won't hold up in court."

"Turner, whatever you want to believe, I am an FBI Agent and I was sent here to investigate you and your band of thugs. And if you're worried about a lawless posse, I'll take care of that right now. Men, I won't ask you to raise your right hand at the moment, but if you will uphold the law just answer, we will."

"We will," they shouted.

"Then I hereby deputize each one of you for this important task of bringing these criminals to justice. Carry on."

"You can't...," sputtered Turner.

Dave continued to walk to Corey. "Are you all right?" he asked. "Sorry I couldn't get to the boat. They jumped me."

"We made it all right," said Roger, "with Corey and Reggie's help."

"Are you all right, Dave?" Corey took in the blue/purple bruises forming around his eyes and across this jaw.

"I've been better," he said. "Susie will be a little upset, but she knows this is my life. How's your father?"

"I think he'll be all right. He's weak and the cold water and air wasn't good, but the farmers took care of him and called an ambulance. Mom was just coming down the alley as I was heading for the warehouse. I sent her to him."

"Sounds like the troops have arrived," said Dave as more sirens and flashing lights poured onto the scene. "The sun will be rising soon, why don't you go home and rest a couple of hours. We'll need information later. I'll call you."

"Why don't you bring Susie and the kids over later this afternoon and stay for dinner. They'll love Reggie."

"I'm sure they will. I would love to have him myself. He'd be a great asset."

"I'm sure he would, but Reggie is Mom's cat – or maybe I should say we are all Reggie's people."

"Whatever. Get some rest. We'll talk later."

"Corey? Roger?"

"Mom, I thought you were with Dad. Is he…?"

"He's fine. The ambulance took him back to the hospital. I'm going over there in a little bit. I had to see that you were all right."

"We're all right – just tired. I hope you don't mind if I invited Dave and his family over later this afternoon for dinner."

"You know I don't mind your friends coming to my house. Are we going to get the complete story soon?"

"I think so."

"Then come on, I'll take you and Roger home then go back to the hospital. I'll spend the rest of the night there – what's left of it."

"My car is here," said Roger. "Turner convinced me that he had a safe hiding place for Mr. Kahlor, but when we started toward this warehouse, I decided something was wrong. I was about to turn around and go back to the hospital, when he pulled a gun and threatened to kill your father if I didn't follow his orders."

"I thought it must be something like that," said Corey.

"Anyway, my car is over there. Mrs. Kahlor, you can go to the hospital and I'll take Corey and Reggie home."

"Thank you Roger. I would appreciate that. See you tomorrow, Dave," Sherylee called as she left. He waved at her.

The State Police and FBI had arrived and were mopping up the scene. Corey tried to act alert, but could not keep from dragging her feet. Even Reggie didn't seem to have as much pep as usual.

"Let's go," said Roger. "You and Reggie both look like ragamuffins."

"Meow," answered Reggie and ran for Roger's car.

Roger took Corey's hand and started after Reggie. "Tomorrow will be another day – or rather today will soon stretch into another unknown round of who knows what."

"Do you want to go to your apartment or your mom's house?" asked Roger as they pulled away from the warehouse.

"It's almost six a.m.," said Corey. "There's no point in going to my place. It's almost breakfast time. We may as well go to Mom's. It's closer and we both need to get into some dry clothes."

Thirty-four

Reggie ran ahead of them when they arrived home, rolling over a few times on the familiar carpet.

"Do you want something to eat?" asked Corey

"Meow."

"Not you, silly. I know you want something. I was talking to Roger."

Roger laughed then said, "I really think we both need to get out of our wet clothes, get warm and have a short nap first."

"I think you're right," she said. "I'll take care of Reggie first."

Reggie ran to the kitchen and waited beside his bowl. Corey followed him, filled his water bowl, and opened a can of his favorite tuna.

Roger waited and walked up the stairs with her. He stopped at her door, hesitantly gave her a light kiss then left her to go to the guest room. Corey went to her bedroom, changed into a warm sweat suit and was just drifting into a deep sleep when Reggie joined her, curling at her feet.

"Thanks Reggie," she mumbled and was sound asleep.

***

Coffee aroma drifted up the stairs into her room. Corey forced her eyes open and took a deep breath through her nose, enjoying the smell of coffee. Reggie had left her door ajar. She rolled over, glanced at the clock and her eyes opened wide. *Ten after twelve?*

Hastily, she dressed and started down the stairs. She heard Roger talking to someone. She didn't hear anyone answer him, so she assumed he was on the phone. He was just closing his cell phone when she walked into the kitchen. Corey reached for the coffee pot, but Roger had a steaming cup on the countertop waiting for her. *Roger must have heard me coming.* She sat down at the table. Roger uncovered a plate of bacon, scrambled eggs and toast then set them before her.

"Thanks," she mumbled still trying to wake up completely.

Roger sat across from her and finished his breakfast. After she had eaten and had her second cup of coffee in hand, he finally spoke. "Corey, I was a complete idiot. I hope you can forgive me."

"Roger, I couldn't believe you were really involved with Turner, but you don't know how relieved I was to find you on that boat with Dad."

"You mean me being tied up to die with him proved I was innocent."

Corey grinned at him. "Not necessarily. Remember he killed his other associates when they failed or he no longer needed them. I was afraid I wouldn't be able to get Dad off the boat with just Reggie's help – although Reggie certainly pulled his own weight – and ours. I needed you to help with Dad, to calm my nerves and to be close to me if I had to die there."

"How can anyone be such an idiot? I trusted him. I thought he was a good role model for a fledgling crime reporter."

"He became a top homicide detective by using people then disposing of them like a used dinner napkin. A lot of people didn't like him, but didn't know why, or what to do about it. He was their superior and they had to obey his orders."

"I understand that, but I've always trusted your instincts. Where did I go wrong on this one?"

"This time it was a person you considered a friend. There was a strong pull between friend and fiancée. I'm sure he gave you many words of wisdom about women and especially highly curious women who stick their noses into things that aren't any of their business."

Roger hung his head and looked sheepish. "You sound like you were listening in on our conversations."

"You don't have to follow a skunk to know what his habits are. I knew he was influencing you with his warped sense of duty – or a need to control – but it hurt to think that you believed him over me. Especially when you accused me of lying to you?"

"Well, you didn't exactly tell the truth, did you? You said you were going to the library and…"

"And I went to the library. I was there all day."

"But he said he called…but of course there was no answer because the library was closed and if it was closed, no one would be there to answer the phone. But there were no lights and no cars."

"I have black-out shades on my office windows – for protection from the sun and for privacy when I want to be alone. You know that. I parked my car over on 6th Street and walked down the alley to the back of the library."

"He called your cell phone…"

"Roger, if *you* had called me, I would have talked to you. I resented him hounding me, wanting to know my every move. And I was angry that you gave him my cell phone number."

"You're right. I shouldn't have given it to him without your permission and I should have called you myself. But if I had, then he would have known you were there and found a way to get inside to see what you were doing."

"Dave called earlier and needed to talk to me. He's been in on the investigation into the diary case since he talked to Dad in Texas. Turner's office wouldn't talk to him or let him use the computers to search for the information that Turner was supposed to find for us. So he used the library computer. Turner suspected that he would contact me and that I would help him in any way I could."

"He did make a big deal of David's involvement and the fact that you and David were *lovers* at one time."

"We were never *lovers*. We dated and half-heartedly talked of marriage, but we were only friends and we both knew it. Then he fell for Susie and no one else existed. We are still friends. I trusted and believed him. I was already suspecting that Turner was involved in some way. He always seemed to be one-step ahead of us in getting to where we needed to be – thus the dead people who might identify him – or who failed him."

"Corey, are you saying Turner is the…?"

"That will be up to Dave to find out, but he's in the mix somewhere. Parker and Dolly got off much too easily. Turner was the only one who knew that Reggie would be home alone. I could go on, but you get the picture. I felt uncomfortable around him and when you sided with him, I had to get out of there before I said or did something that would get us in more trouble."

"Corey, I'm truly sorry and I hope you won't hold it against me forever. I do love you and I don't want to lose you because of my stupidity."

"Roger, I love you very much. As difficult as this last week has been, I think it's made us stronger. I think we should seriously think about setting a date. After all, I now have a father to walk me down the aisle and a mother-of-the-bride to cry at my wedding."

Roger laughed. "As soon as we get this mess all settled, we'll take a look at our calendars."

"Why should we let the activities of others be the determining factor in our lives? Why don't we just set a date to suit us and let the rest fall in step with us?"

"I think that's a wonderful idea. What do you have in mind? I know you've mentioned a Christmas wedding on occasion."

"You remembered," said Corey. "You're right. How about December 20? The church will be decorated and…"

"I think December 20 is on a Monday."

"Then…," Corey counted backward. "…the 17th. That would be a Friday."

"The 17th will be perfect day. We'll tell your parents sometime today when they're together and Daniel is feeling better."

Corey's cell phone interrupted their excitement, reminding them that there was still a mystery to solve. Hopefully, Dave and his men rounded up all of the gang last night. But would they get off on a technicality? Would they be after the diary again? Sherylee took the original diary to the station last night. But…

Reluctantly, Corey reached for her ringing cell phone. "Hello," she answered cautiously.

"Miss Kahlor?"

"Yes."

This is Bernard Vincent, President of the Masontown Library Board. The police called this morning and said it's safe to open the library today."

"Thank you Mr. Vincent. Since it's already afternoon, I think it would be better to wait for tomorrow and proceed with our regular hours for Wednesdays. That will give me time to adjust the schedules. I'll have a couple of the staff to come in today and make sure everything is ready to go."

"You're right, of course. I'm sure you can handle it. I'll drop by tomorrow and see if you need anything."

"Thank you again, Mr. Vincent."

"Good news?" asked Roger as she closed her cell phone.

"Yes, the library is back in business. I need to call Susan and have her and Betsy come in for a couple of hours this afternoon then open up in the morning. We still have some loose ends to gather up here"

Corey called Susan then turned to Roger. "If the library is opening, Dave must be pretty confident that he has everything under control."

"I'm sure he has, but I understand your fear. Will Turner

somehow get off?"

"If we could just tie them in with the bank robbery of 1929…Wait! The papers I was printing when Mom called. They're in my brief case in Dave's car."

"Corey, none of these folks were even born back then."

"But their parents or grandparents were."

"You think these hoods are related to those bank robbers?"

"I know they are. The man who followed Dad for twenty years was a grandson of one of the robbers – Hollister. From what I've read, they never recovered the $50,000 from the heist. They think my grandfather hid the money and put a code in the diary so it could be found."

"But we've read that diary over and over and there is nothing there but family matters and his depression and loneliness."

"Maybe we need to take another closer look at the Bible. I was doing some comparing with it and the diary at the library when Mom called. Everything is in my briefcase."

"It was basically the same as the diary. Entries of the same day were just a shortened version of the diary."

"There were differences. Dave thinks he used the Bible version as a code.

"Is the Bible still in the safe deposit box, or did you remove it when you removed the original diary?"

"It never was in the bank. We hid it downstairs, remember?"

"Oh, I forgot – a good thing, I guess. Had I told Turner it was here…"

"Did you even tell Turner about the Bible?"

"No, I guess I didn't. He never asked if there was anything else and I never thought about it. I guess I thought anything important would be in the diary because the Bible was such a shortened edition. Why don't you get it and we'll give it a quick once over, comparing it with the diary before we meet your mother at the hospital."

"All my notes are in my briefcase, but the Bible is still downstairs. I need to call Dave."

"Meow," said Reggie who had sauntered over to the table. Surprised, Corey and Roger laughed.

"You think that's a good idea too Reggie? I suppose you're going to help us figure it all out."

"Meow," answered Reggie which sounded an awfully lot like, "of course."

Corey laughed again, the went downstairs for the Bible.

205

Thirty-five

With fresh coffee in hand and diary notes spread across the table, Roger and Corey began pouring over them – again. There must be something. Reggie sat on the floor watching, ears twitching and the tip of his tail moving like a caged mouse trying to escape.

"Your great-grandfather seems to read five chapters each day, regardless of what book he starts with," said Roger.

"And he begins in the Old Testament book of Numbers on December 24," said Corey, "a strange place to begin in the first place and on Christmas Eve. You would think he would begin with the Gospels and the story of the birth of Christ."

"Maybe he just opened the Bible and started with what was there."

"Could be. A lot of people do that. But it still seems strange. And why did he begin with days near Christmas when he had been in prison since early fall?"

"Maybe he was just lonesome and homesick. It was a holiday."

"He either began at the beginning of the book or it is a continuation from Leviticus. He begins to date it at Chapter 3."

"Corey, we'll go nuts if we try to understand his mind about seventy years after the fact."

"But there has to be a reason behind his method. The heading in the Book of Numbers is The Fourth Book of Moses, called Numbers. He reads three chapters, dates it, reads five chapters from then on." Corey stopped and pondered the problem. Reggie sat thumping his tail on the floor in a rhythmic pattern: thump, thump, thump, thump – pause – thump, thump, thump, thump, thump.

"Reggie will you stop that thumping," said Roger irritably.

Corey looked at Reggie, who stared back at her as he continued his thumping. Roger turned to say something to him again and saw the look in Corey's eyes.

"Roger, he's trying to tell us there is significance in what I just said."

"What the Book of Numbers?"

"No…the *fourth* book of Moses called Numbers."

"Meow," said Reggie still staring at Corey.

"And…five chapters a day."

"Meow," said Reggie that sounded a lot like, "Now, you're thinking."

"Roger, where's that newspaper article I copied from the Toledo Times dated August 15, 1929?"

Roger shuffled through the pages on the table and pulled out the one Corey wanted. "This one?"

"Yeah, how many men were involved in that robbery?"

Roger skimmed the article. "Looks like four." He gave her a curious look.

Corey frowned. Reggie thumped his tail – five thumps. "There were five. One went to prison, three were never arrested."

"That still is only four."

"Who was the brains behind the attempt? And what happened to those other three men? And…"

"And what?" asked Roger.

"Samuel Miller."

"Meow."

"The farmer who took you and Reggie in? What does he have to do with any of this?"

Corey told him the story Samuel told him.

"But that would mean…"

"The boss – for want of a better term – was inside the bank. But, how could he shoot a man and no one know about it?"

"From what Samuel said, he was standing behind a desk near one of the robbers. He fired and dropped the gun in the desk drawer in the confusion that followed. They assumed one of the robbers did it. Goldmeister, a bank manager, accused Harry Kahlor, but Harry admitted that he drove the car and was not in the bank."

"Goldmeister killed the man? Was he the boss?"

"Sounds like it."

Roger stared at her, mouth open. "Corey, you either have a very vivid imagination or you're on to something important."

"No, Reggie's onto something. I need my notes. I have the names of the other three men in the Bible diary. They aren't mentioned in the notebook diary."

Corey turned to the Bible list. "In early February, 1930 Harry had a letter from Oyler. Two days later, he had a visit from him. Four days later, he received a letter from Mark Hollister. Nothing unusual there, except he said he was surprised to see Fred Oyler. In March, Goldmeister sent a letter telling him Mary Sue would come on Wednesday. On April 7 – apparently Harry's birthday – Mrs. Warren Zurphy sent him a birthday card. On April 13, Goldmeister visited him saying he was in Columbus for the Jewish Easter. I didn't know the Jews celebrated Easter. Must have been Passover or else Harry is trying to tell us something."

"Maybe he was saying that Goldmeister was sort-of Judas – a traitor?"

"Maybe. We have four robbers and the headman. Kahlor went to prison. What happened to the other three suspects who were never convicted?"

"That would be Hollister, Oyler and Zurphy. You Google Oyler and I'll do Hollister."

"I did already," said Corey. "If I remember my notes correctly, "Fred Oyler was found in the Maumee River with a bullet in his back on April 1, 1930. Mark Hollister suffered a similar fate. March 25. Firemen found him in a burned out building that was ruled arson. He also had a bullet in his back. Kahlor was still in prison, Oyler and Hollister are dead; that only leaves Zurphy."

Reggie yawned, turned over, yawned again and turned over and over on the carpet. Corey and Roger laughed at him.

"Are you having fun, Reggie?"

"Meow." He turned over again and began cleaning his paws.

"Did you get to Zurphy?"

"Yes, I'm trying to remember…"

Reggie turned over again and looked at Corey as if to say, "well, aren't you going to praise me?"

"You're a good kitty Reggie, but don't carry the cutesy bit too far," said Corey.

"Meow," he said and sauntered off swishing his tail.

Corey laughed then frowned. "I think Reggie wasn't trying to be cute. He was trying to tell us something."

"You think? What…?"

"I remember Goldmeister…He owned the China Import Business in Toledo, which went bankrupt. Then he bought a warehouse in Masontown to continue his import business under a new name."

"Meow!" Reggie called from the living room.

"What did he buy another warehouse with if he was bankrupt?"

GREAT-GRANDPA'S DIARY

Roger frowned then suddenly his face lit up with understanding. "Let me guess. The new venture was Parker's Wholesale Merchandise, 691 River Road."

"That's right. Parker is probably the grandson of the Goldmeister who accused my Great-grandfather Kahlor of murder and somehow got the money. He changed his name because he was the brains behind the heist in the first place?"

"It would look that way to me. My guess is Great-grandfather Kahlor took the fall and was promised that Goldmeister would pull strings and get him out early. He didn't – or if he did, he killed him as soon as he was released. What about Zurphy? Another name change?"

"Yes, Warren Zurphy was found shot to death behind his place of business – a donut shop in Wauseon – on March 20. His widow married a Marvin Beecher. She was now Dolly Beecher, who also moved her business, Dolly's Donut Den, to Masontown."

"But it can't be the same Dolly we know …can it?"

"I doubt it. Probably the mother or grandmother of our Dolly."

"And what is our Dolly's married name?"

"I didn't get that far." Corey grabbed her laptop and began clicking away. "Aha!"

"What?" asked Roger looking over her shoulder. He let out a long slow whistle.

"It seems Dolly Beecher also had a daughter named Dolly, who married a Simon Turner. She divorced him and was married and divorced several times in the last twenty years."

"Did she have any children?" Roger almost whispered the question.

"We need to call Dave." Before Corey could reach for the phone, her cell phone rang. Surprised, she jumped then put it on speakerphone and said, "Hello."

"Corey, Dave here. Are you folks up to coming down to give your statements not that it will do a lot of good. The DA is already screaming about lack of evidence, abuse of rights, and interference of FBI with local law enforcements."

"Mom is at the hospital. We can stop and pick her up on our way. But I found some interesting information that will put a little different light on the matter. Most of the notes are in my brief case in your car." Briefly, she told him about their discoveries.

Dave whistled softly. "It certainly gives a different perspective. We can nail Turner on conflict of interest if nothing else – not much but..."

"We'll be there as soon as possible. In the meantime, check the printouts in my briefcase." She gave him the combination to the lock and closed her phone. She turned to Reggie who had come back into the room. "I'm sorry, Reggie. You were way ahead of us. Got any more ideas that will help us put these guys away for life?"

"Meow," he answered, stood on his back legs to reach the table and knocked the Bible to the floor."

"We've searched that," said Corey. "Not much there."

Reggie turned and glared at her and began leafing through the book with his tongue. He stopped at I Thessalonians 5. Verses 16-21 dated Sept. 10, 1931. Corey picked the book up and read: "Rejoice evermore. Pray without ceasing. In everything, give thanks; for this is the will of God in Christ Jesus concerning you. Quench not the Spirit. Despise not prophesying. Prove all things; hold fast that which is good."

She paused. He adds to his "diary" around the edge – going home soon. Will mail diary and Bible to Mary Sue in case I don't make it."

"So what does that mean?"

"It means, first of all that we didn't look far enough. We assumed he was dead when he stopped writing in May of 1931."

"Is there anything there to help us?"

"Maybe. Roger see if you can find out when he was released or died. The Rejoice evermore sounds like he is happy because he will soon be free."

"Why don't we call Dave back? He should have that information."

"Good thinking." Corey pulled out her cell phone, ran down the list of numbers, and pressed send."

"Dave, can you find out when Kahlor was released from prison, or if he died there?"

"Sure hold on a minute. I have the folder right here in front of me." There was a pause while he looked it up. "Here it is, September 15 1931."

"Then why didn't he come home? How did he get out? Did he serve his time or was he paroled or did someone pull strings?"

"Let me look...Looks like someone vouched for him and offered him a job."

"Who?"

"Why didn't I think of these things? Would you like a job with the FBI? Corey you just hit the jackpot."

"Goldmeister? Or maybe Parker?"

"You got it. A man named Parker who was just opening a wholesale warehouse in Masontown said he would hire Mr. Kahlor."

"Is there any way you can find out if any unidentified bodies showed up around Masontown around the end of September 1931? I remember something in the Bible Diary – May 31, 1931. He said something about hearing by the grapevine that some prisoners were being paroled. He hoped that he was one of them, but if his "friends" found out about it, he was dead."

"We'll check it out. But I think you are on the right track."

"We'll see you in a little bit."

Thirty-six

Corey and Roger left to go to the hospital. Corey opened the door on the passenger side and Reggie dived over her head, hit the front seat then sprang to the back. Corey got in and turned to look at him. "You know you can't go in the hospital with us. You'll have to wait in the car."

Reggie stared at her and said nothing. Corey glanced at Roger who was grinning. He shrugged his shoulders and started the car.

When they had parked in the hospital lot, Corey turned back to Reggie and said, "Stay in the car, Reggie, We'll be right back with Mom."

Reggie stared straight ahead. Roger and Corey headed for the main entrance. They walked to the elevators, pushed the button and waited for the car. As they stepped inside, Reggie zipped in. The door closed and he slipped to the back of the car.

"Reggie, you can't..." The door slid open before Corey could finish her sentence. Reggie was slinking down the hall, staying close to the walls. Once in Daniel's room, he hid under the bed.

"Coral Rae did I just see Reggie go under that bed?"

"Probably. He didn't want to be left out."

"I hope that's all. I sure don't want to need his help again to save someone's life."

Daniel laughed and dropped his arm over the side of the bed, letting his hand dangle. Reggie licked his fingers and purred loud enough to be heard above their conversation.

"We're on our way to police headquarters to give our statement about last night. When I talked to Dave earlier, he said Turner and his gang seemed to have the DA on their side."

"Jonathan Burke?" asked Sherylee.

"I guess so, if he is the DA."

"But that's a conflict of interest."

"How so?" Corey and Roger asked together.

"He's one of Dolly What-ever-her-name-is-now's ex-husbands."

"And one of Detective Turner's step-fathers," said Roger. "Is

GREAT-GRANDPA'S DIARY

everyone in this town related to one another?"

"Almost," said Sherylee.

Corey told her parents all they had learned and what they believed. "If we just had a little more evidence…Were there any more papers, letters, postcards or anything in the bundle of things you received from your grandfather?" she asked Daniel.

"I really don't know. There was a box – you know a stationery box – with letters, postcards, and greeting cards. I didn't really look because I thought they were love letters and I didn't want to – you know – intrude on personal stuff."

"It might be important. Could we see them?" asked Roger. "We won't read any of their personal letters."

"Sure, but you'll have to find them."

"Where are they?"

"They're in my duffle bag. I left it in a large locker at the bus terminal until I could find someplace to stay. Didn't plan on it being a hospital."

"Our bus terminal?'

"Yes, the key is in that closet with my clothes. It's in my billfold."

Sherylee opened the closet and checked his pants pocket. She removed the billfold and handed it to Daniel. He extracted the key and gave it to Roger.

"Thank you sir," said Roger. "We need to get going. We told Dave we would stop and get Mrs. Kahlor and be there in a few minutes. We'll make a detour to the bus terminal."

"Be careful," said Daniel. "I'm really sorry for all the heartache I've caused."

"But we're ridding the town of a major crime syndicate," said Roger. "We couldn't have done it without you."

"Meow," came a soft answer from under the bed.

"Certainly not without you," said Roger. "Let's get you out of here before we're arrested for bringing a vicious animal into the hospital."

Corey and Sherylee started down to the elevator. When the door was open, Roger said, "Go for it Reggie. I'm right behind you." The Bengal cat streaked down the hall, into the elevator and slinked behind Corey and Sherylee.

***

The bus terminal was on the route to the police station. Roger stopped in a no parking zone. "I'll run in and get it. You two can begin looking while I drive to the station. Move the car if a policeman comes along and insists."

Roger jumped out of the car, Reggie right behind him. They raced into the building, to the locker area. Pulling the key from his pocket, he found the locker with a matching number and opened it. Tugging the duffle bag from it and closing the locker, he turned toward the door. Reggie growled and moved closer to Roger's legs. A man stood on the corner, leaning against the lamppost trying to look disinterested. Roger had the feeling he would take the bag if he had half an opportunity. Reggie barred his teeth and growled like his larger namesake. The man turned away and Roger threw the bag in the trunk. Reggie jumped to the front seat and Roger took off.

"I thought you were going to put it back here so Mom and I could begin to search for the box," said Corey.

"I was, but I think we're being followed again. That man on the corner seemed intent on taking the bag, but Reggie convinced him he didn't want it. I think we need to get it to Dave and let him decide what to do."

***

Roger stopped in front of the police station. "You and your mother go find Dave and get us an armed guard to bring this bag into a safe place where we can open it," said Roger. "Reggie and I will stay here until you come back – and we won't give it to anyone unless you are with them."

Corey found Dave and explained what they thought they might have. "They gave me an office to work in for a few days until we get this mess cleaned up. We can bring it in here. Sgt. Williams, will you accompany Miss Kahlor to her car and make sure there's no mishap with the bag they are bringing to my office?"

"Yes, sir."

Corey and Sgt. Williams went back to the car. Roger carried the bag while Reggie walked close to him on one side and Sgt. Williams, gun in hand walked on the other side. Corey ran ahead, opening doors for them.

In Dave's office, they dumped the contents of the duffle bag on the corner of his desk – clothes, blanket, a skillet and small pan and the stationery box, tied with a strong cord. On the other corner were the contents of Corey's briefcase. While Corey and Dave opened the box, Sherylee carefully folded Daniel's clothes and placed them back in the bag along with his other belongings.

GREAT-GRANDPA'S DIARY

Corey picked up some letters tied with white ribbon and flipped through them. They were all addressed to Daniel's grandmother, so she set them aside. "These look like they are personal," she said. A small envelope with what felt like file cards lay near the bottom of the box. Dave dumped the cards and Corey picked up one with what looked like a locker key taped to it – a key similar to the one from the bus terminal.

"It's a key to a locker somewhere, but where? There's no note with it," said Dave.

"According to the paper he only had an hour or so before they caught him. He didn't have time to go far," said Corey

"The locker has to be in Toledo," said Roger.

"But where? And what's in it?"

"Could be a list of people involved and/or cash from the robbery," said Dave. "The bank claimed none of the money was recovered.

"But how can we find...?"

"Meow." Reggie stated with authority.

"You think you know," said Roger grinning at the cat.

Reggie turned, glared at him and knocked some of Corey's papers to the floor.

"Now what did you do that for?" she said.

Reggie gave Corey a *how can you be so dense* look and started sorting through the papers. Corey, feeling thoroughly chastised, glanced at Roger who shrugged his shoulders. She stooped to help Reggie. Then it hit her. "You're right, Reggie. How *could* I be so dumb?"

"What?" Dave, Roger and Sherylee all looked at her for an explanation. She placed her work paper on the desk – the one with numbers on it.

"Look at the numbers from the Bible pages. They weren't included in the diary pages, so they must have some importance. He gives specific directions for his grandmother's grave Maple Hill, Lot # 243, Sect. 87. Why? Wonder if there is such a place? The only time he mentions specific time of visits is with Fred Oyler – 20 minutes. Although the papers say Professor Snook was buried in Greenlawn Cemetery, he says Snook was buried at the prison at 5:00 a.m. He says his grandfather was celebrating his 82nd birthday on April 1 – the day one of the other men was killed – and yet in the diary he says his grandfather is dead. In the Bible, he says George is 11 on April 12, but in the diary he says his birthday is May 5. The

215

visit from Goldmeister was April 13. Passover was probably not that day. It may or may not have anything to do with the other numbers, but as Roger mentioned earlier it might have had to do with Goldmeister being a traitor, like Judas. And, as Reggie so aptly pointed out, he started reading Numbers – the 4th Book of Moses – the 3rd Chapter, 5 chapters per day."

"Corey, that's interesting, but…"

"Don't you see? These numbers have to lead us to that locker – or whatever it is – in Toledo. Put them together and you have: 234 87 20 82 41211 5511."

"But, what do they mean? How do they tell us anything?" asked Roger.

"I don't know, but… They could be street numbers or locker numbers or…Could we get a Toledo phone book for 1929?"

"You have to be kidding, Coral Rae."

"Maybe not," said Dave who had been listening with a growing look of admiration on his face. He reached over to his intercom, pushed a button and said, "Send Mike O'Malley in here."

A minute or so later, the door opened and a young rookie – tall, red hair, green eyes that sparkled with enthusiasm – stood holding the door half in and half out of the room. "You wanted me, sir?"

"Yes, I'm told you are a whiz with computers and numbers."

The young man's face turned a deeper shade of red – almost matching his hair. "Yes, sir," he answered, looking embarrassed.

Dave laughed. "Sorry Mike, I'm not talking about a youthful discretion. I need your help."

"What can I do for you?" the voice showed more enthusiasm.

Dave gave him the page on which Corey had written the numbers and told him some background and Corey's theory that the numbers were some kind of code. See what you can find out for us."

"Yes sir …eh, how soon?"

"Yesterday," said Dave.

"I'll get right on it," he said and left, taking the paper with him.

"It's getting close to dinnertime," said Dave. "If you folks want to go…"

"Why don't we order in a pizza or something," said Roger.

"We really would like to know what he finds," said Corey.

"Meow," said Reggie and gave them his *I'm not about to move* look.

"Well, there we have it," said Dave. He laughed and picked up

GREAT-GRANDPA'S DIARY

the phone. "Oh, by the way, Corey. The records show that a body meeting the description of Harry Kahlor was found in the Maumee River lodged against some fallen trees, September 20th, 1931. Mrs. Kahlor was contacted, but refused to acknowledge his death. The county buried him in a far corner of the cemetery. There is a grave marker with his name, date of birth and date of death."

"All those years of anguish and she didn't..." Corey's voice choked in anger.

"Don't be too harsh," said Sherylee. "Right or wrong, it was her way of coping."

"She's right," said Dave. "Don't judge her too harshly. Now, I need to call Susie," he said. "One of you order something."

"It's getting too late tonight, but, tell Susie I'd like to see her and the children. Maybe for lunch or dinner tomorrow," said Sherylee.

Roger pulled out his phone and ordered pizza.

***

Corey took her last bite of pizza, lifted her napkin and wiped the remains of sauce from the corners of her mouth as Mike O'Malley knocked and opened the door. He tried not to stare at the pizza boxes on the desk.

"What do you have for us, Mike?" asked Dave.

The young man grinned and began reading from the printout he held in his hand. "In Toledo 1929, there was a Fourth National Bank between 3rd and 5th Avenues – three blocks from Toledo Merchants Bank. At 3:15 p.m. a Mr. George Daniels opened a savings account # 234 8720 with $10,000 in $100 dollar bills. He then got a safe deposit box # 82412 and arranged for the bank to draw payments from his account yearly to pay for the box until such time that he or his heir would come in person to retrieve the contents of the box. He also said he would send a letter to his son, Robert in care of the bank and asked that they place the letter unopened in his box. He placed a small piece of paper and a small package wrapped in newspaper in the box. He locked the box and left.

"The bank has since changed hands several times and is now a National City Bank. I talked to the manager. He said the box is still there. The savings still pays for the box yearly rental. No one has asked about it in almost seventy years. He said they have thought about closing the account and opening the box, but decided as long as there is money in the savings to pay for the box, they would keep it as is. After one hundred years, they will probably put out a search for an heir. He said he would be willing to meet you there in the morning before the bank opens if you want to get to it."

Corey, Roger and Sherylee sat with mouths open. Dave smiled at them. "I told you this man is good. "Good job O'Malley. Take that box with half a pizza with you."

Mike grinned broadly as he reached for the box. "Glad to be of help." He left and Dave turned back to Corey.

But why did he use the name George Daniels?" Dave asked.

"His youngest son – Daniel's father – was named George Daniel," said Sherylee.

"I'll head for Toledo first thing in the morning," said Dave.

"Can you get in the box without Daniel?" asked Sherylee.

"We'll go with you," said Roger. "Corey maybe…"

"You're right," said Dave. "I'll pick you up at 7:00 a.m. Where will you be?"

"At Mom's," said Corey.

Thirty-seven

At 7:00 a.m., Corey and Roger met Dave in the driveway, waved to Sherylee and Reggie and left for Toledo. October was almost over. Frost covered much of the ground and tops of buildings. What few leaves left on the trees after Tuesday's rain, swirled and fell to the ground.

"Do you think there'll be anything in the box?" asked Roger. "Anything that will be of use to us, that is."

"I hope so," said Dave. "With the research you, Corey and I did, we have enough evidence to prosecute, but a good lawyer – or a crooked one – will get them off with a slap on the wrist."

"You can't prosecute Goldmeister for murder now," said Corey. "It's been over seventy years and he's long dead."

"There is no statute of limitations on murder. There won't be a trial, but it will be put in the file and the case of the civilian who was killed will be closed. Also Harry Kahlor will be cleared of the murder charge."

"Will there be something in writing for Samuel Miller?" asked Corey.

"I'll make sure there is. His father was a hero and should be remembered as such."

"We should be there in about ten minutes. I called the manager last night and arranged to meet him before the bank officially opens for business. I didn't want to take any chances of some of the family members we haven't yet apprehended showing up and causing trouble."

"That's a good idea," said Roger. "There's Main Street. Third and Fifth Avenues must be pretty close to downtown."

"There the National City Bank," said Corey.

"And there's Mr. Conrad waiting for us," said Dave as he pulled to the curb in front of the bank.

"Mr. Conrad?" he asked, stepping out of the car.

"Yes, you must be Agent David O'Riley."

"I am and this is Corey Kahlor and Roger Trent. Corey is the great-granddaughter of the man we spoke about."

Mr. Conrad moved to the doors, unlocked them and motioned for the three to enter. He locked the door behind him and led them to his office. He smiled and extended his hand to Corey. "I'm glad to meet someone who is really connected to this mystery that has been with us for so many years."

"Thank you," said Corey. "It was good of you to meet us so early."

Mr. Conrad shook hands with Dave and Roger as well. "I assume you want to open the box. It takes two keys to open it. Do you have the other one?"

"Yes we do," said Corey. She pulled the key from her pocket and handed it to Mr. Conrad.

"Very good. It should still work. If not, we'll have to get someone in here to drill it open."

"How did they open it to place the letter inside? My great-grandfather was in prison by then."

"I went back and read the records on this case. It was unusual and I might add that my grandfather was a young man then. He was newly elected president of the Bank. When I was a child, my dad was president then – Grandpa told us the story. It was written in the historical files also.

"He said the man asked him to make it all legal. He told Mr. Daniels that he could not open the box without both keys, so Mr. Daniels gave him the second key and told him to return it to him when he could. He said Grandpa would know where to find him.

"The next day the story of the bank robbery hit the press. My grandfather anguished over keeping stolen money, but he really didn't know for sure it was stolen. The paper said $50,000 had been taken and Mr. Daniels only had $10,000. The paper said a Mr. Kahlor had been arrested. The man who opened the bank was Mr. Daniels. He decided that if it was stolen money the police would be asking for it and would open the box for them. No one ever came or asked, so he put the letter in the box and visited Mr. Daniels – alias Kahlor – at the city jail before the trial and returned the key on a chain that he could wear around his neck."

"He sure went to a lot of trouble for something," said Roger. "I wonder where the rest of the $50,000 went."

"He must have gotten it to Goldmeister someway," said Corey.

"Well, let's see what's in the box," said Dave.

GREAT-GRANDPA'S DIARY

"The bank boxes are behind the tellers' area." Mr. Conrad began moving in that direction. Walls of metal box fronts lined all sides of the room, leaving only enough space for the door. In the center of the room was a long metal table on which to set the box when it was removed from the wall. Mr. Conrad handed the key back to Corey.

"Put your key in the first slot and turn it. I'll put mine in the second one and do the same. It should open, although the locks might be a little rusty from non-use. I brought a can of oil along just in case."

They tried the keys, applied some oil, tried again and the lock snapped opening the door to the box. Mr. Conrad slid the box out and set it on the table. "I'll leave you alone…"

"You're welcome to stay, Mr. Conrad," said Corey. "I'm sure you must be curious."

Mr. Conrad smiled. "Well, yes, I am. If Agent O'Riley doesn't mind."

"Not at all. I'll even have you sign a form stating what we found. We might need that in court."

"Glad to help."

Corey opened the box. There was a package wrapped in newspaper containing fifty one hundred dollar bills, a small piece of paper and an envelope still sealed with a canceled stamp from Toledo addressed to Mr. Daniels in care of the bank. Dave picked up the small paper that listed several names: Goldmeister, Hollister, Zurphy and Oyler. Corey opened the mailed envelope.

"It's a letter." She glanced over it than began to read:

To George, or whoever finds this letter.

Please make sure it gets into the hands of the police or FBI. I might not be around when you read it.

I am Harry Daniel Kahlor. I drove the getaway car for the robbery of Toledo Merchants Bank in May of 1929. Not much chance of getting off. Looks like I'm the scapegoat. Goldmeister, manager at Toledo Merchants also owns Toledo Wholesale Warehouse. He promised to buy off the judge so I won't go to prison. He won't. Hollister said he killed that Negro who was in the bank and said I did it.

I was an idiot. He said he needed a driver for a small job. I thought he meant handyman job. That's what I did for a living. Hollister, Oyler, Zurphy and I were to pick up something for him, leave it in a shopping bag in the alley behind his warehouse No one said nothing about a bank robbery.

Hollister, Oyler and Zurphy left the shopping bag in the car and went inside the bank to get Goldmeister's instructions. They ran out of the bank like their tails were on fire carrying bank bags and pulling bandanas from their faces. They threw the bags through the open window. Oyler and Zurphy took off in separate directions. Hollister took long enough to shout at me to leave the shopping bag in the alley behind the Goldmeister's warehouse near the side door. Then he ran off in a third direction. I got left holding the bag (Ha! Ha!).

I don't trust Goldmeister. He'll kill me if he don't get the money, but I needed some kind of protection and insurance, so I pulled a reverse robbery – robbed from the robbers. (Ha! Ha!). None of us knew how much money was in the shopping bag – except possibly Goldmeister – so I took $15,000 in fifties and hundreds and stopped at the first bank I saw. I parked my car on a side street, hoping no one would recognize it or me. I walked in as if I did it every day and opened a savings account. Then I rented a safe deposit box and bought my insurance. I wrote the names of the others on a slip of paper and placed it in the box along with $5,000 in $100 dollar bills wrapped in newspaper. I made arrangements with the bank manager to make sure this confession went in that box. Then I left and drove to Goldmeister's warehouse, dropped the shopping bag beside the back door and headed home. Cops stopped me before I got out of Toledo. Tried to lie my way out, but someone saw my car.

Feel bad for Mary Sue and the boys. Shoulda known better, but times are hard and ... trusted the wrong people. Hope they can forgive me.

Harry D. Kahlor

Cory read it through and handed to Dave, who read it and handed it to Roger. Roger then let Mr. Conrad read it.

"I would say that pretty much wraps up the case. Along with Samuel Miller's testimony, we should be able to sort out the past and prosecute the present," said Dave. "We certainly appreciate your help Mr. Conrad. If we need your testimony, we'll contact you. It shouldn't be necessary, but with these guys, you never know."

"I'll be glad to do it if you need me. Will you want to keep the box and the savings account?"

"I doubt there is much in the savings account," said Corey.

"Well, actually, it's been there for almost seventy years. We had some good rates, some not so good and some that were spectacular. Over all, the interest pretty much took care of the box rental and the account has more than doubled."

"Well the original $10,000 was stolen money and the $5.000 in the box is stolen money, but the interest…not sure who that belongs to," said Dave.

"Well, it's my father's responsibility, now. He'll be out of the hospital soon. When he's able to travel, he can take care of it. Why don't we close out the box and keep the savings as is until he does something about it. You'll want the box of money, the letter and the note for evidence."

"I think that makes sense," said Dave. "Thank you again, Mr. Conrad."

"This will be the icing on the cake," said Dave as they walked back to the car. "I've called the State's Attorney because we have too much corruption in Masontown to know who to trust. I can't thank you folks enough," he said.

"Glad we could help," said Roger, "but …"

Dave looked at him and grinned. "I know. You're a freelance journalist. You have first dibs on any of the facts, pictures and arrests. You can start writing anytime you're ready."

"Thanks," said Roger.

Epilogue

Roger and Corey prepared a light lunch for Daniel's homecoming. Reggie watched the driveway from the side foyer window as if he knew what was happening – which of course he did. Before Corey heard the car, he had his paws wrapped around the doorknob. When a car door closed, Reggie was on the porch to meet Sherylee and Daniel.

"Meow, meow, meow!" Reggie watched as Daniel slowly walked up the steps, across the porch and into the house. Leaping into Sherylee's arms, he rubbed her chin and purred. Inside the house, he jumped down and followed Daniel into the living room. Once he was settled in one of the recliners, Reggie took possession of his lap, purring and patting Daniel's chin.

"I think Reggie is happy to have you both home," said Corey. "We'll let you rest a minute then we have lunch ready – unless you would rather have it on a tray in here.

"Oh, no," said Daniel. "I've had enough food trays to last me a life time. I want to sit at a real table and use real plates and utensils."

"It's good to see you out of the hospital and able to be home," said Roger.

"It's good to *have* a home," he said. "It's even better to be wanted."

"Daniel, you were always wanted," said Sherylee.

"I know that now…and I think deep down, I knew that then." He leaned back and squeezed his eyes shut. A tear slid down his cheek, but before he could swipe it away, Reggie's rough tongue lapped it up. Daniel opened his eyes and hugged Reggie close. "Thank you, Sir Reginald. You are certainly a knight in shining fur armor."

"Meow?"

Daniel laughed and Corey threw her arms around both her father and Reggie. "Welcome home, Dad."

Daniel gently squeezed Corey's hand. "Corey, I'm sorry about all the heartache and trouble my return caused for everyone, but especially for you and Roger. I don't know why you do, but I'm glad to know you loved me enough to try for me."

"It was quite an adventure," said Corey. "We all learned something and without Reggie's help we would have been in real trouble."

"Meow," said Reggie.

"Well, I'm glad you and Roger worked out your differences," said Sherylee. "I was afraid I would lose a wonderful son-in-law."

"It was a difficult time," said Roger, "but it made our love stronger. By the way, we've set the date for our wedding now that Corey has a Father of the Bride to walk her down the aisle and a Mother of the Bride to cry at the wedding."

Daniel and Sherylee both looked at them expectantly, saying nothing, but obviously waiting for either Roger or Corey to say more.

Corey laughed at their expressions, then said, "December 17."

"You always said you wanted a Christmas wedding," said Sherylee. "Even when you were only five or six."

"I know," she said. "It's a perfect time of year – a time of peace on earth and good will to all and the birth of truth in a manger. How much more perfect could it get?"

"Well, I hope if you decide to keep a diary of your life together, you won't use a Bible and codes," said Daniel. "Be honest with one another always. Talk things out. Don't run away from trouble."

"That's what I've learned," said Corey giving her father a hug. "Now, if everyone is rested and excited about a wedding in the future, I suggest we move to the dining room and enjoy our conversation over lunch."

"Meow?"

"Yes, you too, Reggie."

"Wonder if he will want to be in the wedding," asked Roger giving Reggie a curious glance.

"Meow!" Reggie said, which sounded a lot like, "Of course!"

"I guess that's your answer," said Corey.

ABOUT THE AUTHOR

Mary Lu (Pennock) Warstler was born in Oak Hill, West Virginia. She is a 1956 graduate of Collins High School.

In September 1957, Mary Lu married Rodney J. Warstler and became a full time Minister's wife. They have four children, nine grandchildren, and six great-grandchildren.

In 1980, Mary Lu received her B. S. in Education with a minor in music from the University of Akron. After teaching learning disabled children for two years, she enrolled at Methodist Theological School in Ohio and received a Master of Divinity in Theology in 1985.

Mary Lu and her husband, Rodney, are both ordained United Methodist Ministers. On July 1, 2000, she joined her husband in retirement where she pursues other areas of ministry – primarily writing. They live in Copeland Oaks Retirement Community at Sebring, Ohio.

Mary Lu loves animals, especially cats. After the deaths of her two Siamese (Nicholas and Sugar Plum) and her "British Blue Wanabe" (Michael), she decided not to have pets again. However, Katy (a four-year old part Siamese) and Charlie (an eighteen-month old female gray shorthair) have stolen her heart.

Mary Lu enjoys reading, writing painting, music and needlework of all kinds.

Made in the USA
Charleston, SC
30 March 2014